FIREPROOF

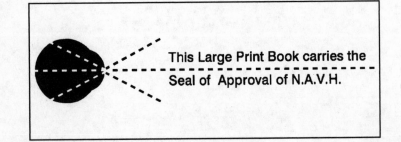

This Large Print Book carries the
Seal of Approval of N.A.V.H.

A MAGGIE O'DELL NOVEL

FIREPROOF

ALEX KAVA

THORNDIKE PRESS
A part of Gale, Cengage Learning

GALE
CENGAGE Learning®

Detroit • New York • San Francisco • New Haven, Conn • Waterville, Maine • London

GALE
CENGAGE Learning·

LIBRARY OF CONGRESS CATALOGING-IN-PUBLICATION DATA

Kava, Alex.
  Fireproof : a Maggie O'Dell novel / by Alex Kava.
    pages ; cm. — (Thorndike Press large print basic)
  ISBN-13: 978-1-4104-5350-1 (hardcover)
  ISBN-10: 1-4104-5350-2 (hardcover)
    1. O'Dell, Maggie (Fictitious character)—Fiction. 2. Criminal profilers—Fiction. 3. Arson investigation—Fiction. 4. Large type books. I. Title.
PS3561.A8682F57 2012b
813'.54—dc23   2012032075

Published in 2012 by arrangement with Doubleday, an imprint of Knopf Doubleday Publishing Group, a division of Random House, Inc.

FOR MISS MOLLY
JUNE 1996–MAY 2011

You were there from the
very beginning,
for eleven out of twelve,
at my feet or at my side.

Sure do miss you, girl.

■ ■ ■ ■

THURSDAY

■ ■ ■ ■

CHAPTER 1

Washington, D.C.

Cornell Stamoran slid his chipped thumb-nail through the crisp seal of Jack Daniel's. He stared at the bottle and swallowed hard. His throat felt cotton-dry. His tongue licked chapped lips. All involuntary reactions, easily triggered.

Back in the days when he was a partner in one of the District's top accounting firms, his drink had been Jack and Coke. Little by little the Coke disappeared long before he started keeping a bottle of whiskey in his desk's bottom drawer, and by then it didn't even need to be Jack or Jim or Johnnie.

He probably wasn't the first accountant to stash his morning fix in his corner office, but he was the only one he knew of to exchange that desk and office for a coveted empty cardboard box, the Maytag stamp still emblazoned on the side.

His first week on the streets Cornell had

9

slept behind a statue on Capitol Hill. Frickin' ironic — he used to sit in the back of clients' limos driving by those same streets. Funny how quickly your life can turn to crap and suddenly you're learning the value of a good box and a warm blanket.

Usually Cornell hid the box out of sight between a monster-size Dumpster and a dirty brick wall when he needed to make a trip downtown. Out here on the outskirts of warehouseland it was quiet. Nobody hassled you. But it got boring as hell. Cornell would make a trip downtown at least once a week. Pick up some fresh cigarette butts, do a little panhandling. Sometimes he'd sit in the library and read. He couldn't check out any books. Where the hell would he keep them? What if he didn't get them back on time? In this new life he didn't want even that little bit of obligation or responsibility. Those were the pitfalls that had landed him on the streets in the first place.

So once a week he'd leave his prized possessions — the box, a couple of blankets someone had mistakenly tossed in a Dumpster. He'd put his few small valuables in a dirty red backpack and lug it around for the day. If he didn't want to walk the five miles he'd have to get up early to catch the homeless bus. That's what he'd done this morning. But he missed the last evening bus. He didn't bother to keep track of time anymore.

What did it matter? Not like he had a meeting or appointment. Hell, he didn't even wear a watch. Truth was, his gold-plated Rolex had been one of the first things he'd pawned. But today Cornell ran into a bit of luck. Actually sort of tripped right in front of it when a black town car almost knocked him into the curb.

The car was picking up some woman and her stiff, both all dressed up, probably on their way to the Kennedy Center or a cocktail party. The woman started to apologize, then elbowed her old man until he dug into his wallet. Cornell didn't pay much attention and instead found himself wondering how all these gorgeous young women ended up with these old geezers.

Never mind. He knew exactly how.

A few years ago he would have been competition for this bastard. Now he was a nuisance to take pity on. Although Cornell convinced himself that the woman had caught a glimpse of his irresistible charm. Yeah, charming the way he picked himself up from the sidewalk, smack-dab between the curb and the car's bumper. Lucky he hadn't pissed himself. He could still feel the heat of the engine.

11

But the woman — she was something. There was eye contact between them. Yeah, she definitely made eye contact. Then a hint of a smile and even a slight blush when Cornell licked his lips at her while her escort wasn't looking. The guy had ducked his bald head to rifle through his wallet. Bastard was probably sorry now that he didn't have anything less than fifty-dollar bills.

In Cornell's mind that smile, that blush, screamed to him that in another place, another time, she'd gladly be giving him something more than her boyfriend's cash. And he took heart in their secret transaction, restoring a small piece of something he had lost but didn't miss until someone like this gorgeous woman reminded him that he wasn't who he used to be. Not only who he used to be, but now little more than garbage to be kicked or shoved to the curb. A small piece of him hated her for that, but he did appreciate the hell out of the fifty bucks.

It was more than he'd seen all month. And as if to prove to her, to prove to himself, that beneath the grime and sweat stains he was still that other person who could be charming and witty and smart, Cornell broke the fifty at a corner diner. He even sat at the counter, ordered soup and a grilled cheese. When he paid the bill he asked for ones. The waitress did a double take, turning the fifty over, her eyes narrowing as she examined the bill and then his face.

Cornell just smiled when she finally handed him his change. He folded and stuffed the ones carefully into the side pocket of his threadbare cargo pants, pleased that the button still closed solid and safe over his new stash.

When his food came — soup steaming, melted cheese oozing onto white porcelain — he sat paralyzed, staring at it. He hadn't seen anything quite so beautiful in a long time. There was a package of cute little crackers and a slice of pickle, utensils wrapped in a crisp white napkin. *A cloth napkin.* All of it seemed so foreign and for a minute Cornell couldn't remember what he was supposed to do with real utensils rather than the plasticware they gave you in the soup kitchens.

He resisted looking around. Dishes clanked, voices hummed, machines wheezed on and off, chairs scraped the linoleum. The place was busy, yet Cornell could feel eyes checking him out.

He tugged the napkin open, laid the utensils one by one on the counter, and draped the cloth over his lap. He ignored the stares, pretending that the stink of body odor wasn't coming from him. He tried to keep his appearance as clean as possible, even making a monthly trip to a Laundromat, but getting a shower was a challenge.

Finally Cornell picked up the soup spoon, stopping his eyes from darting around for direction. He let his fingers remember. Slowed himself down and ate, painfully conscious of every movement so that he didn't dribble, smack, wipe, or slurp.

Now, as he made his long way back to his cardboard home, he took guarded sips from the brand-new bottle. The food, though delicious, had upset his stomach. The whiskey would help. It always did; an instant cure-all for just about anything he didn't want to feel or remember or be. Tonight it sped up the long walk and even helped warm him as the night chill set in.

Cornell had barely turned the corner into the alley when he noticed something was wrong. The air smelled different. Rancid, but not day-old garbage. And tinged with something burned.

No, not burned, smoking.

His nostrils twitched. There were no restaurants nearby. The brick building he kept his shelter against had been empty. It

14

was quiet here. That's all he cared about and usually the Dumpster didn't overflow or stink. All important factors in his decision to take up residency here in the alley, his Maytag box sandwiched between the wall of the brick building and the monster green Dumpster.

That's when Cornell realized he couldn't see his cardboard box. Though hidden, a flap usually stuck out no matter how carefully he tucked it. A sudden panic twisted his stomach. He clenched the bottle tight in his fist and hurried. He hadn't had that much to drink yet, but his steps were staggered and his head dizzy. The only two blankets he owned were in that box, along with an assortment of other treasures tucked between folds, stuff he hadn't wanted to lug inside his backpack.

As he walked closer, the smell got stronger. Something sour and metallic but also something else. Like lighter fluid. Had someone started a fire to keep warm?

They sure as hell better not have used his box for kindling.

That's when he saw a flap of cardboard and a flood of relief washed over him in a cold sweat. The box was still there. It had been shoved deeper behind the Dumpster. The box, however, wasn't empty.

Son of a bitch!

Cornell couldn't believe his eyes. Some bastard lay sprawled inside his home, feet sticking out. Looked like a pile of old, ragged clothes if it weren't for those two bare feet.

He took a long gulp of Jack Daniel's. Screwed the cap back on, nice and tight, and set the bottle down safe against the brick wall. Then Cornell pushed up his sleeves to his elbows and stomped the rest of the way.

Nobody was taking his frickin' home away from him.

"Hey, you," he yelled as he grabbed the ankles. "Get the hell out of here."

Cornell let his anger drive him as he twisted and yanked and pulled. But he was surprised it didn't take much effort. Nor was there any resistance. He didn't stop, though, dragging the body away from the container, letting the intruder's tangled hair sweep across the filthy pavement. Before he released the ankles he gave one last shove, flipping the person over.

That's when Cornell saw why there had been no resistance.

He felt the acid rise from his stomach. He stumbled backward, tripping over his feet, scrambling then kicking, gasping and retching at what he saw.

The face was gone, a bloody pulp of flesh and bones. Raw jagged holes replaced an eye and the mouth. Matted hair stuck to the mess.

Cornell pushed to his knees just as the soup and grilled cheese came up his throat in a stinging froth mixed with whiskey. He tried to stand but his legs wobbled and sent him back down to the pavement right in the middle of his vomit. His eyes burned and blurred but he couldn't pull them away from the mangled mess just a few feet away from him.

In his panic he hardly noticed the smoke filling the alley. He tried to wipe himself off and saw that it wasn't just his vomit he'd fallen into. A slick stain trailed into the alley, as if someone had accidentally leaked a line of liquid all the way to the Dumpster.

That's when he realized the slick stain that now covered his knees and hands was gasoline. He looked up and saw a man at the entrance to the alley, pouring from a gallon can. Cornell slipped and jerked to his feet just as the guy noticed him. But instead of being startled or angry or panicked, the man did the last thing Cornell expected. He smiled and then he lit a match.

CHAPTER 2

Newburgh Heights, Virginia

Maggie O'Dell tried to push through the black gauze, her head heavy, her mind still swimming. There had been flashes of light — laser-sharp white and butane blue — before the pitch black. A steady throb drummed against her left temple. Soft, wounded groans came out of the dark, making her flinch, but she couldn't move. Her arms were too heavy, weighed down. Her legs numb. Panic fluttered through her.

Why couldn't she feel her legs?

Then she remembered the electric jolt — the memory of searing pain traveling through her body.

More panic. Her heart began to race. Her breathing came in gasps.

A gunshot blast and her scalp felt on fire.

That's when she smelled it. Not cordite, but smoke. Something actually was on fire. Singed hair. Burned flesh. Smoke and ashes.

The sound of plastic crinkled under fabric. And suddenly at the front of the darkened room Maggie could see her father lying in a satin-trimmed coffin, so quiet and peaceful while flames licked up the wall behind him.

She had had this dream many times before but still she was surprised to find him there, so close that all she had to do was look over the edge of the lace to see his face.

"They parted your hair wrong, Daddy," and Maggie lifted her hand, noticing how small it was but glad to finally be able to move it. She reached over and pushed her father's hair back in place. She wasn't afraid of the flames. She concentrated only on her fingers as they stretched across his face. She was almost touching him when his eyes blinked open.

That's when Maggie jerked awake.

Flashes of light, tinged blue, came from the muted big-screen television. Maggie's eyelids twitched, still heavy despite her desperate attempt to open them. She pushed herself up and immediately recognized the feel of the leather sofa. Still, her head and heart pounded as her body pivoted, looking for shadows, expecting the embodiment of the wounded moans in the corners of her own living room.

But there was no one.

No one except Deborah Kerr, who filled the TV screen. Deborah's face was as worried and panicked as Maggie felt. She was running on a beach in the middle of a storm. Somewhere Robert Mitchum was hurt, injured.

Maggie had seen this movie many times and yet she felt Deborah's panic each time. *Heaven Knows, Mr. Allison.* It was one of Maggie's favorites. She had just defended it to her friend Benjamin Platt during one of their classic-movie marathons. Which had prompted her to pull it out. But tonight she was alone. At the moment, it was just her and Deborah.

She sat up. Leaned back against the soft leather and rubbed her left temple. Sweat matted her hair to her forehead. Her heartbeat started to settle down but the familiar throb continued. Under her fingertips she could feel the puckered skin on her scalp. The scar no longer hurt even when she pressed down on it like she did now. But the throbbing continued. All too predictably it would lead to a massive headache, a pain that started as a sharp pinpoint in her left temple but would soon swirl around inside her head.

Eventually it would settle at the base of her skull, pressing against the back of her brain, a steady dull ache threatening to drive her mad. Even sleep — which came infrequently and often in short bursts — gave her little relief. She had no idea if the insomnia was the result of her nightmares or if the threat of nightmares kept her awake. All Maggie knew was that any sleep, no matter how short, was accompanied by a film version of her memories — the edited horror edition, looped together. This newest sequel included clips from four months ago. Teenagers attacked in a dark forest, two electrocuted, the rest reduced to frightened and wounded moans.

Her fingers found the scar again under her hair. Just another scar, she told herself, and she wished she could forget about it. If it weren't for the headaches she might be able to put it out of her mind for at least a day or two.

Last October she had been shot . . . in the head. Actually the bullet had grazed her temple. Perhaps it was asking too much to forget so quickly. She did wish that everyone around her would forget it. That's why she wouldn't tell anyone about the headaches.

Her boss, Assistant Director Raymond Kunze, already thought she was "compromised," "altered," "temporarily unfit for duty." So far she had managed to avoid and put off his insistence that she go through a psychological evaluation. Her only leverage in delaying it was that Kunze felt responsible for sending her on the detour that resulted in her almost being killed. Not that he would admit responsibility. Instead he let her off the hook, claiming he had a soft spot for the holidays. Funny, when she thought about Kunze and Christmas, Maggie could easily conjure up the image of the Grinch who stole Christmas. But now that the holidays were long over, she expected Kunze would push for the evaluation.

Deborah Kerr found Robert Mitchum just as Maggie realized she could still smell something scorched and sooty. Was the smoke *not* a figment of her nightmare? Could something in the house be on fire?

In the dark corner of the television screen she saw movement. Not flames but a flicker of motion that was not a part of the movie. A reflection. A figure. A man walking across the doorway of the room behind her.

Someone was in her house.

CHAPTER 3

The dogs were gone.

Maggie should have noticed sooner. They were always at her feet.

Her eyes darted around the dim living room. She sank into the sofa and remained still. It was better if he thought he hadn't been spotted. He may not have seen her. Instead, he stayed in the kitchen.

She kept the corner of the TV screen in her line of vision. If he came up behind her she'd see him.

Or would she?

As scenes changed in the movie so did the corner reflection.

Maggie tried to remember where her weapons were. Her faithful Smith & Wesson service revolver was upstairs in her bedroom. A Sig Sauer was down the hall in a bottom desk drawer. She had never before felt the need for a gun inside her home. As soon as she moved into the two-story Tudor, she had installed a state-of-the-art security system. She'd taken great care to create barriers outside as well. Not to mention two overprotective dogs who would never allow an intruder inside. And for the first time Maggie felt sick to her stomach.

Where were Harvey and Jake?

She couldn't bear the thought of either dog injured or dead.

A quiet *click-swoosh* came from the kitchen, and the room brightened. Her intruder had opened the refrigerator.

Maggie slumped farther down on the sofa. Waited. Listened.

She slid her body off the cushions, dropping her knees onto the floor, now wishing she had carpeting to muffle her movement. Ironically that's why she didn't have a shred of carpeting in the house. Not because she loved the gorgeous wood floors but because floor coverings concealed footsteps. Thank goodness she had on socks.

Maggie kept her focus on the corner reflection, her new angle giving her a new view. She saw his hunched back. He was looking inside her refrigerator. She grabbed a glass paperweight from the side table. Quietly she crawled to the doorway, sliding against the wall and hugging the shadows.

What did you do with my dogs, you bastard?

She let the anger drive her as she inched closer to the door.

She could smell him. He reeked of smoke and charred wood. So it hadn't been her nightmare playing tricks on her imagination.

He reached inside the refrigerator, unaware of her presence, leaving himself vulnerable. She clutched the paperweight tight in her fist and swung it high, ready to bring it down on the back of the man's head. Then she took a deep breath and charged through the doorway. He startled and spun around, and Maggie stopped her arm in midair.

"Damn it, Patrick. You scared the hell out of me."

"That makes two of us."

"I almost bashed your head in."

Her brother squatted down to the floor, obviously weak-kneed, sitting back on his haunches. In the light from the opened refrigerator behind him Maggie could see the soot smeared on his forehead. His fingers clenched the door handle.

"I didn't want to wake you," he said, struggling to his feet. He was a firefighter, young and in great shape, and yet Maggie had reduced him to a frazzled pile on her kitchen floor.

"I didn't expect you until the end of the week."

"We finished early. I should have called." Then he added with a smile, "Sorry. I'm not used to having someone to call."

And Maggie wasn't used to having someone come home.

They were still learning their way around each other. Maggie had invited her half brother, Patrick, to stay with her when he graduated from the University of New Haven in December. Armed with a new degree in fire science, he was anxious to add experience to his résumé and had taken a job as a private firefighter. The company maintained contracts in thirteen states, so Patrick spent most of his time away, using Maggie's house as a home base in between assignments.

They had just found out about each other in the last several years. Maggie's mother had kept her father's infidelity a secret for more than twenty years. Likewise, Patrick's mother had told him only that his father had died a hero. There had been no mention, no hint, no clue that a sister existed, half or otherwise. It was an agreement the two women had wielded after the man they both loved died suddenly, leaving each of them with a child to raise on her own.

So here they were, two fatherless children, now adults, learning to be siblings.

"You mind if I have some of this pizza?" He pointed to the box he had been reaching for on the top shelf of the refrigerator.

"Help yourself."

Maggie knew it wouldn't be easy. She had become an intensely private person. She actually liked living alone, and she liked — no, it was more than that — she *craved* solitude. So it wasn't a surprise when she and Patrick began an ongoing battle almost as soon as he'd arrived. The surprising part was that it had nothing to do with typical issues of sibling rivalry or even territorial roommate disputes. Not about money or food or dirty socks in inappropriate places. If only it could have been something that simple.

No, Maggie didn't approve of Patrick's new employer. Worse than that — she questioned the ethics of the Virginia-based corporation and she couldn't understand why Patrick didn't.

Braxton Protection sold high-end, expensive insurance policies — the Cadillac of policies, offering protection for elite homeowners who could afford it. Part of that special protection included a private crew of firefighters if the need arose. In other words, Patrick had chosen to be a sort of mercenary. Instead of a gun for hire, he was a hose for hire.

Maggie wasn't sure why she couldn't just shut up and pretend it didn't matter. Patrick wanted the accelerated experience. What was wrong with that? Why wait around a real fire station for a fire when you can dive right in to monster wildfires threatening catastrophes? And if people could afford it, why shouldn't they be able to purchase special protection? Or so their arguments, or rather their discussions, went.

"So what happens," she had countered, "when you have to drive around a house that's already engulfed in flames to go hose down a house miles away?"

That's when Patrick would shrug and give her a boyish grin that reminded her of their father.

And right now he looked like a twenty-five-year-old who was exhausted and hungry. He must have come directly from the fire. Soot smudged his forehead and lower jaw. His hair was still damp with sweat from his helmet. The cowlick — their father's cowlick, even on the same side — stood straight up and Maggie fought the urge to reach out and smooth it down, just like she did every single time she dreamed about her father in his casket. That's what had sent her spiraling into the nightmare. She had smelled smoke. Patrick reeked of it.

"Did you drive directly from the site?" she asked, trying to remember where he had been this past week.

"Yeah."

He left the open box of leftover pizza on the island countertop while he popped open a can of Diet Pepsi. He slid onto one of the bar stools, suddenly stopping and hopping off like the seat was on fire.

"Sorry. I guess I smell bad." A slice of pizza in one hand, the Pepsi in the other, he looked back to see if he had gotten the bar stool dirty.

"Don't worry about it. Sit."

Maggie grabbed a slice of the pizza and took a seat next to him, waving at him to sit back down.

He hesitated and Maggie hated how tentative and how polite he still was around her. Almost as if he were waiting for her to change her mind, change the locks. She blamed herself. There were twelve years between them, and she was supposed to be the mature one. What a joke that was. She had no idea how to do this family thing. She purposely kept people at a safe distance. She had lived alone a long time and hadn't

29

shared living quarters since her divorce.

Other than Harvey and Jake.

That's when she bolted off her bar stool.

"Where are the dogs?"

The panic from her nightmare returned, showing itself in her voice.

"I let them out in the backyard." But Patrick was already on his feet again.

In three steps Maggie was at the back door, punching in the security code and flipping on the patio light.

"Jake's been digging out." She tried to calm herself. "One of the neighbors threatened to shoot him if he finds him in his front yard again."

"You're kidding. That's crazy."

But Patrick was beside her as she flung open the door.

Both dogs came loping out of the dark bushes, white and black, side by side, tongues hanging out, noses caked with dirt.

"Looks like he's gotten Harvey to help him." Patrick laughed.

It was funny and Maggie smiled, relieved despite the tightness in her chest. Four months ago Jake had saved her life. She wanted him to feel safe here, to feel like he finally had a home, and yet he insisted on escaping like she had infringed on his freedom. Maybe she had been wrong in tak-

30

ing him away from the vast openness of the Nebraska Sandhills. She had wanted to save him, like she had saved Harvey, but maybe Jake had never needed saving.

The dogs lapped up water, sharing the same bowl, leaving dirt in the bottom. Patrick and Maggie returned to their pizza just as Maggie's cell phone began to ring.

She checked the time — 1:17 in the morning. This couldn't be good. For some reason she thought about her mother, but knew it was just Catholic guilt for not telling her about Patrick staying here. Not like it was a problem. Her mother rarely came to her house. Finally she grabbed her phone and saw the caller's number displayed on the screen.

"Detective Racine," Maggie answered instead of offering a greeting.

"Hey, sorry to wake you."

"No, it's okay. I was already up."

Maggie was surprised. Usually Julia Racine's brisk manner didn't include an apology no matter what time of day. It took a lot to soften up the District homicide detective. Maggie had witnessed the occurrence only a handful of times.

"I already called Tully. Our firefly's been busy," Racine said without much pause. "And this time he's left us a body."

CHAPTER 4

Washington, D.C.

R. J. Tully flashed his badge at the uniformed cop patrolling the first set of crime scene ribbons. The guy nodded and Tully slipped under. He wished he'd grabbed something warmer than his trench coat.

And, damn, when had he gotten a stain on the lapel?

Didn't matter. His choices had been limited. Staying overnight at Gwen Patterson's was still something new. With his daughter, Emma, away and in her second semester of college, there wasn't any excuse to hurry back home, but he hated the idea of having two different sets of clothes at two different houses. He had been married for thirteen years, on his own now for more than five. Maybe he was too set in his ways to be in a relationship.

Gwen had generously given him his own drawer at her house and his own side of a closet, almost twelve inches next to her soft and colorful fabrics. His space looked pathetic with only an extra shirt and an extra pair of trousers. That's all he had hung there. None of it seemed right. It felt like he was playing house at someone else's place and he didn't like it no matter how much he loved Gwen.

When the phone call woke them both, Tully should have been reluctant to leave, disappointed or something — anything, but not relieved.

Thank God, Gwen had been too sleepy-eyed to notice.

He stepped aside. Let two firefighters tromp past him headed into the billowing smoke. Before sunrise he guessed this one would be a two-alarm. In less than a week Tully had learned more about fires than he cared to know.

Another thing about staying at Gwen's — it put him at the scene sooner than perhaps he wanted to be here. This time of night it was a short five- to ten-minute drive from her Georgetown condo. Ordinarily it would have taken him thirty to forty minutes to get to the District from his bungalow in Reston, Virginia.

He took advantage of being early. Found a spot downwind from the smoke. The flames actually felt good against his back, warming the chilled night air, letting him forget the thinness of his trench coat. The days had been unseasonably warm for February but the evenings were still a reminder that winter was not over.

Tully pushed up his eyeglasses. He pulled out a pen, and his fingers checked his pockets for something, anything, to write on. He settled for a sales receipt. Then he found a spot under an oak tree, safely out of the way, and started to examine the gathering onlookers.

Son of Sam had admitted to starting hundreds of fires. Even before he shot his first victim, he claimed to be a serial arsonist. He'd set a fire, then stand off by himself someplace where he wouldn't be noticed. He'd watch the blaze, enjoy the chaos, and masturbate.

Tully studied the faces in the glow of the flames, trying to ignore, to shut out the crackling *whoosh* behind him. A camerawoman and a reporter had already stationed themselves up close to the ribbon.

How did they get here this soon?

Tully jotted down, "Who called in fire?"

Then he looked beyond them, beyond the bystanders. He searched the shadows, scanning the alleyways and sidewalks across the

34

street. He let his eyes move over the rooftops. He checked each window, side by side
and row by row in the neighboring buildings. As far as he knew, these were warehouses, not residences, so it would be
strange, or at least unusual, to see movement or lights on any of the floors.

He moved to the other side of the tree and
started the process again with the adjacent
block. That's when it struck him that the
few bystanders looked like homeless people.
He was used to seeing what he called the
city's "night crew." Drug dealers, prostitutes, overnight delivery men, and cabbies.
They were usually the only ones out at this
time of night. But he never got used to seeing the homeless, with their hollowed-out
cheeks and vacant eyes, reminding him of
walking zombies.

"Hey, Tully."

The voice startled him so much it made
him jump. Probably thinking about zombies
didn't help.

Tully glanced over his shoulder. Detective
Julia Racine wore jeans and a leather
bomber jacket, unzipped — her badge and
weapon on display. There was always something Racine did or said that made her seem
tougher than Tully knew she was. Tonight it
was the unzipped jacket on a cold night,

plus a swagger and now a swipe of her hand through her short spiky hair, which was still wet from a quick shower.

"What are you doing out here in the shadows?" she asked.

She didn't expect or wait for an answer. It was Racine who had called him and this was her greeting. He was used to it by now.

"He's here," Tully said, almost under his breath, and he didn't move. His eyes returned to the adjacent building.

He wasn't sure Racine had even heard him. She came up beside him and stood stock-still, hands in her pockets, so close he could smell coconut and lime. Probably her shampoo, and it was enough for Tully to think that the aroma canceled out her swagger and her unzipped "I'm too tough to get cold" tough-guy message. It was one of the things Tully liked about working with women, though he'd never in a hundred years admit it — they always smelled so much better than men.

"Fifty-five percent of arsonists are under eighteen," she said with no emotion and without a glance in his direction, all business as usual.

She studied the clusters of people while Tully continued to go from window to window, floor to floor.

"You've been reading too many worthless statistics."

He stopped at the third floor of the brick building on the corner. He could have sworn he saw a flash through the window. Did it come from inside the building or was it only a reflection of the flames?

"Body's outside," Racine said. "It's in the alley behind a Dumpster."

"Outside?"

That didn't sound right to Tully. The other fires had had no casualties. A body usually meant the acceleration of an arsonist, the next step. Fire wasn't enough to achieve the same high so they started setting fires to occupied buildings. But if the body was outside, it was hardly a casualty.

"Someone who made it out but too late?"

Racine shook her head and pulled a notebook from her pocket. Started flipping pages. Tully kept his hand in his pocket, fingering his crunched receipts. Why couldn't he ever remember to carry a notebook?

"Separate call about the body," Racine said, finding her notes.

Tully glanced over. Even her handwriting was neat and clean, not the scratches and odd abbreviations he used.

"Person said there was a — quote — stiff

with half its face gone in the alley by the Dumpster."

"By the Dumpster? Not in the Dumpster?"

Racine flipped a few more pages and returned to the same one. "Yep. By, not in. Fire chief told me she's not burned. We have to wait until it's safe for us to enter the burn zone."

"That changes things," Tully said.

"Yep, it sure does."

They stood silently side by side again, eyes preoccupied. Seconds ticked off. Behind them firefighters called out to their crew members. Pieces of soot with sparks floated through the air like tiny fireworks filling the night sky. At the last fire someone had mentioned that they looked like fireflies, and soon after they started calling the arsonist the firefly. Tully figured it made about as much sense as firebug.

It was Racine who broke the silence. "So you suppose the bastard's right here watching and jerking off?"

That's exactly what Tully had been thinking earlier, but he knew it wasn't that simple, especially if this guy had now started to kill and hadn't even bothered to set the body on fire. Again, he didn't glance at her, but he did smile. "You've been reading way too much Freud."

CHAPTER 5

Maggie parked a block away. Her head had started its familiar throb, same side, same place, drilling a *rap-a-tap* into her left temple. She stayed behind the steering wheel of her car. Black clouds of smoke billowed over the area. She stared at the flames shooting out the windows and devouring the roof of the four-story building. Even a block away the sight paralyzed her. It kicked her heartbeat up and squeezed the air out of her lungs.

She tried to slow her breathing. Closed her eyes and gently rubbed her fingertips, starting over her eyelids and moving to her temples. Small gentle circles, trying to ignore the scar.

This is temporary, she told herself. She was going to be okay. How could she expect to get shot in the head and bounce right back?

She tried to focus on why she was here. And yet all she could think about was how angry fire always looked. Flames like this reminded her of those grade school cat-echism books with colorful illustrations of what the gates of hell were supposed to look like. Where killers and rapists were sent. Where evil was punished. Not where loved ones raced in and never came out.

Not for the first time, she wondered about her father, and now Patrick. How could they go charging into the middle of raging fires when her entire body kept telling her to turn around and run?

She knew that fear of losing someone else important to her — that dread knotted at the pit of her stomach — had triggered these recent nightmares. That uncertainty riddled her sleep in between her regular bouts of insomnia. Her self-diagnosis spelled out the simple reason. This latest set of nightmares was caused by Patrick's coming to live with her, the fact that he reminded her of their father, and, of course, his new job, which put him into the same danger that had cost their father his life.

Tonight for a fleeting moment when Patrick stood in front of the refrigerator and looked up at her — right before she almost bashed in his skull — Maggie was struck by how much he looked like their father. Thomas O'Dell had been only six years older than Patrick was now when he ran into that burning building and cemented Maggie's image of him forever in her mind, the mind of a twelve-year-old girl.

Simple enough. Psychology 101.

She was used to having nightmares. It was one of the reasons she didn't sleep. Maybe a good night's sleep was asking too much in her line of work. She chased killers for a living and in order to catch them she sometimes had to crawl inside their heads, walk around in their skin.

Long ago her mentor, Assistant Director Kyle Cunningham, had taught her how to deal with it through his example. He was a master of compartmentalizing, shoving and stacking different killers and victims into different parts of his mind, separating them from one another and from the emotions and memories they caused.

He was a master of sectioning his life into separate cubicles. Such a master, in fact, that when he died, Maggie realized she knew little about his private life. Ten years she'd worked with him, admired and respected him, and yet she'd had no idea if he and his wife had any children, a family pet, or a favorite vacation spot. And now that he was gone she couldn't ask him what to do when some of her carefully sealed compartments started to leak. How was she supposed to stop them from seeping into her subconscious? For the last year Maggie had been trying to keep them from flooding her sleep with nightmares. And now Patrick and these arsons . . .

She took a deep breath and made herself get out of the safety of her vehicle. She cinched her jacket and shoved her hands into the pockets for warmth. At the last fire, she had hated how damp and chilled she'd gotten. Her clothes reeked of smoke despite putting on Tyvek coveralls.

What was worse was getting wet, little by little, spray by spray. She'd never considered that investigating a fire scene could leave her feeling like she'd stepped into a rain of cinder and ice water mixed with foam. All of it dripped from the charred skeleton of the building. From the rafters that dared to hang on and the pieces of ceiling that defied gravity. It was like walking inside the dark hollows of a dying creature. One that still hissed and groaned and bled.

Not that Maggie was squeamish about blood. She'd been sprayed with it, splattered with it, and rolled in it, had even felt her own leaking out. She had dealt with murderers, killers, and terrorists. Had profiled their motives — power, greed, revenge, sexual gratification.

But arson? This was her first experience with arson and she was having trouble deciphering the motives of someone who set fires deliberately.

She and Tully had been called in as profilers. Neither was sure why, but then their director had been sending both of them on strange and wild cases in the last year. Maggie guessed there might be some politics involved. There always seemed to be with Assistant Director Kunze. A favor, a payback, some piece of legislation that needed to be passed or some scandal that needed covering up. She never thought she'd be working for a man she not only didn't respect but also didn't trust.

At first glance this case seemed to be that of a typical serial arsonist. He chose a warehouse in the middle of the night when no one would be inside. That fact made Tully and Maggie believe he was a nuisance offender, setting fires for attention, for kicks. He really didn't want to hurt anyone. Just enjoyed watching the chaos and the sense of power it gave him.

He'd now chosen another warehouse. But tonight was different. Racine had said there was a body. That changed everything.

Maggie walked slowly, approaching the

scene from a distance, giving herself a big-picture view but also trying to calm herself and reverse the strong instinct to flee. She had to physically coax her entire body — from her rapid pulse to her staggered breaths — to go toward the flames. It didn't help matters that she could already feel the heat.

The smell of smoke assaulted her nostrils almost immediately, gaining strength as she approached. She could hear the violent hisses, the crackle and pop as flames ate away chunks of the building, leaving other pieces to crash down. It sounded like trees being timbered — a slight *crack* followed by a *whoosh* and then the crash.

Unnerving sights and sounds and smells.

Stick to your job, she told herself. *Observe. Look for any clues he may have left.*

She walked by an empty lot under construction where the bulldozers and huge equipment with clawed scoops and trucks with dump wagons seemed out of place in this landscape. Her eyes jumped from cab to cab — dark and abandoned for the night. A sign three feet back from the sidewalk announced it to be the future home of something called the D.C. Outreach House. Even if she hadn't noticed the small print "in partnership with the U.S. Department of

Housing and Urban Development (HUD)," Maggie would have guessed that in a neighborhood of warehouses and displaced homeless people, the project was most likely another sleep shelter. For now it amounted to several piles of concrete chunks and yellow monster-size equipment.

She continued up the street, glancing down alleys and into door wells. Her eyes darted up to rusted fire escapes and instinctively her right hand reached inside her jacket. Her fingertips brushed over the leather holster cinched tight against her left side. She settled her fingers on the butt of her revolver as she peered inside vehicles parked along the curb.

She was close enough to the fire now that the hisses and the whoosh of flames were the dominant sounds on an otherwise quiet night. Traffic had been cordoned off. There was no one on this street. No voices or footsteps. Behind darkened windows there were no silhouettes, no movement, no sounds coming from the warehouses that were closed and locked up for the night. Everyone who had been in the area was now pressed against the crime scene tape's perimeter about two hundred feet away. In fact, there was absolutely no evidence of anyone, and yet Maggie stopped in her tracks. Slowly, she turned completely around.

He was here.

She could feel someone watching. A sixth sense. A gut instinct. There was nothing scientific on which to base the claim.

She stood perfectly still and started once again to examine the buildings. She scanned the doors and windows. Was he looking out at her? Her eyes darted up to the rooftops. She looked at the empty lot she'd just passed. But still she saw no movement, no shadows. She heard no footsteps.

"Hey, O'Dell," someone yelled from behind her.

Her head pivoted to see Julia Racine ducking under the crime scene tape, headed in her direction. But Maggie stayed put, her eyes darting back in the other direction, not ready to leave the empty street.

From the corner of her eye she saw a shadow peel away from under a lamppost. A flash of movement, nothing more. But now she wasn't sure. Sometimes the pounding in her temple blurred her vision.

Annoying. But it is temporary. It had to be temporary, she kept trying to convince herself. And she certainly wasn't going to let Julia Racine notice.

CHAPTER 6

He didn't much care about fire. It was a cheap way to get attention.

Sure was pretty, though.

Almost like fireworks on a dark July night. Lighting a fuse, the smell of sulfur, sparks followed by glittery explosions of color. Like a thousand shooting stars. Good memories.

He still remembered his momma frying chicken for their picnic basket. He and his brother would spend the entire morning helping to butcher those poor stupid birds — beaks chattering, beady eyes staring up at him even after the head was chopped off and lying on the ground. So very fascinating to watch.

That's where his mind was when he first saw her.

The street had been empty for quite a while. Everyone had gone to watch the flames like moths to the light. They came out of door wells and pulled themselves off warm grates in the sidewalk just to go take a look, and he shook his head as he watched the pathetic parade of the ragged.

But this woman wasn't one of them. She didn't belong here.

Even before he saw her hand reach inside her jacket he knew she was a cop. She was attractive. No, more than attractive. She was a real looker. Could have been a number of things other than a cop. But he recognized that confidence in her stride, the way she carried herself. Her head swiveled, a constant but subtle motion — up and down, side to side. She took in everything around her as casually as if she were window shopping. She was precise and efficient but with a sort of grace and composure that usually came with the maturity of someone older.

Yeah, she was good, and yet she still missed him.

To be fair, who really paid much attention to a construction site after hours? You just didn't expect anyone to be peeking around the ripper of a bulldozer or standing behind the rubble of pavement it had clawed up that day.

Besides, he didn't need to hide. He blended in most places without drawing suspicion. In fact, he could buy this woman a drink at the local cop watering hole and she'd never think twice about his being anything other than an interested citizen paying his respects. He'd done just that many times. He liked hanging out, listening to them. Got some of the best information directly from the cops. Details that would help him tweak his methods or give him fresh ideas for his future ventures.

Yeah, he liked cops. Respected them. Even admired them. Probably would have been one, once upon a time, if he hadn't become so successful in his own profession. Now he made too much money to even consider something in law enforcement. He was good at what he did, in demand. He liked his lifestyle. It gave him plenty of freedom for his outside interests, for his restless spirit and his curiosity-induced adventures.

He watched her walk the entire block, then suddenly she turned around.

Damn! She was good.

He stayed in the shadows and smiled. He'd never expected to find someone who piqued his interest here. A most unlikely place. He liked this lady cop. Liked that she could sense his presence. Made it interesting. A challenge.

She was confident, smart, strong-minded. He liked strong women. He particularly liked to hear them scream.

CHAPTER 7

"Hey, are you okay?"

Racine was right beside Maggie. Her voice so quiet and gentle, Maggie almost didn't recognize it.

She hated that tone, that look of concern. It grated on her nerves and shoved her guard carefully back into place. Since she'd gotten shot last October, too many people approached her like she might shatter or snap before their eyes. And she was getting sick and tired of it.

"I'm fine."

"You don't look so good." Racine dealt the second blow. At least, that's what it felt like.

Maggie's best friend, Gwen Patterson, had told her to ignore the kid-glove treatment. People were just showing their concern. Getting pissed off by it would only validate their concerns, their suspicions. Actually, Maggie added "suspicions." Gwen had used "concerns."

"I thought I saw someone. Back there behind the lamppost."

She saw Racine glance over to the area but her eyes didn't spend much time there and she looked back at Maggie.

Oh great! Now they'd all think she was paranoid, seeing things in the shadows.

"You said on the phone the body was outside." Maggie needed to change the subject, wipe that look of concern off Racine's face. "Where is it? Can we take a look?"

"It's in between the burning building and the next."

Maggie turned and started walking toward the perimeter, making Racine follow and hopefully transferring the detective's mind back to the scene and off Maggie's newly revealed vulnerability.

"We have to wait until the hose monkeys are finished," Racine said. "Just hope they don't wash away and trample all the trace. Right now they say it's too dangerous for us to be there." Then Racine shrugged and crossed her arms like they were in for a wait.

Maggie wanted to ask her, *Why didn't you wait to call me or say not to hurry?* Her patience ran thin with Racine, sometimes hanging on by a frayed thread. Maggie wasn't quite sure why the woman still pushed her buttons after five years. After all, they'd become friends . . . sort of friends.

In the beginning, Racine's reckless tactics had grated on Maggie. The young detective was all bravado, taking unnecessary risks, smart-mouthing and bullying her way through the ranks as though she believed it was necessary to compensate for being a woman. All the while it was like she was shouting, "Yeah, I'm a woman, you wanna make something of it?"

Even now Maggie wondered if Racine, with her jacket left open, was showing off her badge and gun or her full breasts in the tight knit shirt. Or both, as a way of constantly pushing, constantly daring. Racine's version of Dirty Harry's "Go ahead, make my day."

Maggie had spent her entire career doing just the opposite, trying to draw little attention to herself, wanting to blend in by wearing suits that matched her boss's style. She spent extra time at the shooting range, worked out, and kept in shape so she could defend herself and cover her partner's back. She didn't want special credit. Unlike Racine, the last thing she wanted her colleagues to notice was that she was a woman.

Now Maggie started to glance around,

pretending to assess the scene and trying to hide the fact that she was searching for an escape. She avoided looking into the fire. It could scald your eyes like looking into the sun. She saw Tully and had to hold back a sigh of relief.

Tall and lanky, R. J. Tully was one of the few men Maggie knew who looked good in a trench coat. And tonight, with his jaw clenched tight and his sight focused just as tightly on something or someone, he looked more like a spy out of a James Bond movie than an FBI agent. Something across the street had his attention.

Maggie headed in his direction and heard Racine following behind her.

"What is it?" Maggie asked him when Tully finally glanced over.

He tipped his head back toward the sidewalk, avoiding drawing attention by keeping his hands deep inside his coat pockets.

Maggie saw what he was looking at immediately.

News crews scrambled to find parking spaces. Some pulled and carried their equipment, jockeying to get as close to the crime scene as possible. There had to be a dozen of them. But one camerawoman and one reporter were already filming in a prime location, up against the perimeter. The

cluster of bystanders behind them was
enough to suggest that the news team had
gotten there and set up before other people
noticed the fire.

"How long have they been there?" Maggie
asked.

"They were already here when I arrived,"
Tully said, and both he and Maggie turned
to Racine.

"Now that I think about it, they beat me,
too."

CHAPTER 8

Samantha Ramirez held the camera in position with one hand. With her other she swiped and tucked a strand of wild hair back up into her baseball cap. She'd already tossed off her coat, yet sweat dripped down her forehead. Another line trickled down her back. Being close to the flames for this long made her feel like the Wicked Witch of the West, melting inch by inch. They had plenty of footage, but Jeffery insisted she leave the camera running.

"You never know what might still happen."

That's what he always said. And usually he was right. That's how they got lucky capturing an unexpected rescue off a rooftop after Katrina. Sometimes not so lucky, when they drew unpredictable rage. That's how they ended up recording the skid marks and trail behind Sam as she got dragged into a crowd of young male protesters in the streets of Cairo. The latter should have been enough warning for her to say, "Never again," if not for the additional footage that showed an equally enraged Jeffery Cole racing after her, grabbing a rifle right off the shoulder of a surprised soldier.

The machine gun had spit over the heads of the men who had their fingers dug into Sam's arms. They already had her shirt wadded into their fists, ripping at her, grabbing, poking, by the time the bullets zinged overhead. It wasn't until later, when Sam and Jeffery were safe back in the States reviewing the footage, that she saw the look on Jeffery's face, the one that had made the men drop her to the ground. The look that told them the next round of bullets wouldn't be in the air.

"I got your back, you got mine," he told her that day, and she'd been hard-pressed since then to argue.

Her Spanish-speaking mother, who lived with Sam to help care for Sam's six-year-old son, didn't like Jeffery. She called him "Diablo." Not to his face. Mostly she called him the devil when he woke the household in the middle of the night, like tonight. Her mother didn't know any of the details about the danger zones they traveled, but she suspected enough that she lit candles at St.

Jerome's Catholic Church every single Sunday.

The longer Sam worked with Jeffery, the more she wondered if her mother was right. Sometimes working with Jeffery Cole felt like she had, indeed, made a pact with the devil.

This was the third fire in less than ten days, but their bureau chief had told them to back off.

"No body count," he said. "Registers low on the sensational meter."

He called it an "oh-by-the-way blip," fifteen, maybe twenty seconds, tops.

Not even close to the feature spots Jeffery prized. Tallying seconds and minutes had become an obsession for Jeffery. He claimed he could find the feature in any news, peeling away the leaves like an artichoke until he got to the tasty heart.

That's what a good investigative reporter did, he'd lecture anyone who'd listen. Usually it was only Sam, who was unable to shrug off his bravado and walk away because there was an invisible chain that bonded them together. A chain, like handcuffs . . . actually more like an umbilical cord, because her life, her career, had come to depend on Jeffery's success.

She wasn't exactly happy or proud of that

fact, but she'd started living by the saying "It is what it is." A bracelet she never took off, the leather worn and the pewter pock-marked, had the words engraved on it. It was a constant reminder. Maybe she couldn't always control all the crap that was thrown at her, but she could damn well control what she made of it.

Her mother's version was a little more colorful: "It's your life. Only you can choose what you make with it, whether it's chicken salad or chicken shit."

She noticed that Jeffery had taken a break and gone off somewhere, either to find a responder to interview or to take a piss. She didn't keep track of him when he was off camera. Often she simply got lost in the world through the camera's viewfinder.

Now, suddenly coming up from behind her, he said, "Looks like we have company."

She glanced around without stopping what she was shooting. A tall man in a trench coat and two women were headed their way. They were on the inside perimeter of the crime scene tape. The tall woman in the bomber jacket was definitely a cop. Sam bet the other two were feds.

"Keep the camera running," Jeffery told her. "No matter what, keep me in the shot, too. Remember to get my good side."

Sam wanted to roll her eyes. Instead she repositioned the camera.

Here we go again. *You never know what might still happen.*

CHAPTER 9

"The bastards are like vultures."

Maggie ignored Racine's muttering. It was the fourth time she'd called the news media bastards during the short walk over. She wondered if Racine clumped her partner, Rachel, into that same category. Rachel worked for the *Washington Post.*

Maggie convinced Tully to let her take the lead even though he was definitely the better diplomat.

"Good evening," the reporter said, an announcement more than a greeting, like the opening to the morning news.

Maggie saw the international news station's logo on the side of the camera and now she recognized the reporter's voice as that of Jeffery Cole. She resisted the urge to wince. This wasn't some local affiliate. The camera was rolling and Cole believed he had an exclusive interview.

He moved clear around to the other side,

shifting the angle as if jockeying for a better profile of himself even at the expense of exchanging the flames behind them for the building across the street.

"Detectives, do you have some information about how this fire started? Or who might have started it? Do we have a serial arsonist loose in the District?"

"We're not here to answer any questions at this time," Maggie said. "I'm sure there'll be a media briefing later." She glanced at Tully and Racine, who appeared paralyzed in the camera's laser beam of light.

"Can you at least tell us whether anyone was hurt?" Cole continued. "Any fatalities? We haven't seen any victims brought out yet."

Maggie recognized the tactic. The rapid-fire questions that didn't wait for answers. Reporters did it all the time. Send out a barrage of questions, overwhelm, overload, tax the patience of the already exhausted cops in the hopes of getting a single piece of information. Cops were used to doing the exact same thing to criminal suspects. They just weren't used to having it done to them.

Racine started fidgeting and Maggie hoped the detective wouldn't do something reckless, like tell them to shut the frickin' camera off. Only Racine would come up with more colorful language or gestures that would require plenty of bleeps if ever broadcast. And Racine's comments would probably be the ones that *would* make the 24/7 loop in the cable news cycle.

Maggie also saw Tully's hand come out of his coat pocket, but he flexed his fingers and thankfully resisted the urge to shove the camera away or to put his hand over the lens. Both gestures would ensure a top-of-the-hour breaking news spot.

"Actually we need your help," Maggie said calmly, addressing Jeffery Cole, not the camera. "I'm sure you and your news organization would want to assist us in this investigation."

It was enough to stop the questions. In fact, Cole looked stunned. That's when Maggie realized the camerawoman had, indeed, been including him in the shot. The young woman flinched as she glanced over for his instructions. The camera bobbed just a notch.

"I'm sorry, Detective, but I hope I'm misunderstanding you and you're not really asking us to stop filming." He took several steps forward and so did the camerawoman.

Maggie didn't budge. She tried not to blink, although she now felt the camera's spotlight directly in her eyes. "No, that's not what I'm asking."

"Good, because that would be an infringement of our constitutional rights. There is such a thing, Detective, as freedom of the press. And we are allowed to film this and inform our viewers. It would benefit them if you could tell us if you have a suspect? Or if these random torchings will continue? Should they be afraid that it might be their neighborhood tomorrow night? Look around." He waved for the camerawoman to span the buildings across the street. "It could happen anywhere in the city."

"What an asswipe," Racine muttered behind Maggie and started walking away.

That's when Maggie heard a crack like thunder behind her. A second crack was followed by a *whoosh* that slammed her to the ground.

CHAPTER 10

Maggie felt the heat press against her and kept her face down in the damp grass. Shattered glass pelted a thousand needles into her back. When she dared take a peek over her shoulder she saw debris floating like feathers and leaving trails of sparks. A glittery mist lit up the night sky, only it wasn't rain.

Bystanders ran, some screamed, others were flattened to the ground like Maggie. Some weren't moving. Flames shot out of the gaping hole in the building across the street. More flames spewed from the blown windows, leap-frogging along the outside awnings until a lace of fire strung clear around the corners.

The moans and darkness took Maggie to another place, a too recent experience. The middle of a forest, thunder and lightning in place of roaring flames. Teenagers injured, two dead. A boy wrapped in barbed wire, bleeding and scared.

She shook her head, brought her elbows up to raise herself off the damp grass. She closed and rubbed her eyes. Without effort, her fingers found the scar at her left temple.

Sirens filled the air. She didn't even see the third fire unit arrive. Black boots stomped by with the rustling of heavy gear. She stayed down on her hands and knees, waiting for the swirl in her head to stop, not pleased when she realized it was simply an aggravated version of her new normal.

"You okay?"

Maggie nodded without looking up at Racine. Hadn't she just asked her that a few minutes ago? She tried to stand. The damn swirl dropped her back to her knees.

"Stay put for a while." A new voice.

She saw the hand on her shoulder before she felt it. When Maggie glanced up at Tully his eyes locked on hers, waiting to find assurance, then darted away, tracking the scene, coming back and pausing at hers for another beat or two before they continued their track again. He turned enough for Maggie to see the bloody back of his head, hair matted and red streaks running down his neck.

"You're bleeding." She reached up. Tried to stand, instinct overriding ability.

She didn't wave away his hand from under her elbow. Although for the last several months it was exactly the type of treatment she had resented.

"Careful," he said, the concern creasing his brow. "We're all bleeding."

He reached his hand to the back of her neck and brought it back to show her his fingertips, red and slick with her blood.

"Just take it easy. Are you okay?"

Her knees wobbled a bit. The swirl inside her head blurred her vision.

"I might not be okay," she confessed.

"I don't think you are either."

Again, she saw his arm around her shoulder without really feeling it.

"We need a paramedic over here."

She heard Tully's voice through a wind tunnel now.

The memory flashed in front of her like an old-fashioned film reel caught on a sprocket, jerking from scene to scene. The gun barrel against her head. A blast of light followed by the roar. The pain was intense — a driving pressure, scalding, then peeling off the side of her head.

Perhaps it really was unrealistic of her to think she could be shot in the head and just shrug it off.

Tully was still holding on to her. She

looked around the chaos and saw Racine with a group of uniformed officers. She was pushing back the crowds while standing tall and strong, legs spread, arms out waving, making room for the paramedics like a traffic cop. From where she and Tully stood, Maggie could see that the back of Racine's leather bomber jacket had been shredded. And Maggie's first thought was that Racine would be so pissed. She loved that jacket.

She tried to take a step but Tully's fingers tightened their grip, holding her back.

"Stay put, okay? Let's have a paramedic take a look at you first." His voice was quiet, gentle, and certainly didn't match his grip. "Let the first responders take care of everyone else." He stopped short of saying, *We'll just get in their way.*

She nodded. She understood. They weren't trained to take care of the wounded. It was a fact she had to accept, only recently discovering that it didn't sit well with her. She hated feeling useless, but the truth was, her skills and training couldn't help the living victims. Her and Tully's expertise wasn't needed until the victims were dead and could no longer tell their stories.

She knew Tully was right on both counts. She did need a paramedic. If she didn't have someone give her the all-clear signal, she'd have to put up with those damned looks of concern. So she stayed put.

Chaos surrounded them and an inferno roared on two sides. Rescuers stomped and yelled while they hauled equipment that lurched and whined. They pushed and shoved their way through. Some of the bystanders stood paralyzed and watched. And in the midst of the chaos, not fifty feet away, Cole and the camerawoman appeared totally unfazed by it all.

"This is Jeffery Cole," Maggie heard him say into the lens, "reporting live." He looked remarkably calm.

CHAPTER 11

Virginia

Patrick Murphy had lost track of how many hours he'd gone without sleep, *this time.* So far college had best prepared him for all-nighters. His fire science classes had barely scratched the surface of what Patrick had seen and done for the last several weeks.

That appeared to be true physically, too. He thought his body was well toned from a daily punishment of weights and two miles pounding the pavement, yet each time he returned from an assignment his muscles screamed at him in places on his body he had taken for granted.

Despite the aches and pains, he'd gladly get back on a fire truck for another assignment rather than be here, sitting in the luxurious lobby of corporate headquarters waiting to be reprimanded by his boss, whom he'd never met.

Patrick poked a finger into his collar, hoping to relieve the stranglehold. He'd also prefer wearing seventy-five pounds of gear rather than a suit and tie.

He checked his wristwatch. It probably cost more than a semester of tuition. It had been a signing bonus. Maybe they'd ask for it back. What was taking so long? Yet, according to the Swiss precision, it had been only eleven minutes.

Felt like forty-five.

At least Maggie hadn't come back to the house before he had left. He wasn't sure how he'd explain where he was going. Not that he had to. Their arrangement was more like roommates than siblings. They had to get to know each other, learn their quirks and pet peeves. Patrick had been on his own for a long time, even growing up. His mom had worked two jobs, leaving Patrick to fend for himself since he was the legal age to be left alone. Total latchkey kid.

She was a good mom, still was. And he understood she did what she did for both of them. As a result he'd grown up a bit sooner than his peers. While his friends were playing video games after school, Patrick sorted laundry and fixed grilled cheese for another dinner alone. He never minded. He liked that it had made him independent. And he knew all kinds of stuff that other guys his age didn't have a clue about. His mom called him an "old soul," and recently told him she regretted that she hadn't given him a chance to be a boy.

Maggie told him she had also been on her own since she was twelve, but Patrick saw in her eyes and heard in her voice a sadness that told him it wasn't the same.

She'd been great so far about his staying with her. Earlier this morning he wouldn't have blamed her if she had conked him over the head. It was totally rude not to let her know before he came barging in, especially during the middle of the night. He'd been too upset to even think, yet he had told her they finished their assignment early like it was no big deal. Like it was true.

Instead, he had been sent home early and was probably lucky he hadn't been fired on the spot.

"Mr. Murphy." The receptionist's voice was so soft and quiet Patrick wondered if she had called to him before and he just hadn't heard.

He started to stand. Stopped. Corrected himself and, despite a bad case of the nerves, managed to make his eagerness look like a scoot to attention, to the edge of his seat.

"Mr. Braxton can see you now." She

smiled and nodded at the door to his right.

Then she swiveled to pick up a ringing phone while Patrick stared at her, expecting further instructions.

He stood and waited a second. The door was closed. Was he supposed to knock? But her eyes were back on the computer while she talked into the phone. Even her attention was not coming back to him. After his mistake of not warning Maggie of his presence and since he was already in hot water, he chose to knock.

"Come on in," a voice with a Southern drawl answered.

The voice and the man who stood beside the sleek iron and glass-top desk were nothing like Patrick expected. The bank of floor-to-ceiling windows showed treetops and blue sky, and Braxton looked like he was posing for a photo with one of those fake too-good-to-be-true backdrops.

The mountain of a man with a sprinkle of silver in his hair offered Patrick a beefy hand. "You must be Murphy."

The unexpected grip crushed Patrick's hand.

"Yes, sir."

"I'm golfing in an hour, so you'll have to excuse my attire." The Southern accent made "attire" sound like two words, "a tire."

"My wife buys these shirts for me with the little polo player on them."

The knit shirt was bright blue, the khakis well pressed. The tops of the leather moccasins were well polished.

"Guess she's always hoping she can make this ol' boy look fashionable." Again, "fashionable" was drawn out into separate words. He gave Patrick an easy, genuine smile as he waved him to take a seat in front of his desk. "You married, son?"

The question disarmed Patrick, though he tried to conceal that. "No, sir."

This wasn't anywhere near the conversation he'd had going through his mind all morning.

"When you find the right one, son, don't let her go."

Braxton's eyes were on the framed picture that took up the left front corner of his desk's pristine glass top. The woman looked young and small compared to her husband, tanned, with lean arms and friendly crinkles at her eyes. Both of them wore khakis and polo shirts, hers pink, his a different version of today's blue.

Patrick had no clue what the correct response was, so he simply said, "I'll try to remember that, sir."

This time Braxton's eyes found Patrick's

and held them. "You be sure and do that, son." But the playfulness had been replaced with something sober. There was almost a sad tinge to his voice. "Hands down, that's the best advice I can give anyone. You find a good thing, don't let go."

Not hesitating, he tapped his index finger on the one file folder on his desk. "Well then, let's see what we've got here," he said as he opened it.

Patrick's palms began to sweat. Was it possible the man didn't know yet why he was meeting with him? He realized he was holding his breath as he watched Braxton slip on reading glasses and start to thumb through the contents.

"Master's degree in fire science," Braxton said without looking up. "Impressive."

This wasn't supposed to be a job interview. Patrick already had the job. The question was, Would he be allowed to keep it? Or did his background somehow help plan his punishment? Perhaps Braxton had decided to go easy on Patrick because he knew how serious he was about being a professional firefighter. The man had to have already looked over his file, didn't he?

"Worked your way through college as a bartender. Even volunteered for a community fire station. Very admirable."

Patrick eased his back into the chair, relaxing a bit from being on the edge. He set his sweaty palms on his thighs. All those extra hours and all-nighters would finally pay off. Someone finally saw the value. He could breathe again and had to stop an almost audible sigh of relief.

"You must want to be a firefighter pretty bad?" Braxton looked up, gave him a tight smile.

"Yes, sir."

Patrick had relaxed just enough that he didn't see the undercut coming.

"Son, I catch you saving another pansy-ass's house who's not a paying policyholder of ours, and you won't just be without a job, but this two-bit degree of yours won't land you another. You know why? Because I'll make sure no one — and I mean no one — will hire you ever again, as a chimney sweep let alone a firefighter."

The tight smile showed bright teeth but the eyes were cold blue marbles when he added, "You think you can *try* and remember that, son?"

"Yes, sir."

CHAPTER 12

Washington, D.C.

R. J. Tully fingered the small cartridge in his trench coat's pocket. The camerawoman had handed it over too easily. Even offered that the live feed would have been recorded at the station and could be viewed there.

Now, as Tully looked down at the body beside the Dumpster, he doubted there would be much to see on the film. This killer had done all his dirty work well in advance of the fire. Tully didn't need any experts to point out the trail of accelerant that had been poured along the side of the building. Black cinder marked the brick wall and he could still smell gasoline.

Judging by this and the timing of the second blast, both fires had been carefully orchestrated. Chances were, the guy was long gone. Maybe even home watching on TV, enjoying from the warmth of his living room the same film footage Tully now had in his pocket. But gut instinct gnawed at Tully. He still believed the guy who started the fire was here tonight, watching and enjoying the chaos.

"We can't assume she belongs with the building."

Really? Tully wanted to say but stayed quiet.

He'd met Brad Ivan, the investigator for the Bureau of Alcohol, Tobacco, Firearms and Explosives, only last week, and already the man's talent for stating the obvious grated on Tully's nerves. It didn't help matters that he had an irritating nasal voice. His upper lip disappeared when Ivan was deep in thought. He tucked it under his bottom teeth, a nervous gesture that made him look like a horse chomping down on a bit.

"I don't think he killed her here," Racine said, and both men stared at her. It took her a minute to realize that they were waiting for an explanation. She waved a thumb over her shoulder to the opening in the alley. "This whole block is hotel homeless. Same as last week's fires." She said it like she couldn't believe neither of them had noticed. "First of all, she's not homeless." She pointed to the woman's feet. "Not with that pedicure. It took some time to bash the face in like that. Somebody would have heard or seen it."

"And they wouldn't have heard someone dragging and dumping a body?" Ivan blew out a breath of disbelief.

"No dragging necessary. Pull a car up to the Dumpster. Open the trunk. Lift and dump." She brushed her hands together. "Takes five, ten minutes. Not much to notice. He just drives out the other side of the alley and is on his way."

Tully nodded. Times like this he appreciated Racine's no-nonsense theories. It made Ivan's slow, analytical process sound as off-key as Ivan was. Sometimes a spade was a spade even after all the tests and assessments and studies.

Ivan put his hand to his chin — another mannerism that grated on Tully's patience — closed fist, bent index finger jutting out, creating a perfect shelf for the square dimpled chin. No answer. Not even a nod.

"I've got a couple uniforms already talking to the regulars." Racine didn't wait for agreement. Tully knew she could care less what Ivan thought.

"Think they'll be willing to share information?" Tully asked.

"Those who aren't too stoned or tripped out will. These alleys are their homes. May seem odd, but it's not all that easy for them to relocate. Downtown's gotten awfully crowded and businesses have cracked down. The Martin Luther King Jr. Memorial Library is close by. That's where the buses load."

"Buses?" Ivan asked.

"The District operates a free mini-Metro for the homeless."

"You're kidding."

"Most of the soup kitchens and social service offices are still downtown. It's about a five-mile walk. When the District moved some of the sleep shelters here they added the buses because there's no place to get a free meal out here."

"So they come to this neighborhood to sleep, then have to commute downtown if they want a meal?" Tully just shook his head. Only in the District did that make sense. He remembered thinking his trench coat hadn't been warm enough. The weather had been nice for February, but he couldn't imagine sleeping on the street all night.

"The homeless have to work at staying homeless, huh?" Ivan actually smiled.

Tully and Racine did not.

The ATF investigator didn't notice and continued, "That sort of blows your theory. Nobody's gonna hear anything in this alley if they're all sleeping in shelters."

"That's just it," Racine said, unfazed. "There are nowhere near enough beds. Drive around here at two in the morning and you'll see what I'm talking about. There's construction for a new shelter about a block away, but that's months from completion."

"You just made me glad I live in Virginia," Ivan said. "I need to start the walkabout inside. I'll let you two start your work out here."

And that was the extent of Ivan's interest. His focus remained on the fire and how it started. That was his job. Dead bodies were an inconvenience, a nuisance, especially ones that didn't belong to the building or the fire. Dead bodies were Tully and Racine's job.

Without another word Ivan turned and sauntered down the alley, his gait slow and thoughtful.

Tully glanced at Racine. He knew the eye roll was coming but still caught himself smiling when it did.

"That guy gives me the creeps. What rock did the ATF find him hiding under?"

With Ivan gone, Racine moved in closer to get a better look at the victim. Tully pulled on a pair of shoe covers and followed. He kept the latex gloves in his pocket.

The woman lay in a heap like discarded rubbish that hadn't quite made it into the Dumpster. Her arms were tucked under her torso and her legs tangled over each other. He wondered about Racine's theory. Rigor mortis sets in twelve to thirty-six hours after death, but what most people don't realize is that after thirty-six hours the body becomes pliable again. This woman had been dead for almost two days. Racine was right. No way was this body lying here unnoticed for that long.

Tully suspected her killer dumped her body just before the first fire. It wasn't unusual for arsonists to hide their murders among the ashes. But if that was the case, this guy had really screwed up. How could he choreograph two fires in two different buildings and fail to burn his murder victim?

Right now that was the least of Tully's concerns. Especially when he got a good look at the damage under the tangled hair. It was difficult to guess the woman's age. Her face had been beaten so badly the left eye socket and nose were practically gone. Her mouth gaped open, a black hole where her jaw and teeth had been successfully shattered. Hair color was impossible to determine, since the hair was caked with blood and tissue. Her clothes were dirty and stained but not torn or ripped.

Did she have a chance to fight back? Tully wondered.

"First body," Racine said. "Last week the buildings were unoccupied. Think he's accelerating? Or just reckless?"

"Maybe he didn't know about this one."

Racine raised an eyebrow. "You think someone else did this? Not the arsonist?"

"Just keeping an open mind." Gut instinct, but he wouldn't say that to anyone except maybe Maggie. Whoever did this was much more brutal than a nuisance fire starter.

"So what? The killer catches a big break that the building he dumps his victim next to goes up in flames? Too much of a coincidence."

Tully shrugged. That's exactly what Maggie would say right about now. He still couldn't believe she hadn't argued with him about going to the ER to get checked. He was pleased but concerned. In the years he had known Maggie O'Dell there was only one other time he remembered seeing such uncertainty in her eyes. Uncertainty that bordered on fear. And that one other time Maggie hadn't admitted her vulnerability to him or anyone else. So how bad was *this* if she was willing to go to a hospital?

He wished he could convince himself that she had agreed just to appease him. But he knew better. The fact that she admitted she might not be okay was unsettling.

They hadn't worked together for more than a year. Not since their director, Kyle Cunningham, had died. The case that led to his death had been their last one. And actually, Maggie wasn't supposed to be on that case after both she and Cunningham were exposed to the Ebola virus. Maggie had ended up in the Slammer, an isolation ward at USAMRIID (U. S. Army Medical Research Institute of Infectious Diseases) at Fort Detrick. Ebola Zaire — the virus she and Cunningham had been exposed to — was nicknamed "the slate cleaner." About 90 percent of those exposed died, with only a slightly better chance for those given an unregulated, unapproved vaccine.

That Maggie had survived amazed her doctors and the experts at the army research facility. Since then Cunningham's replacement, Raymond Kunze, had been sending both Maggie and Tully on wild-goose chases, either impossible or simply ridiculous cases, brazenly telling them that they needed to prove their worthiness to him.

It was ridiculous. Both of them were

veteran FBI agents. Both had gained hard-earned reputations as expert profilers. It was Kunze's way of interjecting his authority over a department that held their previous director in high regard. Maybe Kunze felt he couldn't possibly function in Cunningham's shadow, so his solution was to tear the agents down and rebuild them in his image, to his standards.

Tully had little respect for the man. He viewed him as a bully more concerned with power and politics than with solving crimes or deflecting criminals. Kunze slid down even further on Tully's scale when the last wild-goose chase the man sent Maggie on ended up getting her Tasered, left in a forest, and shot in the head. All because the man wanted to repay a political favor.

Which made Tully wonder — what was it about *this* case that had Kunze sending in two of his top profilers? Who did he owe or want to please? Had he already suspected last week that the case would take a violent turn?

"Hey, Tully, Racine," Ivan called out, interrupting Tully's thoughts as he waved at them from the opening of the alley. "We just found another one for you inside."

CHAPTER 13

Maggie already regretted her decision.

A nurse had poked and cleaned and prepped her wounds, murmuring a few "uh-huhs" with the appropriate inflections for the bloodier ones. She left Maggie with a sterile towel to hold against the back of her head.

"Don't be lifting this off now to take a look," she warned.

As soon as the nurse cleared the doorway Maggie lifted the towel and took a look. There was enough blood on the towel that it looked as if someone had wiped up puddles of it. She fingered the same wounds the nurse had just cleaned. The one on her neck would require sutures. The others were minor scrapes. Scalp wounds bled a lot. Didn't mean much. None of it was worth a trip to the ER. The guy sitting next to her in the waiting area had had his lip hanging down on his chin. Now, he needed to be here.

In the waiting area Maggie had spent the time watching the others, checking for burns, especially on the hands. Sometimes criminals made mistakes, got hurt, and didn't think twice before going to an ER. Gunshot or knife wounds would require a police report, but burns were easily explained away. It wouldn't be the first time an arsonist sat in an ER waiting room while a blaze he'd started still burned.

Now Maggie considered getting up and leaving the exam room to continue looking at the other patients. At least she'd be doing something. Would anyone notice if she left? The place was crazy busy. The fact that she was law enforcement moved her up the list. However, she had insisted they treat the man with half his lip ripped off before they took her.

She had scooted to the edge of the table, ready to hop down, when the door opened.

"I am Dr. Dabu. You are O'Dell, Margaret?"

The man was short, had an Indian accent, and looked too young to be a resident, let alone a doctor.

"Yes. It's Maggie actually."

He looked at her over the computer tablet, then back at the screen as if checking to make sure the name hadn't changed.

"Explosion, yes?" He sounded eager, like a contestant on a game show.

"Right."

"We need sutures, yes?"

We need our head examined, was what she wanted to tell him, but she simply nodded.

Regret suddenly became a lump in her stomach. She realized she wouldn't be able to put off Kunze's psychological evaluation now. She wasn't sure which was worse — listening to her career regurgitated in psychobabble or seeing that scared concern on R. J. Tully's face.

She paid little attention when Dr. Dabu pulled open a suture tray. She could feel the needle poke into the back of her neck. The nurse had returned to assist and Maggie tuned out their bits of communication. Neither asked about her blurred vision or the jackhammer at her temple. Had she mentioned either to the paramedic who had shined the tiny laser-beamed flashlight into each of her eyes? He had asked her a series of questions. She couldn't remember any of them or her answers.

All she remembered was that look on Tully's face and the panic in his voice when he said, "I don't think you're okay either."

It was the fire, the flames and the heat. All

of it too much like a gunshot. She closed her eyes. She'd be okay. It would just take time. She never had patience. Hated feeling vulnerable, out of control. But not to have control over her body . . .

No one needed to know how disoriented she really had been at the fire site. She didn't have to tell anyone about the blurred vision or the scent that permeated the lining of her memory, that smell of scorched flesh from the bullet scraping her scalp.

The gunshot wound had happened four months ago. The fire's blast had simply been a reminder. It threw her off her game. That's all. But this little slip-up would be enough to trigger Kunze. It'd be enough for him to justify his psychological tests.

So let him. Bring it on.

There'd be nothing to report. Maggie had a degree in psychology. She knew exactly what they'd be looking for and she simply wouldn't give it to them.

Just then she realized she could still feel the needle as the doctor pulled it through her skin. The local anesthesia hadn't been enough to numb the area. Her jaw clenched and her eyes stayed closed. This pain — this prick of the needle sliding through, the tug of the suture thread following — *this* was nothing. She wanted all of it to be over. To get back to the crime scene. This was just a distraction.

When they were finished the doctor quietly left. The nurse told Maggie she had some papers to get for a signature and she left. She hadn't been gone long when the examination room door opened again.

Benjamin Platt wore his military dress uniform, had his hat tucked under his arm, and his stance was that of a soldier delivering dreadful news. The look on his face wasn't much better. Worry creased an indent between his eyes.

"Are you okay?" he asked in almost a whisper.

"I can't believe Tully called you."

"It wasn't Tully."

"Racine?"

"I wish it had been you."

CHAPTER 14

"This isn't unusual," Stan Wenhoff, the District's chief medical examiner, told them.

Tully stared at the blackened skull. The pile of rubble didn't appear to include a body. He took a couple of careful steps closer. Something about a fire scene made him expect the floor — what was left of it — to still burn all the way through the fire boots and the soles of his shoes.

The scent of smoke and ashes hung in the air. Water and foam dripped from the skeletal rafters that remained. He wished he had a baseball cap. Stan had brought an umbrella and looked ridiculous, like an English gentleman in from a stroll along the countryside. That is if the English gentleman wore Tyvek overalls.

Something wet and solid slopped onto the back of Tully's neck. He snatched at the debris and flung it aside, drawing a few scowls from Ivan and the fire chief, who had stopped their own inspections to hear what Stan had to say about their latest "not unusual" discovery.

The skull looked as if someone had taken a fist-size rock and bashed a hole into the top of it. The fire investigative team had just begun moving and raking smoldering debris into ridges along the concrete floor, where they would later sift and examine it.

"Think of the skull as a sealed container," Stan explained to his audience, ignoring the pitter-patter hitting his umbrella. "Like a ceramic jug filled with liquid. Heat it up and it doesn't take long for the liquid inside to reach a boiling point. That creates pressure."

Just when Tully envisioned the ceramic jug bursting apart, Stan put an end to his own analogy and added, "The cranium explodes. Boiling blood, brain, and tissue expand and have nowhere to go. The skull literally explodes into pieces. Sometimes it can blow a head right off a body."

"It was a hot fire," the fire chief admitted, nodding. "This thing burned upward of a thousand degrees. That doesn't happen without some help. Definitely used an accelerant. May have been a chemical reaction. We found the start point at the back door. Actually on the *outside* of the back door."

All of them continued to stare down at the rubble as if expecting more bones to appear, like one of those picture puzzles that if you looked hard enough and long enough you'd see the hidden objects.

"The intense heat makes the blood boil inside the bones, too," Stan said. "Same kind of pressure builds up as in the skull. Makes bones fracture and break apart. Could be blown all over the place."

Which set them all looking around.

"There are other floors." Ivan pointed up. "Is it possible the rest of the body's still up there?"

And again, as if on cue, all heads swiveled upward to the smoldering, dripping rafters.

"Chief," one of the techs interrupted.

He held up a finger to tell the man he'd be right there. As he turned to leave he told them, "Give my folks time to sift through this mess. We should have some answers for you, but remember I've got two sites here." And he walked away.

Ivan followed close behind, his neck still craning up as if he expected body parts to fall down from the second floor.

"What are the chances of IDing this . . ." Racine paused, searching for words as she referred to the skull. "This victim?"

Stan set aside his umbrella, dug in his Tyvek pocket, and pulled out a pair of purple latex gloves.

"Teeth don't burn. They might have broken or been jarred off from the pressure." He picked up the skull and carefully examined the jaw. "Well, this is unusual." He turned the skull to get a better look inside the jaw. He scraped at the soot with his gloved thumb.

"What's wrong?" Racine asked.

"The bone doc will need to examine this. But I think the teeth may have been shattered."

"The fire couldn't do that?"

"No. Not that I know of." He was studying the top of the skull now and turned to show them the hole at the top. "Usually when a skull bursts from heat pressure, it shatters. It is a bit odd to have a hole this big without fracturing the skull into pieces. Unless the skull was compromised before the fire."

"What do you mean 'compromised'?" Tully wanted to know. "Are you saying the victim may have been bashed in the head and teeth before the fire?"

"It's possible."

Tully and Racine exchanged a look and

Stan noticed.

"What is it?" he asked.

"The victim out by the Dumpster. Her face is bashed in."

CHAPTER 15

It was complicated. That's what Maggie wanted to tell Ben.

In just a little over a year Benjamin Platt had gone from being her doctor to her friend to her . . . what? What were they exactly?

Boyfriend, girlfriend sounded sophomoric. And although they had shared a hotel room — *and a bed, once* — as well as many intimate thoughts and conversations, they weren't lovers. *Yet.*

Just when both of them confided that they wanted to be more than friends Ben had put the skids on. All it took was his admission that he wanted children, and Maggie found herself backing off, way off.

His only daughter had died five years ago, ending his marriage and causing him to focus all his energy on his career. Maggie had buried herself in her work, too, ever since her divorce. But Ben still ached for his daughter. And while he longed to replace that ache, Maggie wanted to shield herself from another potential loss. Being alone was safer than feeling too much.

Yes, it was complicated.

But she was glad to see him. So why didn't she tell him that? He was still her friend. Partly because he had reverted to acting like her doctor as soon as he crossed the exam room threshold.

"An occupational hazard," he had said when he saw her impatience with his incessant questions. But then he continued, "Did you lose consciousness? Any blurred vision? Dizziness?"

"I'm fine." And she finally put up her hands in surrender. "Tully insisted. That's all."

And she convinced herself that this lapse back to a doctor-patient relationship was enough reason *not* to tell him that her head still throbbed, that she'd been getting killer headaches for months now.

Ben had been her doctor at USAMRIID after Maggie was exposed to the Ebola virus. She had been in the Slammer, an isolation unit. No one could talk to her without an inch-thick glass wall in between. No one could touch her without wearing a blue hazmat suit. Her conversations with

97

Ben had kept her from panicking, from diving deep inside herself. When they discovered they both loved classic movies, Ben had used them to entertain and transport her to another world outside the Slammer's walls. He had shown her how to escape reality to gain a grasp on sanity.

Dr. Benjamin Platt — army colonel, scientist, soldier — was one of the strongest, most gentle men she'd ever met. There were times when he looked at her and she felt as though he could see so deep inside her that he must have gotten a glimpse of her soul. He understood her, sometimes more than she understood herself. And for the last several months what she had started to feel for him scared the hell out of her.

He offered to take her home. Her car was still at the fire site and she asked if he would drop her there instead. Besides, she wanted to get back to the investigation. She didn't want Kunze to have any more ammunition against her than this little trip to the ER had already given him.

Ben suggested breakfast first. Before he could slip back into his role as doctor, Maggie asked, "Are you sure you have time? You look dressed for something important."

She wanted to lighten the mood and almost added, *Who died?* Then she was very glad she had not, when Ben said he had a funeral to attend later. Another soldier, another comrade coming home in a box.

She didn't know how he stayed strong and positive with so much death around him. She told him that once and he said he wondered the same thing about her.

"But my dead people are usually strangers," Maggie had told him. Which wasn't exactly true. By the time she closed the file on a murder case she often knew more about the victim than his or her family did. And sometimes the victims had been people she knew. Always, she knew much more about the killers than she ever cared to know.

She chose the McDonald's just off the interstate. Maggie let Ben order while she found a quiet corner table where she could sit with her back to the wall. It was an old compulsion, one she hadn't recognized until she started sharing meals in restaurants with Ben. He wanted to do the same thing — they laughed the first time they realized each of them wanted — needed — to sit where they could see the doors and where no one could come up from behind them.

They were quite the pair: a woman who expected killers in every corner and a soldier who looked for grenades or suicide bombers. And yet the similarities were a surprising comfort to Maggie. She'd never met a man who understood her so well and, more surprisingly, who accepted her and all the insane components that made her who she was. But this morning there was a disarming quiet between them. She knew he was disappointed that her first instinct hadn't been to call him.

It wouldn't help to explain. He knew the reason and grudgingly even accepted it. That didn't mean he had to like it. Being a loner and being alone were two separate things. Maggie had been alone since her divorce but she'd been a loner since she was twelve. She had learned back then not to count on anyone other than herself. If you didn't count on anyone, they couldn't let you down. More important, they couldn't hurt you.

She watched Ben standing in line from across the room. He was so damned handsome. She glanced around, noticing the looks he was getting from the other women customers. There was something so graceful in the way he moved, broad shoulders back, chin up, eyes intense and aware of the surroundings.

Racine said he was too "spit and polish," but after working with Ben on a school contamination case last fall, even Racine had a new respect for him. The uniform did make him look pressed and proper, but Maggie had seen him out of uniform enough to know that this man had a keen sense of who he was and what he valued, and he knew it without the uniform, without a stitch of clothing on.

That's when it hit her. The obvious smacking her in the face. Ben didn't consider a phone call from her a courtesy or an obligation. He hoped it would be an extension of herself. An instinct, second nature. Of course he did.

And why wasn't it?

Was she simply not capable of allowing someone else to be a part of her?

She watched him let a mother with a little girl go in line before him. She saw him smile down at the girl. The mother looked like she was giving her daughter instructions to thank him.

Even from across the restaurant Maggie could see the sadness in his face. That was where the major difference lay between them, like a thick wedge. Both of them had scars from their pasts, but the hole Ben's daughter, Ali, had left in his heart was not one Maggie would ever be able to repair.

For the first time Maggie realized this was

why she hadn't called, why she hadn't allowed him to get any closer. Rather than lose him, she was already pushing him away. And suddenly that revelation made her feel terribly sad and empty.

CHAPTER 16

Patrick unpacked the last of the groceries that he'd picked up on his way back from his official slapdown. At least it didn't come with a suspension. Since he was fifteen he had had some kind of job. Money was always tight, but he had always pulled his weight, paid his way. He promised — no, he swore — he wouldn't take advantage of Maggie's generosity.

He stood in front of the open kitchen cabinets trying to figure out her system. She was neat and tidy, but it looked like she didn't cook beyond the basics. Patrick had been cooking since he was ten. During college he volunteered at the fire department in a nearby community outside of New Haven, Connecticut. Firefighters were some of the best cooks and Patrick had learned how to experiment and improvise, building a repertoire that included everything from chateaubriand to a killer jambalaya. Tonight he'd fix pan-seared scallops with a rice pilaf, a baby-greens salad, and a peach-raspberry crisp for dessert. Hopefully it wouldn't make her suspicious.

Maggie had already made it clear that she didn't like him working for a private fire-fighting company. Like government-run departments were any more ethical? He did have to hand it to her. She listened, heard him out, even refrained from commenting many times when he could see her pretending not to wince, not to clench her teeth. As a public servant, she believed it was wrong to decide who to save and who not to save depending only on whether they could afford it.

"Are you saying you wouldn't stop to put out a fire at a house because the owner wasn't on your roster of policyholders? You'd drive your truck and equipment and special skills right on by? Could you really do that?"

"It isn't my decision," he'd argued. Reasoning that if he hadn't been paid by the policyholders he would not be driving by that house in the first place. Even he didn't quite believe that logic, but that's exactly what had been drilled into him during training.

Yet that's exactly what had happened during this last assignment. There hadn't been just one house — there were dozens. The fire had spread quickly, like liquid racing over the grass. The policyholders they had been sent to protect were a good ten miles away from the fire. They had spent the day cleaning gutters, removing flammables from the yards, hosing down the houses and the perimeter with fire-retardant chemicals and helping to evacuate. They were finished with all their preparations. There was nothing more to do except sit back and wait until and unless the fire got closer.

So Patrick and his partner, Wes Harper, drove back to their staging area. To get back they had to maneuver around the burn zone. Patrick was team captain for the day. Switching built confidence, fairness, and reliability. You didn't screw with your partner because tomorrow it was his turn to screw with you. That's not exactly the way they explained it in training, but that was the basic idea. And that was what happened. Because Patrick made the team decision to stop. And Wes made the team decision the next day, to rat Patrick out.

Harvey, Maggie's white Lab, stood whining and watching even though Patrick had filled both dog bowls. That's when Patrick realized that Jake hadn't come in from the backyard. Then he remembered Maggie's concern earlier. Jake had been escaping and a neighbor had already been complaining. Actually, now that Patrick thought about it, Maggie had said the neighbor had been threatening, not complaining.

It wasn't hard to understand. The black German shepherd looked menacing, and from Maggie's brief explanation as to why the dog made the trip back with her from Nebraska, it sounded like Jake had proved to be not only menacing but also dangerous. It was obvious the dog had a fierce loyalty to Maggie. It cut both ways. Maggie had panicked this morning when she thought Jake had dug his way out of the backyard.

Patrick felt his stomach drop. After all that Maggie had done for him. Damn if he'd let this dog get out on his watch. He left the cabinets open, grabbed a leash and a jacket, and ran out the back door.

CHAPTER 17

Maggie arrived back at the scene just as Tully and Racine were walking out of the blasted wall of the second site. She almost wished they had left for the day. Anything to avoid those looks of concern. Tully had already called to check on her, offered to pick her up and take her home. She had declined. Told him she was on her way back, and yet the two of them looked surprised to see her.

"Just a few stitches," she told them before either had a chance to ask. She said it in midstride and in a tone that closed the subject. "You mind catching me up?"

Racine gave her details about "the stiff" behind the Dumpster, including her theory that the kill had been made somewhere else.

"Stan's office bagged and carted her," Racine added. "He promised to do the autopsy himself first thing tomorrow morning."

"Any chance she was homeless?" Maggie asked.

Racine shook her head. "Feet were exposed. Looked like a professional pedicure."

"We did find the remains of a cardboard box," Tully said. "Ganza's back there seeing what trace he can find."

Keith Ganza was the director of the FBI crime lab. Maggie wondered why this case suddenly warranted the director's presence instead of a crime scene tech. Their boss, Assistant Director Kunze, lived by a political code Maggie abhorred. Twice in the past year that code had almost gotten her killed. She hoped Ganza was on the site simply because he wanted to be here instead of sending one of his techs. He was good. She liked working with him. If there were any answers in the rubble, Ganza would find them.

"I've got uniforms talking to the locals," Racine continued. "They're checking deliveries to the area and cab drivers. Maybe we get lucky and one of them saw something."

Maggie stopped outside the opening Tully and Racine had just exited. The scent accosted her and she pretended it didn't bother her. Why had she thought the scorched stench would have dissipated? She knew better. What she didn't know, what still surprised her, was her body's involuntary reaction to it. She caught herself wanting to hold her breath as the smell seeped into her throat, her lungs. Even her mouth tasted the charred remains like the black carbon on an overdone charcoal-grilled steak.

Don't think about it, she told herself.

Tully kept his fingers at the top of his Tyvek overalls' zipper, almost as if waiting for Maggie's signal whether they were going back inside.

That's when it occurred to her that she didn't need to go in. What could she possibly learn that Tully and Racine hadn't found? Her jaw relaxed. To insist on going for a look-see would be overkill. She didn't need to drive home any point here.

She saw the fire department's crew still sifting and raking the ashes and rubble.

"Any signs of the timing device?" she asked, not making a move.

Tully shook his head. "Not yet."

"Fire chief believes they found the start point on the outside of the first building," Racine said. "Preliminary guess is some kind of chemical reaction, because of the intensity of the fire. Said it looked similar to last week's."

"There was gasoline poured along the alley from the front of the building to the Dumpster," Tully told her. "It was against the brick wall. Burned up the line of accelerant without going anywhere else."

"The alley wasn't the start point?"

"Not even close. It might have been an afterthought. And a poorly executed one."

"The killer didn't even try to burn the body?"

Tully shrugged. "If that was his intention he didn't do a very good job. The guy torches two buildings but his murder victim doesn't quite catch fire. Doesn't make sense."

"Oh, and there was another body inside the first building," Racine said casually, almost absentmindedly. "Or at least someone's head. They haven't found the body yet."

"Stan said something about pressure in the skull building up enough to blow it off the body."

"Yeah," Racine added with a roll of her eyes. "Gives new meaning to snap, crackle, and pop."

"Only the skull looks bashed in. Has a hole about the size of a fist." Tully held up his own to emphasize how big.

"You're thinking he killed the person inside, too. But then why leave one body

110

out by the Dumpster?"

"Maybe the one inside was some poor schmuck who was sleeping there. Maybe a homeless person who saw him." Racine's turn to shrug.

Truth was, they couldn't answer any of those questions until they started piecing together the trace evidence or found out who the victims were.

Maggie's phone started ringing. She pulled it out and was going to send it to voice mail when she saw the caller ID. She shot Tully a look. "You told Gwen?"

"I haven't talked to Gwen since midnight."

"Racine?"

"Gwen Patterson is not on my speed dial."

"But Ben is?"

Racine's eyes went wide. *Busted.* Her head turned, hands went up in surrender. No denial.

Maggie finally answered her phone.

"Hey, Gwen."

"Are you okay?"

"I'm fine. A few stitches. That's all. How in the world did you find out?"

"I'm watching the news. They were showing the fire. Then you were trying to take away some TV crew's camera."

"They showed that on the news?" Maggie glanced at Tully. He pulled a small plastic

111

cartridge from his pocket.

"Just as you're trying to ask them something, a building explodes into flames behind you. They said you were rushed to the hospital. Are you sure you're okay? And why am I hearing about this on TV? Or do I need to wait for Jeffery Cole's profile piece on you tonight to find out?"

"Profile piece?"

"An hour long. You either intrigued him or really pissed him off."

That's when Maggie's call waiting started beeping in her ear.

"I've got another call, Gwen. I'll talk to you later."

"Are you really okay?"

She hesitated too long, and before she responded Gwen added, "Please be careful."

Maggie took the next call without looking at her caller ID.

"This is Maggie O'Dell."

"O'Dell. I just heard what happened."

It was her boss. But Assistant Director Kunze didn't sound angry. It was worse — he sounded concerned.

CHAPTER 18

"You didn't tell me anything about a profile piece."

Sam Ramirez paced the narrow space in the sound studio. Their feature on this morning's fire had made the national circuit.

"Big Mac loves the idea," Jeffery told her from his perch beside Abe Nadira, whose long fingers were playing the computer keyboards as smoothly as if they belonged to a musical instrument.

He was referring to Donald Malcolm, the bureau chief who had taken over programming when ratings dropped last year.

To Nadira, Jeffery said, "You can search and use footage from our affiliates, right?"

"Yes, I can. As well as any syndicated sources."

"Jeffery, the feds are already going to be pissed I didn't give them this morning's film. Do you really want an FBI agent gunning for you?"

"She already has it bad for me, Sam. You saw her. She has a major hard-on for me."

"No, somehow I missed that."

Sam rubbed her hand over her face. She was tired. She wanted to go home. Her clothes and hair — hell, probably her skin, too — all reeked of smoke. Jeffery had showered and changed. He kept spare shirts and trousers in his locker, all of them immaculately pressed.

The man was a neat freak when it came to his appearance. Probably an occupational hazard from being in front of a camera. Even in third-world countries he managed to have creases in his trousers and gel in his short-cropped hair. In fact, she had been surprised this morning when he showed up with a brown stain on his shirt cuff. He'd shrugged when she pointed it out, but she saw him tuck it up into his jacket later.

Sam brushed at the grass and cinder stains on her jeans when she really wanted to peel them off and throw them in the washing machine. She shouldn't have taken off her ball cap. Her unruly curls flew around her face, wild snakes of hair that smelled like burned toast. She wouldn't blame Nadira if he threw her out of his editing studio, but Jeffery's excitement could be contagious and Nadira had it bad. Though you'd never be able to tell. The man looked perpetually bored. His mouth remained a thin line. His knobby shaved head stayed put while his half-lidded eyes darted along from one computer monitor to the next in line, three rows of them, five screens in each row.

In fact, neither man noticed her presence despite her pacing behind their captain chairs. Their attention was focused on the computer images.

"By the way," Jeffery said without looking at her, "good job on keeping the film. Even I didn't see that coming."

"I learn from the best." Actually her mother would say that the Diablo was rubbing his evil off on her. "Ever since Afghanistan I keep a spare."

Two years ago, when Jeffery managed to get them embedded with some U.S. troops, Sam shot some amazing footage of a tribal court carrying out justice on two of the village's women, a mother and daughter. Their Afghan sponsors were not pleased. A huge argument started, and in the middle of the drama Sam sensed what was coming. Without anyone noticing, she inconspicuously switched out the footage in her camera with film she already had in her pocket. When one of the Afghan soldiers demanded the film, Sam opened the camera and grudgingly handed it over. She watched as he destroyed it, smashing it to bits with his rifle butt, right in front of them.

That footage ended up winning a feature for her and Jeffery, sweeping award after award but also winning the assurance that they could never return to Afghanistan.

"So what footage did Dudley Do-Right end up with?" Jeffery asked.

"I had extras made of that zoo feature we did last year."

He swiveled back to grin up at her. "Lions and tigers and bears? Oh my. And what will you tell him when he comes knocking?"

"It was an honest mistake." She shrugged, palms out, mimicking a gesture Jeffery recognized as one of his, and he nodded with a bigger grin. "You're always telling me it's better to ask forgiveness than permission. I told you, I learn from the best."

"Now you're giving me a hard-on." It was Jeffery's highest compliment.

But he was already spinning back to the computer monitors.

"Why don't you go on home for a few hours, Sam?"

"You sure?"

"Yes, you deserve it. You did good. We don't have anything until the documentary interview later."

When she still didn't make a move he waved his hand over his shoulder. "Go. Get a shower. You don't want to smell worse than the prison inmates. Take a nap for all I care."

"Okay, I will."

She could use the break. Jeffery had woken her shortly after midnight. She had gotten only an hour of sleep. She was starting to feel it, but Jeffery hadn't gotten any more sleep than she had and the man looked energized.

Sam could see his latest obsession unfolding on the monitors. Like a dog with a bone, it was too late to tell him to let go of this one. But something told her *this one* wasn't the same as his other obsessions. It could make or break his career. It was a waste of her time to say anything. She knew Jeffery Cole well enough to know he'd do whatever he wanted.

Sam started for the door before Jeffery could change his mind. She shook her head, glancing one last time as monitor after monitor began filling with different images of Agent Margaret O'Dell.

CHAPTER 19

"I'm fine," Maggie told her boss, repeating the mantra as her breakfast did an unpleasant flip. "Just a few stitches."

Tully caught her eyes and frowned. Racine stepped away. Okay, so she wasn't that convincing.

"I heard you made a trip to the ER. Are you okay?"

But had he seen the news yet? He actually sounded concerned, so no, he probably hadn't heard about the news clip.

"If this assignment is too . . ." He paused as if looking for the correct wording. "If it's too difficult considering the circumstances —" And he let the rest hang.

This was not typical Kunze. For more than a year he had berated, dogged, and insulted her. Several times Maggie had considered transferring to the Department of Homeland Security at the suggestion of Deputy Director Charlie Wurth. He and

Maggie had worked together on several cases. She liked Wurth, respected and trusted him, which were three things she could not say about Kunze.

But in many ways DHS would be starting over for her. She had worked long and hard, fought battles beyond those with killers, to get where she was. She had not run from anything or anyone in a very long time, and she had decided she wouldn't start now. She wouldn't let Kunze push her out.

Ever since the case last fall, the case in Nebraska, Kunze's crash tactics appeared watered down. He pulled punches and held back his ordinary slew of criticism. If Maggie didn't know better, she'd swear he'd gone a bit soft, even to the point of sounding conciliatory.

Now, as she let too much dead air float between them, her eyes met Tully's. In his eyes she saw the same distrust, the suspicion. And she realized, of course, it couldn't be that simple or easy with Kunze. Trust was something earned. Kunze hadn't gotten close to being there. Immediately she felt her guard come back up into place, just as it had earlier with Racine.

"I'm fine with the case, Director Kunze." She gave the lie her best shot but still couldn't bring herself to call him "sir."

"Good, I'm glad to hear that. Part of my job is to make sure you're fine."

Maggie winced and tightened her grip on the phone, preparing herself for the punch. He had spun it just the way she expected. Same ol' Kunze. *Spider, welcome to my web.*

"So, in order to make certain you are fine, I've made an appointment for you," he said. "To start the psychological evaluation we talked about. Your first session is tomorrow afternoon at four o'clock. I'll leave it to Dr. Kernan to decide how often and how long he thinks you'll need."

"Dr. Kernan? Dr. James Kernan?"

"That's right. If you have any questions, call my office."

More dead air. Only this time Kunze was gone.

He was good, Maggie had to admit. She didn't see that coming. And James Kernan. Who knew the old geezer was still alive? This would be worse than she'd even imagined.

CHAPTER 20

She was back. He was surprised. Even more surprised by the flush of sexual excitement he felt. That hadn't happened in a long time.

He had spent the morning watching the investigators parade in and out of the alley. A rare treat. Something he didn't get to do very often. And the risk he'd taken to dump the body was reaping greater rewards than he'd expected.

He wished he could see what they were bringing out in the brown paper bags. How could there possibly be so much? But of course they would be collecting evidence for the fire. They were even checking the Dumpster, going through the garbage piece by piece. He wanted to venture closer. He wanted to see everything.

He had an insatiable curiosity. That was partly what had gotten him to start his little habit. More like a hobby, really. Though it wasn't until recently that he'd begun keep-

121

ing track of some details after discovering what a sense of accomplishment it gave him to go over the kills weeks later.

In his logbook, he tried to record as many interesting tidbits as he could. Changing things up was so much easier when you could look back on the details and think about them. Sometimes remembering was almost as exciting as doing.

Well, not really as satisfying. But it placated him during those days or weeks — sometimes months — when he knew he'd have a dry spell and wouldn't be able to get on the road.

Just this morning, after they found the body in the alley, he had pulled out his logbook and flipped to a page from another kill about a month ago. He had read his notes, memorizing the passage as if it were a poem or a psalm: "Cold night. Steam rises when you pull the guts out of the body. The blood is so warm on my hands."

Actually, it did sound poetic.

The log helped control his curiosity. Allowed him to have patience. Even now, remembering that image and recalling how the blood felt on his skin were enough to soothe him. Enough to stop him from letting his curiosity push him to do something reckless just to get more information. After all, he knew how close he could get to a scene, where he could stand, how many different places he could move around to without drawing attention. There was a point where blending in crossed over to suspicion, and he had always been very good at sensing where that line was.

He watched the alley until they took away the body. Interesting how it looked in that bag, like a long black cocoon. He liked the look of body bags. They were so much better than garbage bags — strong, more efficient. Definitely wouldn't leak. Sure would keep his vehicle cleaner. He was wondering where he could buy one of those when he saw the woman cop back on the scene.

Earlier he'd seen her getting into an ambulance. It made him smile because he was close enough to get a glimpse of her face. She hadn't been pleased with the tall guy in the trench coat helping her. And she wasn't pleased about getting inside the ambulance either.

Confident and stubborn. Sort of like him. A rebel. A kindred spirit.

He definitely needed a closer look at her.

CHAPTER 21

Tully didn't like what he saw. Maggie looked battered, her skin washed out, her eyes a bit glassy. He could tell Racine noticed, too. Maggie claimed she had "grabbed some breakfast with Platt." He was the one who had dropped her back at the crime scene, but Tully could hardly believe that either. How could Benjamin Platt, army colonel, MD, Mr. Button-down, have decided Maggie was good to go?

But then Tully reminded himself that no one — not even the good doctor — could tell Maggie what to do. That she had listened to Tully earlier and gone to the hospital had been some kind of fluke, a blip on the O'Dell stubborn scale.

He had kept his eyes on her while she talked with Kunze. He watched as their boss took her on his usual roller-coaster ride before depositing her back on the ground, dizzy and spitting mad. Actually, spitting mad was preferable to the hollowed-out look that had preceded it.

"You knew he wouldn't let you off the hook," Tully said. "He made me do the same thing last year. Just as well to get it over with."

Yet the whole time he was telling Maggie this, Tully was thinking Kunze couldn't have chosen an absolute worst time. She still looked vulnerable and now was dealing with new wounds. Seemed like a low blow.

After Assistant Director Cunningham's death, Tully had been on mandatory suspension for shooting and killing the man responsible for exposing Cunningham and Maggie — as well as hundreds of others — to the Ebola virus. It was Tully who Kunze should have been upset with. The killer, an old rival of Tully's, had meant for Tully to be the target. He'd even sent a note at the bottom of a box of doughnuts, knowing his old friend wouldn't resist the temptation, especially since it had been sent to their offices at Quantico.

But Tully hadn't been there that morning and Raymond Kunze — Cunningham's replacement — felt it necessary to remind Tully of his absence as often as he possibly could. If that's what he wanted to do, that was fine. But Tully wished Kunze would leave Maggie out of it. He could take care of himself. He couldn't take care of Maggie — she'd never let him.

Gwen said that both he and Maggie were suffering from survivor's guilt. That's what they called it. Seeing a shrink wouldn't rinse it from the system. Even Kunze had to understand that. It was just another form of punishment on the assistant director's long list.

"But James Kernan," Maggie said, still obviously rattled by Kunze's order. "The man was ancient and loony when I had him for Psychology 101."

"He knows the guy can get under your skin. So don't let him."

"Who's James Kernan?" Racine wanted to know.

The three of them were making their way back to the alley and the Dumpster.

"He's a psychiatrist. Old school. His method of analysis is to badger, trick, and insult his patients."

"Isn't that what all psychiatrists do? Some are just more subtle than others."

"She has a point," Tully said, thinking how Gwen could get him to admit to things without his realizing it — and he was her lover, not her patient.

The barricades erected that morning

remained. Crime scene technicians and fire investigators still worked both buildings. Small groups of law enforcement officers huddled by the vehicles. Some packed evidence bags for transport. Others were on their cell phones. Several took cigarette breaks, the smoke rising into a cloud that Tully found himself thinking was just a bit too reminiscent of the one that had just been put out.

Keith Ganza stood at the back of his van, which was parked in the entry to the alley. He looked ready to leave, back in street clothes, his Tyvek coveralls wadded up under his arm as he loaded brown paper bags sealed with bright red evidence labels.

"Did you find anything that might ID the victim?" Tully pointed to the stash of bags already packed in the van.

"Ask me tomorrow," Ganza said. "Right now it's just a bunch of charred garbage. I think I got a couple good chunks of material I can test for residues. He obviously poured gasoline back there. Wood, fabric, insulation are highly absorbent. Chromatography should break down the chemical composition of the hydrocarbons."

Tully pretended he understood the technical mumbo-jumbo, but he was tired. It'd been a long day and he was sure his face registered that his mind was blank.

"So you'll be able to give us a blueprint of what exactly he used to start the fire?" Tully asked.

"If it's gasoline, the chromatography is so accurate I should be able to differentiate between makes and grades." Ganza said this matter-of-factly. "Each grade has a different chromatography fingerprint, depending on the proportion of various chemicals present. Refineries make gasoline according to café standards for a variety of state and federal regulations."

"Are you saying you'll be able to tell where the gasoline was refined and possibly where it was distributed from?" Racine asked.

"In some cases the chemical breakdown can be so accurate we've been able to identify and trace the gasoline to a specific gas station. In one case we were able to trace it to a particular vehicle."

"Smells like diesel," Maggie said, walking around Ganza's van.

Tully sniffed the air. Smelled like the bottom of his kitchen oven. One of these days he needed to learn how to clean that burned crispy gunk that stuck to the rack.

"Good nose," Ganza said. "If it is diesel that'll explain why the body didn't burn.

Diesel fuel is combustible, not flammable. Doesn't burn as easily. Soaks in or dissipates before giving off enough vapor to ignite. Also narrows it down a bit. Not as many inner cities sell diesel. But the interstate is close by."

"Interesting choice. Why make it harder for him and easier for us?" Racine asked.

"Maybe he just used what was handy," Tully guessed. "Most criminals don't go out of their way to buy something special. They use what's available. What they already have."

"Or find at the scene," Maggie added.

"But someone who's done it before and is most likely planning on doing it again?" Racine didn't buy their explanation. "Wouldn't he be more careful?"

"Serial criminals don't expect to be caught," Maggie told her. "The fact that they've gotten away with it several times usually makes them more reckless, not more cautious." She turned toward the alley. "Can you show me exactly where the body was?"

Tully led the way. Everyone else had gone. Ganza was the last to collect his samples. That's why the movement at the other end of the alley was so easy to spot.

The man was hunched down, sneaking

underneath the rusted stairs of a fire escape, staying along the far wall. He was about twenty feet from the alley's exit. He froze and stayed low in the shadows, apparently unaware that Tully had seen him.

Maggie thumped the back of her hand into Tully's arm. Racine stopped cold.

"So the body was by the Dumpster," Maggie said casually, keeping her gait steady, her voice even.

Each of their steps came with a crunch, telegraphing their approach. Had the arsonist come back? It wouldn't be the first time. He must have been waiting around and thought they were finally finished.

Racine reached inside her jacket. Maggie touched her elbow and shook her head. She waved her thumb over her shoulder and Racine got the hint.

"Hey, I've got to make a call," she said. "I'll catch up with you two later."

She turned a bit too quickly on the balls of her feet, but otherwise Tully thought she did a fine acting job. Racine had just cleared the corner to the entrance when they got to the Dumpster.

The guy started slithering along the wall again, and Tully wanted to stop him. If he got to the exit a few strides ahead, he might get away. Tully tried to remember what was on the other side of the alley. Another street. He could hear the traffic.

He didn't need to make the decision. The guy stood and broke into a full-throttled run. Tully did, too. The guy was fast. Not so fast that he couldn't sling a backpack under Tully's feet, and Tully came down hard. His elbow smashed against the pavement with a sick crack. Pain shot up his shoulder, all the way to his back molars.

CHAPTER 22

Maggie hurdled over Tully's long sprawled legs. She glanced back and heard him yell, "Go, go. I'm okay."

His face was contorted in pain and Maggie knew he wasn't okay, but she kept going.

"FBI, stop," she yelled at the man as he got to the end of the alley.

He didn't even flinch. Slowed just enough to skid around the corner.

Maggie followed. Depending on which building Racine was coming around it could be Maggie's footrace to lose.

The man looked over his shoulder. He saw how close she was and jolted into the street. He danced through traffic. Brakes screeched. Horns blasted. The hydraulics of a Metro bus whined and the man bounced off its bumper. He didn't look hurt. If anything, it had propelled him a few steps more ahead of her.

Once back on the sidewalk the guy broke into a sprint, weaving and shoving his way through. There weren't many people. Most were homeless. They moved slowly or simply stood and watched. Maggie was a runner, tracking ten to twenty miles a week. Ordinarily this footrace would be a cakewalk. Not today. The thump in her head was accompanied now by a ringing in her ears. But she stayed with him.

He darted around a corner. Just as Maggie got there a shopping cart came barreling into her. She grabbed the front. Kept the cart from tipping and spilling all the tattered possessions inside. Its owner came next. The poor woman screamed at Maggie, fists raised, ready to do battle. Maggie swung the cart over to her and started running again. She had taken her eyes away for only a second or two, but now she couldn't see the man.

She stopped. Waited. Let her eyes check over the door wells. There were no alleys in this block. He couldn't have made it around the corner and she didn't see him across the street.

She was breathing hard. Adrenaline pumping. Ears now a high-pitched hum. The thump at her temple had accelerated. Between it and the hammering of her heart, she couldn't focus. Her vision blurred a bit. She leaned a palm against the cold brick building. That's when she realized that she could see her reflection on the windows across the street.

She started out again, slower this time. Walking and watching the reflections ahead of her. She stayed close to the building. Still, she didn't see him. Could he have darted into one of these buildings?

She craned her neck to look for a business sign and noticed there weren't any fire escapes on this side, not even a rusted ladder. There were no low windows. Only one doorway, and it looked bolted. All of these buildings appeared to be warehouses or storage facilities.

How could he have just disappeared?

Maggie bent over, hands on her knees, catching her breath, trying to quiet the rumbling in her head. That's when she realized she was spending too much time looking up.

Steam billowed from the grates of a manhole cover. Steam was always billowing up from the District's sewer system, especially on chilly days like today. But this cover lay askew, the lip overlapping the concrete. Someone hadn't set it back correctly. Someone in a hurry.

Maggie stared at it for a moment, then looked up and down the street one last time. She noticed an old woman going through a garbage receptacle, picking out aluminum cans. Across the street a man in coveralls leaned against the corner of a building, tapping on his cell phone. Another man was chaining his bicycle to a lamppost. Otherwise there was no one else around. Even traffic had been intermittent.

She stood with hands on her hips. Stared at the manhole cover again. Why would the guy run if he wasn't the arsonist? Did he come back to see if the dead body had been removed? The one that he put there. If he got away now, they might never catch him.

Maggie released a long sigh. Then she squatted down to shove off the manhole cover, letting the metal clank and thump against concrete. Just as well let the bastard know she was coming down after him.

CHAPTER 23

He wanted to tell her the guy with the backpack was a waste of her time. He was a nobody. One of those street people, a real loser. Still, he'd been keeping his eye on the man since before the fire. He hadn't realized that he had used the poor bastard's home — a crappy cardboard box — for his dump site. So he'd been keeping an eye on the raggedy man, though the guy hadn't even noticed him.

In fact, he had sort of forgotten about him, until the footrace.

Wow! She could sprint.

Her body looked like it was used to running, prepped and trained for the chase. He wondered how much faster she could run if she was the one being chased. There was that tingle again and suddenly he wanted very much to watch that. To see what her stride would look like when fear propelled her.

He didn't need to follow too quickly. He knew exactly where the homeless man was going. He knew his routine. Wasn't like the guy was bright enough to change it up. And usually when someone was frightened he always resorted to the predictable. That was one of the reasons he had started doing a double now and then. Of course, the conditions had to be right for doubles but that just added to the challenge.

By the time he rounded the corner she was already there — exactly where he knew the guy had dropped into his underground world. Actually an interesting world. He had followed the guy once before. A bit too confining for his taste, and the squirrelly bastard didn't add much to the game. He moved like one of the displaced sewer rats, always looking over his shoulder. Nosier than hell. He was too annoying and stupid to kill. Much more fun to follow, let him know that he was being followed, then watch him squirm.

Just as he tucked himself into a dark shadow ready to observe, the woman cop did something he hadn't predicted. She dropped down into the hole.

CHAPTER 24

Maggie texted Tully and Racine. She gave
them her location. Told them she was going
down under. She should wait for backup
but the guy would be long gone by then.
She could still hear the crack of Tully's
elbow hitting the pavement. Did that consti-
tute assault? He was certainly fleeing after
an order to halt.

No, she couldn't wait. She gave one last
glance around and then she started her
descent down the brick-lined hole that
reminded her of an oversize drain.

God, how she hated closed-in spaces.

The metal ladder crumbled rust under her
palms and felt slick under her shoes. Hot,
fetid air rose to meet her. She didn't expect
the bottom to be so deep, and halfway down
Maggie glanced back up.

Big mistake.

Nausea churned her stomach and she
pressed her body against the rungs while

she steadied herself.

She'd just take a look. That's all.

Finally the hole spit her out into a dimly lit tunnel, concrete and brick, pipes snaking alongside. Steam hissed. Valves cranked. Water slushed. She stepped off the last rung and put her foot into water, jerking it back and almost losing her balance.

Of course there would be water down here. What was she thinking?

A steady trickle soaked the bottom half of her leather flats, but she was relieved to have some space.

Two feet above her head a maze of monster pipes hung from the ceiling. The concrete walls swallowed any sound from above the street and replaced it with drips and gurgles and the swishing of water. Air hissed and Maggie could feel bursts of steam. Somewhere overhead metal clanked and scraped as valves opened and closed.

She told herself it wasn't any different from a big furnace room. *Pretend it's not twenty feet underground. Pretend there are no moving vehicles and brick buildings right on top of you.*

Incandescent bulbs lit the tunnel in front of her. Two others branched off to the left and to the right but those remained dark. Maggie's fingers found the butt of her gun.

She waited. And listened.

Her first impulse was to follow the brightly lit tunnel. But isn't that what he'd expect her to do? Did he know the tunnel system well enough to use the darkened routes? Despite the twists and turns, she'd probably be able to see illumination if he was using a flashlight down one of those pitch-black tunnels.

Maybe he didn't expect her to follow him down. Maybe he expected her to do the sensible thing, like wait for backup. Only now did she realize the wheeze she kept hearing was actually her own breathing. She tried holding her breath. Listened again. She could hear a faint echo of footsteps walking away from her, down the lighted tunnel.

She started to follow, slipping her gun out of its holster. She stayed close to the concrete wall, pressing against it in places to keep from touching the pipes and to avoid dripping water. She stopped before every bend, holding her breath and listening. She planted her feet, making sure they didn't slip. Cringed when she saw the greasy water getting deeper. Damn! It was starting to seep inside her shoes.

But she could hear him up ahead, the thump of a steady pace. He was walking.

Not running. He didn't know she was behind him.

She paid little attention to how many corners she turned. She followed the lighted tunnel, trying to keep as quiet as possible. Something black in the water moved across her foot. Maggie stifled a gasp and kicked out her leg. The toe of her shoe caught the rat under its belly and flung it away.

Rats. Of course there'd be rats.

She took a couple of deep breaths, despite the smells that were getting more rancid. Then she started forward again.

A sudden pop behind her echoed through the tunnel.

A valve switching on? A pipe bursting? She couldn't tell. She ignored it. Took another step. Another pop. This time she noticed the light behind her dim. Just as she glanced back, the third pop she recognized. Incandescent bulbs made a sound like that when they broke.

Could steam or water pop out a lightbulb?

That's when she heard footsteps again. Only this time they came from behind her.

CHAPTER 25

Maggie tightened the grip on her revolver. Kept her finger on the trigger.

A brick ledge ran along the wall, about six inches wide and almost twelve inches above the water. Maggie stepped up onto it. Pressed her back against the wall and ignored dirt and concrete crumbling down into her collar. She could still feel the sting and pull of the stitches on her neck.

The popping sound stopped. She was sure it had been lightbulbs. She could see the tunnel she had just come from had become dark. Someone had smashed the bulbs as he came up behind her.

How the hell was he able to backtrack?

It didn't make sense that the tunnels would wind in a circle. And now she couldn't hear any footsteps. Only water gushing through the pipes. A drip started over her head. She didn't move. Tried to focus on the sounds beyond the pitter-plat.

Within seconds the familiar throb began at her temple. That's when she saw his shadow. He had stopped to listen for her. Just around the last corner, unaware that she could see a piece of his shadow.

She held her breath, trying to quiet the pounding in her head and in her chest. She readjusted her grip on the revolver. It didn't matter. She couldn't fire down here. The bullets would ricochet. He had to know that. Probably counted on it.

She watched the shadow inch forward and she pressed tighter against the wall. The drip found her forehead. Damn! It wasn't just water. She could smell it now. With a slow, smooth motion she switched her grip on the revolver, slipping her fingers down around the barrel, converting it from gun to club.

"O'Dell, where the hell are you?" Racine's voice echoed through the tunnel, almost making Maggie fall off her ledge.

The shadow bobbed and ducked back out of sight. She heard a shuffle, a swish of water, and retreating footsteps. Maggie jumped off the ledge, jogged, and sloshed to the corner.

He was gone.

She tried to listen while her eyes adjusted to the dimmer light. He had to have escaped down one of the dark tunnels. He could be standing halfway down in the pitch black, staring right at her, and she'd never see him. She felt a shiver. It didn't help matters that her feet were soaked and her hair damp.

"O'Dell?"

"I'm here." She finally yelled when she saw a flashlight beam dancing along the wall.

She sidestepped her way to Racine, keeping an eye on the black mouths of the tunnels. Now she realized that to catch him down here would be impossible. He obviously knew his way around. But he was still there in the dark. She could feel him. Almost certain she could smell him. But there was nothing she could do.

CHAPTER 26

"What the hell did you think you were doing?"

Safely back aboveground, Maggie let Racine lecture her. A bit ironic — Racine was usually the one doing something reckless, running off half cocked. It didn't matter. All Maggie could think about was that her feet were freezing. And even in the fresh cold air, she could tell she smelled bad.

"Do you have any idea how dangerous it was to follow him down there?"

"He probably knows his way around," Tully said, holding his arm tight against his side.

Maggie had asked about his arm when she first came out of the manhole. He had looked at her like she was ridiculous, considering she was the one coming up out of a hole in the ground. But he had assured her that nothing was broken. She wasn't so sure about that from the pale look on his face.

"You don't want to go down there if you don't know where you're going," Racine continued her lecture.

"You've been down there?"

"No, but I've heard stories. The tunnels go all over the place. You need higher security clearance these days to work in the sewers than to work in the Pentagon."

"You think he's our firefly?" Tully asked the obvious.

"Why else run?"

"Did you see him?" He wanted to know.

She shook her head. It was true. She hadn't seen him. Now she wondered if she had really seen his shadow or heard footsteps. It didn't make sense. Maybe she'd talk to Tully about it later. She wasn't going to talk about it with Racine. That would be another lecture.

"He could just be some homeless guy," Racine offered. "He was probably scavenging around after the fire and we scared the shit out of him."

"What's in the backpack?" Maggie asked Tully, just realizing that he had it with him.

"I don't think it's his. He may have found it. Or stolen it," Tully told them as he lowered then dropped the bag from his shoulder. The whole time Maggie could see his jaw clenched against the pain.

He tugged open a zippered pocket to show them the small blue booklet inside.

"How many homeless guys do you know carry around their passport?"

Racine pulled out a pair of latex gloves from her bomber jacket pocket and snapped them on. She slid the passport from the bag and carefully flipped the cover open.

"Cornell Stamoran. Nice, clean-cut, professional young man. Blond, blue eyed. Suit and tie."

"The guy we're chasing had a beard. Long dirty hair." Maggie looked at the photo as Racine held it out. "And he looked older."

"The backpack might have been dropped in the alley." Tully turned it over to show them the soot-covered flip side. "Maybe our bearded man found it where Cornell dropped it right before he got his head bashed in."

"You think Cornell could be the victim we found inside the building?"

"We have his address." Racine tapped the passport closed. "I'll send a uniform over to see if he's home. Might be a simple explanation. I've gotta get back downtown. I'd rather Ganza processes that." She pointed to the pack.

"I'll get it to him," Tully said, but kept it on the sidewalk next to him.

Still, Racine hesitated. "You two gonna be okay?"

"Of course we're okay," Tully snapped.

"Hey, just checking."

The exchange made Maggie smile. She was glad to see someone else was annoyed with that question. But Tully's forehead was damp with perspiration and it was chilly here in the shadows of the warehouses, the sun already down low in the sky.

Maggie stood on the sidewalk beside him, watching Racine leave. Neither said anything about the back of her shredded leather jacket. It seemed the perfect symbol for this crazy day.

"This isn't some harmless guy who's been living on the streets."

"I don't think so either," Tully said.

"There was someone else down there."

"City maintenance?"

"I don't think so. He was smashing out lightbulbs."

This got his attention. And his concern.

"Do you know if the tunnels loop around?" she asked.

"I'm not sure, but it wouldn't make sense. The purpose is to move water and sewage from point A to point B, not swirl it back around."

Maggie took a deep breath of fresh air.

148

That's what she had thought. "I heard our guy running away in front of me and I followed. But then I heard someone behind me."

"I suppose he could have crawled back out onto the street and backtracked. But why come back? And smashing out lightbulbs? Doesn't sound like someone who's afraid and running away."

"No, it doesn't."

"So who do you think it was?"

She shrugged. "All I know is that for once I was really glad to hear Racine's voice bitching at me."

This made him smile. "Are you okay?"

"I've got a pain in the neck." Unconsciously her fingers found the sutures, checking to make sure they were intact. "Are you going to be able to drive with that shoulder?"

Finally he allowed a grimace. "I think I may have dislocated it. Can you fix it?"

It had been a long time since the two of them had worked together. She'd forgotten what it was like to have someone covering her backside. Someone who hoped for the same from her.

"Yes, I can. We need to find someplace for you to sit. You're too tall for me." Plus, she failed to add, she didn't want him falling down if he passed out. "It's going to hurt like hell."

"Already does." He followed alongside her. "Don't tell Gwen, okay?"

Maggie smiled. She was usually the one asking *him* not to tell Gwen.

CHAPTER 27

Sam hated riding anywhere with Jeffery. As meticulous as the man was about his physical appearance it certainly didn't carry over to his car. Before she could even climb in, she had to remove a stack of newspapers from the passenger seat, several empty cups, and a jug labeled "swimming pool cleaner" from the floor. It was disgusting. She shook her head while she readjusted the seat, thinking to herself that Jeffery didn't even have a swimming pool.

Of course he didn't notice any of this. He was primed for their interview, breezing through each security checkpoint without even flinching at the trunk check or the excessive pat-downs or the warden's snarky comments.

She had been with Jeffery for every single interview, enduring the body searches that seemed to get more invasive with each visit, with each security check. What bothered her more was how they handled her camera equipment, purposely smudging the lens with their fingerprints. Once a guard even licked the palm of his hand before pressing it against the viewfinder. It was their way of showing they didn't approve of the interviews.

Jeffery shrugged it off when she told him about the harassment. All she got from him was a raised eyebrow when she showed him the used condom they had left inside her equipment bag after one visit. Of course he *could* shrug it off. He was the celebrity who charmed them and told them how important they were, sometimes offering to interview them as well. A safe offer, since he knew the prison rules wouldn't allow it. Still, the guards appeared flattered. The warden, however, was a tougher sell.

So this time Sam took pleasure in the warden's being put out. They'd bent over backward — not necessarily a good choice of words in a prison — but they had worked hard to get interviews for the documentary. Each step of the way, the warden had made it as unpleasant and uncomfortable as possible.

This time Jeffery had been invited, actually "summoned," to the prison by one of the inmates. From Jeffery's vague explanation, an arsonist named Otis P. Dodd had been sending him letters for the last three weeks, insisting that Jeffery talk to him and giving Jeffery details of his crimes as some sort of testament to his expertise.

Sam understood why Jeffery had put the man off. All of the others they had interviewed were murderers. Poor Otis P. — as he liked to be called — had not caused a single death with any of his fires, despite setting about thirty-seven across the state of Virginia. It wasn't for lack of trying. His last one had been a retirement center. Twenty-three residents miraculously made it out alive.

Otis P. was serving the first year of a twenty-five-year sentence. Sam suspected he was missing the attention and excitement. Truth was, he probably wouldn't have garnered Jeffery's attention if it hadn't been for the warehouse arsons. In fact, Sam wondered if Jeffery even intended to use Otis P.'s interview for the documentary or if he simply was curious what insight the man might share about arson.

Sam was still setting up her equipment when a guard brought the prisoner into the room. He and Jeffery exchanged greetings while his shackles were being connected to iron hooks in the concrete floor. She had already seen a photo of him, yet his large physique and lopsided grin surprised her. If you ignored the receding hairline, Otis P. looked like an overgrown teenager uncomfortable with his size. His boyish face had a look of genuine curiosity and a disarming smile.

"Will I have one of those itty-bitty microphones clipped on my collar?" he asked in a soft, gentle — almost childlike — voice, his eyes looking away from Jeffery and over to Sam.

She pulled a wireless from her case and held it up. "Do you mind?"

"No, I'd like that." He licked his lips.

To Sam's relief the guard reached for the microphone to put it on.

She nodded at Jeffery when the camera was ready but it was Otis P. who took her cue.

"I have a gift for you," he told Jeffery.

The statement drew a stunned look from the veteran newsman that unnerved Sam. She had witnessed plenty of Jeffery's performances. This was not one.

There was the smile again and another lick of his lips. Then Otis P. added, "I want to tell you where there's a dead body. A pretty little thing wearing only orange socks."

CHAPTER 28

Sam reminded herself that criminals lied all the time. During some of the previous interviews, she and Jeffery had listened to bizarre tales that murderers claimed as truth. Stories of how they stalked and killed their victims. They'd describe details as though they were proud craftsmen revealing trade secrets.

Some even shared horrible rituals of torture that they endured as children, as if to explain or excuse their compulsions. It was almost impossible to determine what was fact and what was fiction. They were lifers with little hope of parole, so they had nothing to lose by sharing.

But Otis P. Dodd? Sam couldn't figure him out. What reason did he have to confess? He wasn't asking for an attorney to be present. He didn't seem concerned that this new revelation might cut some time off his sentence. About the only thing Sam could think that the man had to gain was attention. And he was certainly getting that.

Jeffery leaned in and stayed uncharacteristically quiet, more patient than Sam had ever seen him. He was allowing Otis P. to take his time and Otis P. was doing just that, enjoying every second.

"He told me she asked him for a ride. Said she was real pretty. Blond hair, blue eyes. Itty-bitty thing. But not a girl. He made sure I knew that. He doesn't do little girls. Or little boys. No challenge in that." He sat back and grinned, pleased to have an audience. "That's what he said anyways."

He started to cross his arms over his chest before he realized his wrist was shackled to the floor. It didn't deter him. "Her car broke down. She was stranded at one of those rest areas off the interstate. He took her to a place in the woods. Bashed her head in. But not so that she was dead. Just part dead. So when he cut her open she'd still be warm."

He paused with that silly grin on his face, like a little boy waiting to see their reaction, wondering if he'd be punished or praised.

"That's what he said. He liked it when the blood was still warm on his hands. Then he pulled her guts out just to see what they looked like. What they felt like."

When neither of them flinched, he continued. "He took everything off her so nobody'd know who she is. Everything except her orange socks. He wanted her to keep those for some reason. I don't remember if he told me why. Then he stuffed her in a culvert."

Otis P. looked away for the first time, up at the ceiling as if trying to think if he had forgotten something.

"At first I thought, *Well, this guy is full of it,* you know. I could tell he wasn't a drinker and we were doing shots. But my daddy wasn't a drinker and some of his biggest truth-telling came out after a shot of whiskey."

He shifted in his chair and looked from Jeffery to Sam and back at Jeffery. He was finished. And now he did look as though he was waiting for praise.

"What did he look like?" Jeffery asked.

"Oh, I don't know." Otis P. shrugged and shook his head. His tongue darted out to lick his lips again and Sam realized it was a nervous habit, not meant to be salacious, as she had thought earlier. "He looked like a pretty ordinary fella to me."

And that was all he was going to tell them. This wasn't about the other guy. This was about Otis P. getting attention. He wasn't going to share his time in the spotlight, not even with the murderer whose tale he was telling.

"I can show you where she is. He told me."

"What makes you think she's still in the same place?"

"Oh, she's still there."

"You've been in here, what? Almost a year?"

A nod. The tongue did a quick poke out of the corner of his mouth and slipped back inside.

"What makes you think the body's still where he said he dumped it?"

"Oh, she's still there. Ain't nobody found her."

"How do you know for sure?"

"I've been watching." Another shrug of his shoulder. "I know she's still there. It'd be somethin', wouldn't it? Have a camera right there?" He waited to make sure Jeffery knew what he was talking about before he added, "You let me know. I'll take you there."

Then he was finished. He had told them all he was prepared to say.

It was dark outside when they made their way back to the car. Both of them had been quiet while they went through the halls and waited for the doors to unlock.

Now out in the open, walking side by side,

with no one to eavesdrop, Sam asked, "What do you think?"

"He just wants a free road trip."

Sam could tell Jeffery had already dismissed the idea and she was surprised. It sounded like the sensational crap he loved. "You don't believe him?"

"When it comes to arson, I think Otis P. Dodd knows just about every single way to start a fire. He's a master and his letters share all sorts of details. But this?" He waved his hand. "This is bullshit. I thought he'd give me something I could use for the warehouse fires. I'm not going to help him fly the coop or, worse, pull a Geraldo and go live only to get a frickin' empty crypt."

"So what about the woman in the orange socks?"

"If she ever existed, she's been dead for over a year. There's nothing we can do to help her now."

CHAPTER 29

Patrick had spent the afternoon racing all over the neighborhood. He had gone door to door. Even met the asshole who, again, threatened to shoot Jake if the dog ended up anywhere on his property.

"Wouldn't it be easier to just call me?" Patrick had asked the man.

"Not much point after the third or fourth time. My solution keeps that bastard out of my yard permanently."

That's when Patrick went back, put Harvey on a leash, and the two of them set out to canvass the entire neighborhood, again. He even checked the empty house that was for sale next door to Maggie's. Canvassed the backyard. Peeked inside the windows after he saw a light on. Lamp on a timer. People hated leaving empty houses dark, but they didn't think about lights being a fire hazard.

Three hours later, it was dark and still no

sign of Jake.

The thought of telling Maggie nauseated Patrick. She had gone out of her way to let him into her home and he'd let her down. How could he have been so negligent? He'd let the meeting with Braxton rattle him too much. It was just a job. Could the man really destroy his entire career over one mistake?

Harvey jerked to the left. The Lab wanted to cross the street. His nose was in the air.

"You smell him, Harv?"

He let the dog lead him, allowed him to tug hard on the leash and guide him. Harvey trotted up and over the sidewalk, continuing along a ridge of pine trees, dragging Patrick to the back corner lot of a huge colonial. Before they made it to the fence Patrick could smell what had piqued Harvey's attention. It wasn't Jake. Someone was grilling steaks.

They trudged home as the moon peeked from behind that same ridge of pines. Maybe Jake had come back on his own. As a boy Patrick had always wanted a dog but his mother always said no. She said a dog was too much responsibility. He longed for the company, someone to greet him at the door when he came from school to an empty home. He hated to think his mom

might still be right — that he couldn't handle the responsibility of another living being.

He saw Maggie's Jeep Grand Cherokee parked in the circle drive and he hoped he'd find them together. No such luck. She was at the kitchen island checking the Crock-Pot he'd left simmering.

"Did you take the boys for a long walk?" she asked when they came around the corner. She was in her robe, her hair still wet from a shower. As she turned to look at Patrick he saw her face fall when she saw he had only Harvey. "He got out, again," she said. Not a question. She knew.

"I'm really sorry." He didn't know what else to say. "We looked everywhere. Twice."

She was trying to hide the panic he'd seen earlier, but he caught a glimpse in her eyes before she purposely turned away.

"Maybe I should never have brought him here. So far away from everything he knew."

"He's a smart dog. He'll find his way back."

"That's if he wants to." She still avoided his eyes, but he heard the emotion in her voice. This was more than just concern for a lost dog. It cut deeper, and she didn't want to share it. Besides that, she looked exhausted.

She pointed to the oven, where he had left the scallops on warm. "This smells wonderful."

"I wanted to treat you. Are you hungry?"

"I'm starved."

She bent down to take Harvey's leash off and hugged the big dog. He sniffed the back of her neck and suddenly started a low whine.

"Is he okay?" Patrick pulled the pan out of the oven, tipped the lid, then, satisfied, slid it back in.

"The smell of blood makes him nervous." She petted the dog, trying to calm him.

"And why would he . . . Oh crap, are you okay?"

"I'm fine. Just a few stitches."

"What happened?"

"A second fire blew out some windows along with the front of the building."

"I hate when that happens," he joked.

"Yes, I suppose you are familiar with that sort of thing," she said, as if she only now remembered that he was a firefighter.

Patrick tried to shrug it off. He pulled a bottle of Shiraz from the fridge and held it up for Maggie.

"Not an expensive vino, but very tasty. I thought you'd get a kick out of the label."

"Shoofly?"

"It's Australian." He tipped the bottle for her to see the decal on the cork and on the label.

"It looks like a blowfly."

"Aussies have an interesting sense of humor. So what do you say, mate," he attempted his best Australian accent, "would you like a glass?"

"Sure."

She watched him set out an antipasto plate with olives, cubes of cheese, and Genoa salami. Then he worked the corkscrew and poured two glasses of wine.

"You went all out," she said, plucking up an olive and popping it into her mouth.

"Hey, I know you're trying to be nice and calm about Jake, but the truth is I should have paid closer attention. You're allowed to be mad as hell with me."

He handed her a glass of wine. She gulped almost half of it like she was chugging water. Patrick stopped, surprised. He hadn't seen this side of Maggie. He suspected that she was being careful and selective in what she let him see.

"It isn't your fault, Patrick. He's done it when I've been here. Sometimes immediately after I've let him into the yard. I see my fenced fortress as security. Jake sees it as a prison."

164

She emptied the rest of her glass before Patrick even took a sip of his.

CHAPTER 30

"This is the longest he's been gone," Maggie told Lucy Coy over the phone.

"Jake's used to taking care of himself. He always ran off for days when he was with me."

"But that was in the country, where he had the forest and cornfields and fresh rabbits. He doesn't know about traffic and neighbors with guns." She tried to keep the panic from her voice. She wasn't sure why this upset her so much. Maybe it was simply that she was exhausted. Too little sleep. The fire, the stitches, her strange adventure down in the sewer. Jake escaping and not coming back was just the break point in a long day.

"Jake saved my life," Maggie said, "and how do I repay him? By taking him thirteen hundred miles away from everything and everyone he's ever known."

"You're taking his leaving as an affront."

"Isn't it?"

"He's checking out his surroundings."

"It's been almost four months. They're not that new anymore."

"Marking his territory. Staking his claim, if you will."

"Escaping from the prison I keep him in."

Lucy Coy laughed that melodic sound that came rarely but, when it did come, sounded natural and heartfelt. It was also contagious, and Maggie laughed, too.

She rubbed her eyes. Took a deep breath. Yes, she was being melodramatic and ridiculous. The physical exhaustion of the day had spilled over into her mind. It had taken twenty minutes in the shower to get the smell of smoke, hospital antiseptic, and the sewer removed from her skin, out of her hair.

"We cannot tame the wild spirit that lives within Jake."

This was the philosophical side of the woman that had mesmerized Maggie while she was a guest in Lucy's home in the Sandhills of Nebraska.

"Is it possible," Lucy continued, "that you find it so unsettling because you wrestle with the same nonconforming spirit within yourself?"

Maggie smiled and attempted to shake

that "aha" feeling that Lucy so often triggered. Her preintroduction to Lucy Coy was a county sheriff who called her "that crazy old Indian woman." The retired death investigator for the Nebraska State Patrol was nowhere near crazy or old. Instead, words like "graceful," "contemplative," "disciplined," and "wise" beyond her sixty-plus years better described the woman whom Maggie recognized as a kindred spirit. When Lucy mentioned Maggie's nonconforming spirit, Maggie took it not as an accusation but as the compliment it was meant to be.

"Didn't you tell me there's a stream that runs behind your property?"

"Yes."

"Sounds like the perfect hunting grounds for him."

It was one of the reasons Maggie bought the place. The steep ridges on both sides of the stream made it a natural barricade, almost like her personal moat.

Lucy's voice and manner had started to soothe and calm Maggie until she heard the *tap-tap* of rain begin to hit the glass of the patio door. Immediately she was on her feet, Harvey beside her, looking out into the dark backyard. Leafless trees waved skeletal branches.

"It's starting to rain," she said. "It could be sleet by morning."

"I remember him being out last winter all night after a snowfall. It must have been freezing. I have no idea how or where he kept warm."

"And when he came back he was okay?"

"Brought back a half-eaten rabbit and left it on the front porch for me. Sharing's never been an issue with him. In fact, I think it was his peace offering."

"You make him sound as if he has supernatural powers."

There was silence. Maggie had grown accustomed to Lucy's contemplative pauses.

"Go ahead and get some rest, Maggie. Jake will be fine." And then she added, "And so will you."

"I hope you're right."

"Just prepare yourself for whatever peace offering he brings back. Let's just hope it's not the arm of your gun-toting neighbor."

She smiled. Tapped the phone's End button. But before she could put the phone down, it started ringing.

It was Racine. Maggie's body tensed at the thought of the arsonist hitting again so quickly.

"Do we have another fire?" Maggie asked

without a greeting.

"A different kind of fire. Turn on CNN."

CHAPTER 31

"Where did he get all these photos?"

Maggie didn't feel angry as much as betrayed and a little sick to her stomach.

"What's the cocktail-dress occasion?" Racine had stayed on the line and they watched together as Jeffery Cole revealed Maggie's life for the world to see. He even had a photo of her father and mother.

"I don't think I've ever seen you in a dress," Racine said when Maggie failed to answer.

"It was a New Year's Eve party for my ex-husband's law firm. They were congratulating me that night, welcoming me to the firm. Greg got me a job as their claims investigator."

"You wanted to investigate lawsuit claims?"

"No, not at all. I had no idea. It was supposed to be a surprise. Greg hated my being an FBI agent."

"Maybe he just hated your playing rough-and-tumble with killers."

"He hated that he couldn't control me, keep me neat and tidy like the rest of his life."

There was an uncomfortable pause.

"You look totally hot in that little black dress." Racine's attempt at humor only made it worse.

Years ago Julia Racine had made a pass at Maggie. Somehow they had managed to get past it and become friends. Part of their journey to friendship had to do with Racine saving Maggie's mother from a suicide attempt and Maggie saving Racine's father from a killer. Both women had grown up without one parent; perhaps it was this absence, this sense of loss that continued to bring them together.

Now that Maggie thought about her mother she couldn't help wondering if that's where Jeffery Cole had gotten some of the photos.

"Why do you suppose he's doing this?" Maggie asked.

"You ruffled his feathers. Piqued his interest. I didn't know you were a forensic fellow at Quantico. Impressive. They don't even have that program anymore, do they?"

"Is this legal? Can he do an exposé like

this on an FBI agent?"

"Your ex-husband might know."

"Very funny."

"I wasn't trying to be funny. He might actually know."

"It's too late. They're already airing it."

"Yeah, but it could stop part two."

"Please tell me you're kidding."

"No, really. Tomorrow night is part two. The whole thing runs back-to-back this weekend. I figure I'll tape it."

"Unbelievable."

"So here's something interesting." Racine must have sensed it was time to change the subject. "Cornell Stamoran used to be an accountant with Greevey, Miles and Holden up until eleven months ago. They're one of the major financial consulting firms in the District. Their client list reads like a who's who directory."

"So how did he get his passport stolen?"

"Don't know. He wasn't home to ask. Landlord said he ducked out on his rent months ago. Nobody at the consulting firm knows where he is either. Greevey said he just didn't show up one day. Said he had a bit of a drinking problem."

"Any chance it's his bashed-in skull that was found inside?"

"Anything's possible."

Maggie's phone beeped.

"I have another call coming in. Autopsy still on for the morning?"

"Stan said nine o'clock. I'll see you there." And Racine clicked off.

Maggie checked her caller ID, saw that it was Benjamin Platt, smiled, then connected.

"Do you still have that little black dress?"

It wasn't exactly the greeting she expected. She felt the annoying but pleasant flip in her stomach.

"Racine already beat you to that punch line."

"Goes to show we both have impeccable taste."

She thought about telling him how sexy he looked this morning in his dress uniform. For some reason she stopped herself, stood up, and began to pace the living room. She glanced out the patio door, the glass still rain-streaked. It was coming down harder now.

"How are you holding up?" Ben asked.

Of course, Maggie realized, he was worried about her. That was the real reason for his call. Not such a bad thing, she reminded herself.

"Jake got out again this afternoon," she said, changing the focus from her. "He hasn't come back yet."

"You want me to take a look around for him?"

"Patrick checked all over for him." Suddenly it occurred to her that Jake probably wouldn't come to Patrick's voice or command. Why hadn't she thought of that sooner? Maybe if she went out and called for him. "It's late," she told Ben. "And it's raining."

"I don't mind," he said. "I can be there in fifteen to twenty minutes."

From the patio window Maggie could make out the ridge at the back of the property, beyond the privacy fence. Pine trees stood like sentries guarding the corners. Streetlights didn't reach back that far. Her subtle landscape lighting was only enough to create shadows.

"Lucy says he'll be fine. That he'll come back on his own. I can't keep racing after him and dragging him home."

A spot of light flashed on the other side of the fence. She could see it through the wood slats. It flickered, then moved along her property line. As suddenly as it appeared, it was gone.

Maybe it was a reflection? Maybe her imagination was playing tricks on her.

She rubbed the back of her neck, fingering the sutures. Patrick's wine had actually settled the throbbing in her head. It was quiet, contained for the time being, but her neck ached.

"Lucy's probably right," Ben finally said, only Maggie had already forgotten what it was that Lucy might be right about.

She shut off the lamp and paced from window to window, trying to see the light again. The house was dark except for the muted television. Red and blue reflections of her life according to Jeffery Cole lit up the corners of the living room. Maggie moved to the kitchen and the back door. That's when she saw another flash.

"I'll have to call you back," she told Ben. "I need to check something." She clicked off before he could ask any questions.

The spot of light bounced behind the fence and skipped a path to the edge of the ridge. Despite the mist, Maggie could see the silhouette of a person following the beam of light.

"What's going on?"

Patrick's voice made her jump. He stood in the entrance to the kitchen in pajama bottoms, nothing else.

"Someone's out there," she whispered, noticing that her heart had already started hammering in her chest.

Patrick was looking over her shoulder

before she said, "It's probably nothing. Someone looking for a lost dog." The exact thing she was contemplating doing just minutes before.

"Or that asshole neighbor tracking Jake."

He spun around and darted for the stairs.

"What are you doing?"

"Putting on some clothes and shoes." He stopped halfway up the stairs just long enough to add, "Bring your gun."

CHAPTER 32

Jeffery had begged Sam to get the photos he needed for part two of his profile piece and have them ready for him first thing in the morning. She should have done it earlier but Otis P.'s tall tale, whether fiction or fact, had freaked her out. She couldn't help wondering if there was some poor woman's body stuffed in a culvert, her orange socks hidden by mud and leaves.

When they left the prison all Sam wanted to do was go home. All week she had gotten home late, after her mother and son were already in bed. After Otis P.'s tale, Sam wanted to be with her family. She had decided to go home instead of straight out to get the photos Jeffery ordered. For once she'd put work second.

She had dinner with her mother and son, almost like a normal family. Then she cuddled up next to little Ignacio, or Iggy as most of his friends called him. He read to her as they snuggled in his bed, roles reversed. They both fell asleep. When her mother woke her, Sam wanted to stay put. The day had already been a long and crazy one, but she had promised Jeffery.

She was used to his giving her a laundry list for background photos or footage that he absolutely had to have. She had given up asking questions a long time ago. She'd clock the extra hours and he'd make sure she was compensated. These days she could use the extra cash, and taking photos at all hours was still better than waiting tables, which is what she did for too many years while she went back to school. She'd never have been able to do any of it without her mother taking care of her precious son.

Rained slowed interstate traffic. By the time she arrived at the address Jeffery had given her it was late. On nights like this one, crawling out of a warm bed and going out into a cold driving rain made it a bit harder to remember that this was her dream job.

She slipped the plastic covers over her equipment and zipped up her rain jacket, pulling the hood over her head. The rain had let up a bit. She parked two blocks away from the housing development on Jeffery's directions. There was no way she could leave her car on the street and not be noticed. It was a neighborhood that was used to BMWs, Lexuses, and Mercedes-Benzes. Her ten-year-old Chevy would have had the local sheriff checking it out and maybe even towing it before she got back.

She followed a path behind the huge fenced-in lots alongside a steep drop-off. She flicked on a flashlight to get her bearings, then turned it off. Now that the rain had changed to a steady drizzle, she could hear water rumbling over the rocks below. She caught a glimpse of the stream and the rocky walls.

She paused and squatted down, resting her camera bag on the wet grass. She'd prepared her equipment in the car, pulling on rain sleeves, though her camera was supposed to be waterproof. The hood over the lens and the infrared strobe were expensive additions, courtesy of Jeffery.

When he had given her the new pieces she joked about turning her into a paparazzo. Jeffery didn't find it amusing. He was an award-winning journalist, soon to be anchor-slash-host of his own daily news show — or at least that was his hope. Sam wondered if he realized he was getting too old to run with the young bulls in this industry.

He'd come a long way from what he called

his humble beginnings as a high school teacher. Sam didn't know why this wasn't enough for him. But his own show had become yet another obsession. He seemed determined to make it happen no matter what he had to do. No matter what Big Mac demanded. He didn't care how many hurdles Sam had to jump, because he knew her future had become intertwined with his.

She just wished she could make him understand why requests like this one, in particular, certainly made her feel like a paparazzo. He was doing this sort of thing more and more. The line began to blur between real journalism and sensational reality TV. If only he could see her now.

Sam was fumbling in her pocket for her flashlight when she noticed a beam of light ahead of her about a hundred yards. The shadow of a man followed.

Sam froze.

Maybe it was a resident walking his dog, though this was much too bumpy and steep to be a walking path. And she didn't see a dog. The man seemed focused on the house on the other side of the fence. The brim of his baseball cap pointed in that direction.

Who was Sam to judge? Here she was, late at night, sneaking around to get photos of that very same house.

Twigs snapped in front of her. Something stirred in the tall grass that lined the ridge. She slipped to her knees and held her breath. She tried to reassure herself that wildlife probably lived down closer to the stream. It was probably a beaver or raccoon. Whatever it was, it was moving away from her and in the direction of the man.

She eased her camera up, slowly, quietly, keeping her eyes on the grass. The zoom lens made the camera heavy enough that she had to use both hands. She started to raise it to eye level.

"Put down the gun."

The voice from behind startled her so much she jumped. But instinct made her grip the camera tighter. At first she thought the warning was meant for the man ahead of her, but when she looked up for him, he was gone.

"Put it down." The woman's voice came with measured breaths.

"It's not a gun." Sam's hands shook but she kept them from moving, from flinching under the camera's weight. Would the woman really shoot her? In the back? "It's a camera," she tried to explain. "I'd rather not put it in the grass."

Oh God, she couldn't believe she'd said that. Jeffery would certainly say she had grown a pair of cojones.

"What the hell are you doing back here?"

"Wildlife photography," Sam said without missing a beat, realizing Jeffery had taught her to be an instinctively good liar. "There was something in the grass." Not entirely a lie. Even her mother would agree that lying for self-preservation was forgivable.

"At night?"

Sam shrugged. She was already going to hell. Then she said, "I have an infrared filter."

The woman came around to face her, shining her flashlight into Sam's eyes. She could still see the outline of the gun aimed directly at her face. Suddenly she realized this wasn't a suburban housewife with a neighborhood watch group.

"Since when does a cable news station sponsor wildlife photography?"

Now Sam recognized the woman's voice. The target of Jeffery's documentary had just made Sam a target.

CHAPTER 33

Back in the warm, dry kitchen Patrick suggested coffee to distract Maggie from still wanting to shoot the woman with the camera. He'd never seen Maggie so angry and wondered if she'd rather have found a serial killer stalking her than this photojournalist.

He insisted that Maggie prepare the coffee, pretending he didn't know where she kept the filters. Fact was, he'd made coffee in her kitchen more in the last month than she probably had in the last several years. Since they'd come in out of the rain Maggie hadn't put down her gun. She did so now, stuffing it into the back of her jeans' waistband so she could make the coffee.

Patrick grabbed a stack of towels from a linen closet in the hall and offered one to the woman who had introduced herself as Samantha Ramirez. As she thanked him, her eyes — a gorgeous mocha brown — held his for a second too long before she probably realized he wasn't on her side. He still wasn't clear how this woman and Maggie had met. Maggie kept mentioning a hit piece on CNN. Ramirez didn't offer any explanation. She seemed to recognize the situation was volatile enough and that it was best to say as little as possible.

"I don't get it," Maggie said as she smacked the coffeepot into its slot. "What's so fascinating about me?"

She pushed the START button, then realized she didn't have the machine plugged in. She yanked the cord free and shoved it into the nearby electrical outlet.

Before Ramirez could respond, Maggie continued, "I've gone through so much trouble to protect myself from killers — the fence, the security system, the stream at the back of the property — and you and your partner rip open my life for everyone in a matter of . . . what? Twenty-four, thirty-six hours?"

She pounded the coffeemaker's START button again, and this time the machine sputtered and began to hiss.

"Why?" Maggie asked, and came to a standstill in front of Ramirez, who sat at the kitchen's island across from her. "Why me?"

"Believe it or not, it's not personal."

Ramirez looked from Maggie to Patrick.

It seemed as though she was imploring him to understand. Maybe she thought he would be more reasonable. Maybe she realized he couldn't take his eyes off her. She toweled off her shoulder-length hair and sent the dark curls and waves into a wild cascade around her face. She reminded Patrick of some beautiful creature from Greek mythology.

"No, I don't believe it's not personal," Maggie told her. She stared at Ramirez and crossed her arms over her chest. Then in almost a whisper she said, "Do you have any idea how close I came to shooting you?"

Ramirez's head jerked up. Her hand with the towel froze in midair.

No, Patrick thought. She didn't have any idea how close; neither did he.

Patrick continued to stay back like a spectator, watching the two women, close enough to intervene but far enough away that Maggie could ignore him.

Was she bluffing? Had she almost fired at the camerawoman?

In the fog and the mist it had been difficult to differentiate whether or not the camera was a gun. And Maggie had been upset, wound tight. He'd watched her once before confront a gunman. He'd seen her in action. He had watched Maggie shift into survival mode. It was like she had this ON switch that when activated, she jumped into motion, single-minded and determined to do the right thing, whatever it took, no matter the consequences, no matter the risk to her own well-being.

It was one of the things he admired about his sister. She was a hero, just like their father had been. She was so much braver than Patrick. Yet at the same time, he understood how easy it was to let your emotions, your fears, your imagination get the best of you and drive you to panic. A panic that could prompt reckless assumptions and misperceptions. But despite this wave of uncharacteristic anger, he knew Maggie O'Dell would never have fired without being sure.

Samantha Ramirez, however, was not sure at all. "Look," Ramirez began, and Patrick thought he saw her hand shake. "Jeffery's an asshole sometimes. I honestly have no idea why he does half the things he does."

"You just go along?"

"Basically, yes."

"You have no journalistic integrity?"

Patrick could see Ramirez's back go straight and her nostrils flare. "You know what I have?" she said, fear quickly firing over into anger. "I have a six-year-old son and I want him to grow up without having to clean toilets or wait on some asshole like Jeffery Cole. I have a Mexican mother who watches *Jeopardy!* as faithfully as she prays to the Virgin Mary so she can learn English well enough to pass her citizenship test. I have a shitload of bills and a mortgage twice the amount my tiny little two-bedroom home will ever be worth. So excuse me if I can't afford your precious integrity just yet."

The two women stared each other down. Rain began to pelt the windows again, only now it sounded more like sleet. The coffeemaker sputtered to an end, filling the kitchen with its fresh-brewed aroma.

Just when Patrick wondered if Maggie would throw Ramirez out into the storm, Maggie said, "Do you use cream or sugar?"

CHAPTER 34

Maggie tried not to give in to the hammering inside her head. She had thought once she was back inside, out of the rain and the cold, that the *thrum-thump* would subside. She was wrong.

She had not shot at Ramirez, but how close had she come?

She unleashed her anger on the woman, but, quite honestly, she was angrier with herself and a bit unnerved that the pain at her temple could blur her vision and challenge her judgment.

The rain had turned to sleet. When Maggie offered Ramirez the sofa for what little of the night was left, the woman stared at her as if looking for a trap. Finally she relented, calling her mother to explain while Patrick, almost too enthusiastically, went to fetch blankets and a pillow.

Ramirez was on the phone in the living room and Patrick in the upstairs linen closet when Maggie heard a thump and a scrape against the back door. She grabbed for the gun tucked against the small of her back. Still, she jumped when she saw the face at the back-door window.

Benjamin Platt's hair was soaked, his smile anxious. Immediately Maggie realized she had forgotten to call him back. But how crazy to come all this way just to check on her. It wasn't until she opened the door that she saw he had Jake with him.

"Oh, my God! Where did you find him?"

She pulled them both in and saw that Ben had his own dog, Digger, tucked under his arm. Harvey came running into the kitchen, whining and nosing and butt-welcoming the huge black shepherd and the small white Westie.

Maggie threw a towel around Jake along with her arms, hugging and wiping at the sleet that stuck to his fur, for as long as Jake would allow. Ben wiped down Digger before he started on his own head.

"How in the world did you find him?"

"You forget that Digger earned his name. I figured he'd know where to look."

The dogs started tussling with one another, and Maggie stood back and watched Ben.

"The first time Digger got out and didn't

190

come back, Ali was crushed. She took it so personally."

"It's hard not to."

"I know. I could hear it in your voice."

Rain dripped from his chin and he wiped it with the sleeve of his jacket, which was equally drenched. Ice crystals stuck to his hair and eyelashes. Maggie pulled a fresh towel from the pile that Patrick had brought earlier. Instead of handing it to Ben she came to him, held his eyes, and gently began wiping his hair, his face, his neck.

She felt him shiver under her touch when she unzipped his jacket. Her hands hesitated on his chest before she pushed the jacket off his broad shoulders, easing it down his arms and enjoying the feel of his muscles going tense beneath her fingertips.

His button-down shirt was soaking, too. She started unbuttoning it with no resistance from Ben. The look in his eyes made her fingers eager. Of course, she had forgotten about Ramirez until the woman cleared her throat behind them.

"Sorry." Ramirez looked genuinely apologetic. Then with a forced smile she added, "I hope you're not going to wish you'd shot me."

Maggie stepped back and introduced the two by first names only, not wanting to share any more information than necessary for the photojournalist to take back to Jeffery Cole.

Ramirez pointed to the wet dogs. "So you must be the guy in the ball cap I saw out back. I thought you might be looking for a dog."

"Out back?" Maggie asked.

"I saw him just ahead of me. Right before you busted me. For a minute I thought you were casing the property."

Maggie glanced at Ben, who had already spun around and was looking out the back window.

"I wasn't at the back of the property," he said as he ran a hand up over his soaked head. "And I didn't have a ball cap on."

CHAPTER 35

The TV profile had finally put a name to the woman cop. Margaret "Maggie" O'Dell. Actually, he wasn't surprised to find out she was an FBI agent. That only contributed to the intrigue.

A couple of hours earlier he had tracked her all the way home after their encounter underground. Though brief, he got to watch her in action and it only fueled his desire to see more. So he followed her. His vehicle was one that she'd never suspect. No one did. It made him almost invisible, and he was able to drive practically to her front door.

He had stayed for a while, parked in an area where he could continue to watch until the guy with the dog came up the front lawn. He thought he was her husband. Decided to leave. He thought he'd scout the neighborhood, maybe go pick up some fast food. That's when he found the motel.

It was just off the interstate, not far from her house, and he had an intense urge to stay close to her for the night.

He was settled in bed, almost dozing, when he saw her face on TV. He was sorry the television didn't have a larger screen so he could get a really good look at her. It was an old TV, not the sleek flat-screen he was used to. Everything about the motel was old, but he learned when he was on the road that sometimes he couldn't be choosy. Besides, the room was clean and he liked that it had a front and back door.

The show had made him antsy. He'd never sleep now that her image had been inside this motel room. Almost without realizing it, he had dressed and was back in his vehicle, back on the road, driving through the fog and the rain. Heading back to her neighborhood.

It was impossible to see inside her house, even from the back. He might have ventured closer if that damned dog hadn't been crouched in the tall grass, growling like some rabid animal ready to pounce. A black creature with snarling white teeth, standing guard.

His mother used to talk about black creatures of the night that warded off evil. That Margaret O'Dell should have one of these guarding her made her a worthy adversary indeed.

His outing stirred him up more than ever. Driving away from Margaret O'Dell was like pulling away from a magnetic field.

He passed by the exit for the motel and kept on driving, despite the sleet. He knew the only thing that would help calm him.

■ ■ ■ ■

FRIDAY

■ ■ ■ ■

CHAPTER 36

Maggie thought the dead body looked almost artificial, splayed out on the stainless-steel table, gray and waxy under the fluorescent lights. A brutally murdered body could sometimes bear little resemblance to anything human. This was one of those times.

Maggie and Racine stood side by side, gowned up and waiting now for Stan. One of his dieners had already photographed, washed, and X-rayed the dead woman. Stan had been interrupted shortly after he started, called away to take an important phone call. He'd already cut and spread opened the victim's chest. The woman's heart lay on a tray, her lungs on another, and the stomach on a third — all in a row on the counter like some freakish display.

Since she hadn't been at the scene, Maggie flipped through photos that had been taken of the body back in the alley beside the Dumpster. Some of the woman's clothes had been singed and covered with cinders, but Maggie didn't see any burn marks on her flesh.

"Had to be someone who knew her, right?" Racine said. "Strangers don't usually bash in the face like that."

"Unless he wanted to destroy her identity. It's possible he knew her. That she wasn't a random victim."

"The cardboard box definitely wasn't hers."

"She wasn't homeless," Maggie said. "Her legs are shaved."

"Doesn't cross off prostitute," Racine said. She pointed to the purple bruising that colored the woman's entire left side, from arm to hip to leg. "Livor mortis — she had to be on her side for several hours after she died. Wherever she died, it wasn't in that alley."

Racine was right. Livor mortis, called the bruising of death, was often a telltale sign of the victim's last position. After the heart stops circulating blood, gravity pulls the blood down to settle at the lowest spot where the body meets a surface.

"Even left an imprint," Racine added. "Looks like she was on some kind of a grate."

Maggie took a closer look. The skin on the woman's hip was embossed with a meshlike pattern.

"Anything found in the alley that would match that?"

"Not unless they pulled it out of the Dumpster. I'll check later."

They were quiet again. Maggie looked through more of the photos. Racine glanced over her shoulder for Stan. She crossed her arms over her chest. Her foot tapped out her growing impatience.

"So what are you getting Ben for Valentine's Day?"

"Excuse me?"

It wasn't the strangest question ever asked over a dead body. Maggie had learned long ago that law enforcement officers talked or joked about some of the oddest stuff. Their way of releasing the tension of the moment.

"Valentine's Day," Racine repeated. "It's next week. This is the first time I've ever been with someone long enough to give a Valentine's Day gift. I'm like Houdini when it comes to relationships — constantly looking for the trapdoor or an escape as soon as the 'L' word is exchanged."

"Really? What about Jill?"

"I forgot you met her. Nope. Four months."

"She seemed nice."

"She was psycho."

"I thought she was an MP in the army?"

"Yeah, I should have taken that as a warning. So what are you getting Ben?"

"Ben and I aren't there yet."

"Right."

"We're friends."

"For real? I thought for sure you two were doing it."

The automatic door buzzed open and Maggie tried not to look relieved as Stan returned.

"Ladies, my apologies for the delay. Where were we?"

"Weapons," Racine said, going from Valentine's Day to murder without missing a beat. "What does that to a face? Baseball bat?"

"No, not a bat. It had to be something with a sharp end. Maybe a claw of some sort. It gouged her flesh. Didn't just create flyers but pulled out chunks of tissue, some of which we found in her hair and on her clothes. We didn't find it all, though, which makes me certain she wasn't killed in the alley."

"Anything under her fingernails?" Maggie asked.

"No. Actually there are no defensive

wounds. Something like this would have left her arms and hands with tremendous bruises, not to mention possible broken bones. Teeth and jaw are pretty much shattered. They won't be much help with ID. I do think she was spared and wasn't conscious for long."

"You think the first blow incapacitated her?"

"That's my initial thought. I won't be able to confirm that until I finish."

"So what the hell did he use?" Racine asked.

"A crowbar or a claw hammer?" Maggie offered.

"Either's a possibility. It didn't splinter. Something metal makes sense. There's a bit of residue inside the nasal cavity, or what's left of it. Something oily. Hard to tell with all the caked blood. I've sent a swab to the lab."

"If her fingerprints aren't on file and we don't have teeth, you're not giving me much to work with, Stan," Racine told the medical examiner. "No one's going to be able to make a visual ID."

Stan shrugged. That wasn't his problem. He was finished with the outside for now. He walked over to the counter, where he had left the extracted organs. He was methodical in processing the body. It was up to Maggie and Racine to take those facts and piece them together as evidence of what happened.

Maggie watched him take what looked like a bread knife and slice open the stomach, tugging back the lining.

"Full house here," he said.

Racine covered her nose while both she and Maggie stepped closer.

"So she'd just eaten," Maggie said.

"Within two hours of dying." Stan poked at the contents, slipping a glob of it onto the tray. "Actually I'd say within an hour. Kind of an odd combination here. Looks like maybe doughnuts. I'm guessing until we can test it. Maybe potato chips." He pushed a red piece around the tray. "Licorice."

"Licorice?"

"Sounds like road food," Racine said.

Stan and Maggie both stopped to stare at Racine.

"I eat crap like that when I drive up to see my dad," she explained. "Stop for gas, pick up something to munch."

The automatic door wheezed open and Stan's diener hurried in with the X-rays.

"Dr. Wenhoff, I think you'll want to take a look at this."

He slapped the pieces of film onto the front of a light box. Secured them in place and turned on the light.

Maggie immediately noticed the white oval in the chest X-ray.

Stan tapped it with his pen. "The killer evidently didn't know the victim very well."

"Is that what I think it is?" Racine asked.

"But there's only one," Maggie said.

"A single breast implant usually indicates cancer rather than just cosmetic surgery. Good news is, we should be able to figure out who she is. It's considered a surgical device, so it'll have the manufacturer and a serial number."

"So they can match it in a database?" Maggie asked.

"The bastard didn't count on that when he was bashing in her face and teeth."

"Should be able to give us the name and address of the surgeon," Stan said. "You'll need to convince him to give you the patient's name."

"Simple as that," Racine said.

"Not quite so simple. I'll need to cut it out completely. The serial number's on the other side."

CHAPTER 37

Tully settled into the editing studio, surprised at how small it was. His long legs folded uncomfortably, his knees against a panel of knobs, switches, and keyboards. The space reminded him more of a cockpit than a television news studio.

The engineer Samantha Ramirez introduced as Abe Nadira was not pleased to have Tully beside him. He glanced at Tully, eyes only, head straight forward. His lips pressed together, a thin line that barely moved when he talked. He gave one-word replies most of the time. Tully was relieved that Sam stayed. He didn't get the whole story of what had happened last night at Maggie's, but it had changed the young camerawoman's attitude. Suddenly she was willing to do whatever she could to help them.

She stood behind them, directing Nadira like a backseat driver, only with a quiet and gentle patience.

"I think you might need to go back all the way to a minute, forty seconds. I did a brief test," Sam said, "then a full sweep of the area."

She was referring to her film footage from the fire, the minutes before the rescue teams arrived. Tully still didn't buy her reason for getting to the fire so quickly. She claimed she and Jeffery Cole were supposed to meet for a late dinner after finishing up what she called a "puff piece" on the District's homeless. They had spent several hours shooting in front of the Martin Luther King Jr. Memorial Library, where the evening buses unloaded the homeless who had commuted downtown for the day and were returning.

That he believed.

Racine had mentioned the program. He had checked and found that the last bus dropped off passengers at about six thirty. Even if Sam and Jeffery had hung around to do more filming, the time stamp on her footage displayed 11:10. That was a pretty late dinner for a thirty-two-year-old woman who had a six-year-old son at home.

He'd checked out Samantha Ramirez last night, too. As remorseful as she seemed about switching cartridges on him, there was something this woman wasn't telling him. Something she didn't want him to know.

Nadira had started playing the film and Tully sat forward, resting his elbows on his knees, since they were up to his chest anyway. He pushed his glasses up and settled his chin on his fists. The position pulled at his shoulder, reminding him that it was still tender from his fall in the alley.

There were very few people in Sam's initial sweep with the camera. She caught them wide-eyed, crawling up off the sidewalk or wandering into the street from the alleys and door wells. The first flames were encased behind the windows, which were still intact. It was almost as if the fire had just started. Was it possible that they had been there that soon?

"Do you know who called in the fire?"

"No idea."

"How did Jeffery find out?"

"He has a police scanner. He always knows stuff before anyone else. Sometimes I think he must be psychic."

"Jeffery psychic. That's a scary thought," Nadira said, and he and Sam laughed.

"What exactly are you looking for?" Sam asked Tully. "Some guy jerking off? Isn't that what Berkowitz did?" But she didn't wait for Tully to answer and continued, "Or that arson investigator in California during the 1980s where the fires were always close to conventions he just happened to be attending."

"Seriously?" Nadira asked. "Criminals can be such stupid bastards."

"Who was the guy in Seattle that started like seventy-some fires before his father turned him in?"

"Paul Keller," Tully said, and turned to look at her. "How do you know so much about all these cases?"

"Are you kidding? Haven't you watched any of Jeffery's investigative pieces on these fires? He has more background trivia than Nadira will ever be able to squeeze in."

Tully saw Nadira smile, if you could call it that. The corner of his mouth lifted a notch.

"He'll be able to use some of it in his behind-bars documentary," Nadira said. "Because he's already pushed Big Mac to the limit on these arsons."

"Big Mac?" Tully asked.

"Donald Malcolm. Our bureau chief," Sam explained. "He's lost interest in the fires. They're not a big enough story."

"Really? How can this not be a big story?"

"No body count."

Tully checked his watch. They would already be started on the autopsy. He didn't agree with holding back the information that they had found a body in the alley and a skull inside one of the buildings. It wasn't his call. Instead, he watched the chaos unfold on the monitor in front of him.

He wondered who called in the fire. Then he realized Racine had never really told him how the body in the alley had been found. Did the firefighters find it? Or did the person who called in the fire know about the dead body? He made a mental note and pushed up his glasses again. That's when he saw a block of red in the middle of the bystanders.

"Stop the film."

Nadira hit a button. The screen froze.

Tully pointed. "Is there any way to zoom in on this?"

Without a word, Nadira tapped several keys.

"What is it?" Sam leaned in over their shoulders.

Tully watched the red block grow larger. It took several seconds for the blurred image to come into focus.

It was difficult to make out the item, seeing only a slit of it between the bodies, but Tully thought it might be a red backpack.

"Can you pull back on the zoom but keep this red block in the center and start the film again?"

More taps and movement began, though subtle. The cluster of people stood still, watching. Soon the red started to move, snaking slowly through the group and inching away from the action. Before the man carrying it reached the corner of Sam's viewfinder he disappeared.

"Stop it," Tully said. "Can you rewind and zoom in on this guy before he moves away from the crowd?"

Nadira obeyed.

"Who is he?" Sam asked.

"I don't know, but I have his backpack."

CHAPTER 38

Maggie drove to Quantico to meet with Keith Ganza while Racine worked on identifying the victim. Tully didn't answer his phone and Maggie suspected he might still be at the television station.

Even if Racine was able to find out who the woman was, there were still the questions of who killed her and why and where. How did she end up in the alley? Why did the killer set two buildings ablaze but fail to burn her body? And whose skull was inside? A homeless person looking for shelter? Or another murder victim?

Ganza was getting his lunch when Maggie came into his lab. He pulled a couple of containers from the refrigerator, containers that Maggie could see had been sandwiched between vials of blood and packaged tissue samples. When he saw her, he raised one of the container's lids.

"Join me? Homemade lasagna."

"Did you make it?"

"Oh God, no."

He placed it in the microwave, then retrieved two forks from a drawer. Maggie tore off several paper towels for placemats and napkins and set them on a table in the middle of the room while Ganza brought out paper plates and pulled a Diet Pepsi out of the fridge to set in front of her.

It looked like the silent ritual of an old married couple and Maggie realized they had done this many times. Ganza had shared his lunch often and yet Maggie knew little about the man's personal life. In fact, now that she thought about it, she had no idea who could have made the lasagna. He didn't wear a wedding ring and had never talked about a family. She'd always assumed he was a bit like her — married to his job.

At first glance he reminded her of Ichabod Crane, his tall, skeletal frame hunched over, his long, mostly gray hair tied back in a tight ponytail that seemed to make his face look more haggard than it was.

"Let me show you something interesting that I found." He pointed to the electron microscope that occupied a corner.

Maggie put her eye to the viewer. The slide contained something long and thin, tubular with a scaly pattern.

"I'm guessing animal hair, but it doesn't look like a dog or cat."

"Correct. Her clothes had plenty of primary transfer, which I've already cross-checked as her own. The secondary, however, is a bit tricky."

"She was found in the alley. There could be all kinds of critters. Even if she wasn't murdered there, how do you know if this strand is from the alley or the actual murder site?"

"I'm sure it's *not* from the alley. This animal most likely was never in the middle of the District."

"Dumpsters attract all sorts of wildlife — raccoons, rats, possums."

"But probably not deer."

Maggie stared at him for a moment, almost waiting for him to say "Just kidding." But Ganza didn't kid or joke about evidence. She pressed her eye against the viewfinder again.

"Are you sure?"

"Yes, I'm sure. The scale patterns are unique features to determine different species. I had several samples to examine. All had roots, which discounts the idea that maybe they came from a fur coat. Pelts made into clothes are trimmed and usually dyed. These hairs have characteristics of being naturally dislodged, most likely by shed-ding."

The microwave's buzzer went off and Ganza stepped aside to check on the lasa-gna. He opened the microwave door and the aroma of garlic and tomato sauce made Maggie's mouth water. Ganza set the timer for another couple of minutes. He fingered a set of slides on the counter and brought another over, changing out the deer hair on the microscope's faceplate.

"This was also attached to the folds of her clothing."

Maggie stared down at what looked like a dusty yellow seed with traces of green.

Centaurea diffusa," Ganza said. "It's a typical knapweed."

"You know where this grows?" she asked.

"It grows wild in the Midwest."

"That's an awfully big area. And a lot of miles between here and there. Are you sure? Maybe someone grows it closer? In their backyard or garden?"

"They'd be in violation of the law."

"It's a weed."

"It's on the federal noxious weed list. There are penalties for moving invasive plants."

"Okay, so where in the Midwest would this have come from?"

"It's common along the roadside or in pastures and meadows. You know . . . where the deer and the antelope roam." He offered a lopsided grin.

"Why would he kill her somewhere in the Midwest and haul the body halfway across the country to dump her in an alley in the District?"

"Wouldn't be the first time a killer drove around with a dead body in his trunk. You know these guys do strange things. Remember Edmund Kemper left a severed head in his trunk while he met with two state psychiatrists, who after that meeting pronounced him 'safe' and good to go."

Maggie pulled out the set of autopsy photos Stan had allowed her to take. She flipped through and found the imprint stamped into the dead woman's flesh. She handed it to Ganza.

"I was thinking this might be a grate in the pavement of another street or alley," she told him. "But now I'm wondering, could it be the bed lining in a truck or SUV?"

Ganza took the photo and moved to a counter, sliding it under a magnifying glass. He switched on an overhead light and examined it, his nose practically touching the glass.

"May I keep this for a day?"

Maggie glanced at the magnified image. "Do you see something?"

"I'd like to scan it into the computer and break it down. Sometimes those liners have the brand imprinted on them."

Maggie thought about what Ganza had said about Edmund Kemper. Kemper was a textbook case every profiler hoped they never ran into. Nicknamed the Co-ed Killer, the giant of a man had murdered his grandparents when he was only fifteen. He would hang around university campuses and pick up female hitchhikers in the Santa Cruz area. He murdered and dismembered six of them. It wasn't until after he killed his mother and her friend that he turned himself in to authorities.

She looked over at Ganza just as he glanced up. The lines on his forehead bunched together in a frown when he saw something in her face that prompted him to ask, "What is it?"

She shook her head. "Nothing," she said, but felt a sudden chill as she thought about the dead woman's battered face. "I was just thinking of Edmund Kemper. He used a claw hammer to beat his mother to death while she was asleep."

She didn't add that she was also thinking of Albert Stucky, another serial killer whose signature was to put dismembered pieces of his victims into take-out containers and leave them to be found on café tables, truck-stop counters, and hotel room service trays.

As if he could read her mind, Ganza said, "Let's hope we don't have another psycho bastard like Kemper on our hands."

CHAPTER 39

Sam told herself it wasn't a lie she had told to Special Agent R. J. Tully. It was simply omitting the truth.

Jesus! Jeffery had taught her some bad habits. But he'd call them survival tactics. With the types of assignments and the caliber of assholes they dealt with on a regular basis, lying — and being good at it — was an asset, not a bad habit.

Sam had insinuated that she and Jeffery were in the warehouse district when the fire started. But the truth was, Sam had been home for several hours. She had tucked in her son and shared a cup of tea with her mother. She had been fast asleep when Jeffery's phone call woke her.

Now she tried to remember if he had told her how he'd found out about the fire. Usually she didn't bother to ask. The man had more contacts and informants than the CIA. She just presumed he'd been tipped off.

Although she had told Agent Tully that Jeffery had a police scanner — and he did — Sam knew he couldn't have heard about the fire that way. She knew because she didn't think the police or fire department had even been called yet by the time she and Jeffery arrived. Her own film footage seemed to verify that. Hell, the street people were just crawling out of their cardboard boxes and stumbling from their warm corners.

So how did Jeffery know so early?

Sam didn't really care, or maybe she didn't want to know. Same thing with Jeffery's decision to do absolutely nothing about the story Otis P. Dodd had shared with them. It wasn't her call. She needed to concentrate on doing her job, a job she loved and wanted to keep. The way Sam looked at it, Jeffery helped put a roof over her family's head and food on the table. That's all she needed to know. Jeffery had made that happen. Better than that, he had made sure she was rewarded with bonuses that she stashed away for her son. If things continued to work out the way she planned, her son would never have to struggle the way Sam and her mother had all those years without Sam's dad.

She wasn't too stubborn to realize that her success and financial stability depended on Jeffery Cole's success and financial profitability. He was one of the top paid investigative reporters in the country and would become even more famous when Big Mac gave him his own show. So when things got a bit crazy, Sam reminded herself that she had attached herself to his star and had to be ready for the journey. Maybe her mother was right. Maybe she had sold her soul to Diablo.

She pulled her car off Interstate 66 and immediately found the diner where Jeffery had asked her to meet him. As far as she could tell, it wasn't anywhere on the way to their next interview, but again, rather than question Jeffery, she simply followed instructions.

Sometimes he liked to eat at out-of-the-way dives, once driving them down the Virginia back roads to what looked like a two-room clapboard shanty on the river. One side sold bait and tackle, the other side served some of the best barbeque pulled pork Sam had ever eaten. Of course, there were also those places that ripped up Sam's stomach, like the bamboo hut in Jinja, Uganda, overlooking Lake Victoria. Never again would she let anyone talk her into eat-ing monkey.

Today's diner looked a bit too commercial for Jeffery, but Sam found a table by the window and waited for him.

When he came in, his face was flushed and his shirt wrinkled, the sleeves shoved up instead of neatly rolled up. He must have left his tie and jacket in the car, even though the day was a bit chilly. Sam thought he looked out of breath.

"Are you okay?"

He sat across from her, grabbing a menu before he got settled.

"Of course, I'm fine. Why wouldn't I be?"

He scooted the wooden chair in, scraping the floor and arranging himself so he could see out the window. Without looking at her, he said, "They have excellent cream of asparagus soup here."

Sam shrugged it off. Jeffery was an interesting study in contrasts: hot then cold, black and white, up and down. Like a sports car, he could go from calm to enraged in less than sixty seconds. However, she had no inclination to study him. It was tough enough keeping up with him and staying out of his way or on his good side.

"What can I get for you two?" A waitress appeared and slammed down two glasses of water. The one she set in front of Jeffery splashed over the rim.

Jeffery stared at the puddle like it was toxic waste while he held the menu, his elbow planted on the table not far from the spill. Immediately Sam's jaw started to clench. She had witnessed him blow up at a waiter for bringing him a salad fork when he had asked specifically for a dinner fork.

"I'll have a bowl of the cream of asparagus soup," Sam said quickly, in an attempt to distract Jeffery.

"Oh honey, we don't have the asparagus. It's chicken and rice today."

"I just told my colleague how delicious the cream of asparagus is, Rita." Jeffery read the waitress's nameplate with what Sam recognized as his best fake smile, the calm before the storm. "You sure your cook can't whip some up for us?"

"Asparagus is on Mondays, sweetie. I can bring you a couple bowls of chicken and rice."

"You know what, I bet the chicken and rice is just as delicious," Sam said. "I'll have that. And a grilled cheese."

She closed the menu and slapped it down, hoping to distract Jeffery. She tried not to wince, tried not to look at him. It was never pretty. First, he'd tell the waitress that she obviously had no idea who she was waiting on. Then he'd ask to speak to the cook. Once in a Miami restaurant he made Sam translate his complaints into Spanish along with instructions on how his entrée should be cooked and served.

Sam looked away, glancing out the window to avoid watching the education of Rita. She didn't even see the stream of smoke until Jeffery's arm shot out across the table, pointing it out.

"What the hell is that?" He was already on his feet and headed for the door.

CHAPTER 40

"One body doesn't mean it's a serial killer," Maggie told Ganza. "And thankfully the Edmund Kempers of the world are still a rare breed."

He nodded and took a bite of lasagna.

"I just can't figure out how the arsons play into the murders," Maggie said. "Kunze wants Tully and me to profile this arsonist, but so far he blows away — no pun intended — all the typical motives."

"ATF's ruled out insurance fraud, from what I've been told," Ganza said.

"Did they bring you evidence from last week's fires?"

He shook his head. "Kunze asked me to take a look at these two. Said no one could connect these warehouses. Told me to see what I could do."

"All of the warehouses are owned by different companies, so revenge seems unlikely. They've all happened in the middle of the night and in the same vicinity. Racine said the cops have canvassed that whole area and have come up empty-handed."

"Nobody's seen anything?"

"Or they're not willing to talk about it."

"Looked like a homeless district."

"It is. But if he's targeting the homeless why dump the body of a victim from somewhere else? Someone who's not homeless? And then not burn the body?"

"You're sure she wasn't homeless?"

"Shaved legs, manicure, pedicure."

"He could have picked her up somewhere on a road trip."

"Racine said it looked like road-trip food in the woman's stomach. Are you thinking she may have gotten stranded?"

"Actually, I was wondering if she could have been a prostitute."

"Somewhere along the highway?"

"I believe they call them love lizards . . . Wait, that's not correct." He held up his empty fork like an orchestra conductor, as though the gesture helped conjure up the correct term. "Lot lizards. It's a whole subculture at interstate rest areas and truck stops. They say it's impossible for a regular traveler to detect them but if you're a trucker with a CB radio there are certain channels you can go to and order up prostitutes, drugs, whatever you want, wherever you want it, and any time of the day or night."

He proceeded to fork off another piece of lasagna and stuff it into his mouth.

"And you know all this because?"

"I read about it in *USA Today.*" Ganza smiled as he continued to chew. "Actually I'm working with ViCAP on the Highway Serial Killings Initiative."

The Violent Criminal Apprehension Program and its database had become a national repository for violent crimes. Law enforcement officials from across the country could access it to find or submit similar patterns.

The Highway Initiative had been created in 2009 in response to more than five hundred murder victims dumped along or near highways, rest areas, and truck stops. Maggie knew about it only from what she had read, despite it being an FBI-driven program.

"I'm surprised Kunze doesn't have you working on that task force," Ganza said. "Seems like the perfect matrix — impossible to solve, impossible to profile — just the type of assignment he loves to send you on."

It didn't please Maggie that so many of

her colleagues saw what Kunze was doing. That reminded her. She glanced at her watch. She needed to get back to the District for Kunze's mandatory psychological evaluation.

"You seem convinced he picked the victim up somewhere along the interstate in the Midwest."

Ganza scratched his long, narrow jaw. "Maybe along the interstate system. I have the breakdown of the gasoline. Remember I told you that gas chromatography reveals the chemical composition of the hydrocarbons?"

"Right. Like a blueprint."

"In this case, almost a fingerprint."

"What are you saying? That you can tell us what company made it?"

"Better. I can tell you the gas station where he bought it."

"And let me guess. It's one along the interstate?"

Ganza nodded just as Maggie's cell phone rang. It was Racine. She couldn't possibly have the victim's ID yet.

"Are you still at Quantico?" asked Racine.

"Just finishing."

"Looks like he's moved across the river."

"It's the middle of the day."

"Off Interstate 66 on Fort Myers. You'll

probably see the smoke. They said it's slowing down traffic."

"Any chance this one isn't related to our guy?"

"Two separate fires, three blocks apart and within about thirty minutes."

"Sounds like our guy," Maggie agreed.

"One difference. No warehouses this time. And there might be casualties."

"What did he set on fire this time?"

"Two churches."

CHAPTER 41

Tully had Abe Nadira print a photo of the last frame before the man with the red backpack dropped out of sight. He also got a print of the man's face. The zoom had reduced his features to shadowed pixels. A short beard and shaggy hair were the only decipherable characteristics. Eyes, mouth, and nose were blurs of gray and black.

Several fire investigators and crime scene technicians, along with their equipment, were still processing the rubble. Yellow police tape had been stretched around a wide perimeter to cordon off the area, but less than forty-eight hours later a couple of the homeless already had crawled under the barrier, taking up residence in the shelter of new Dumpsters and equipment that had been brought in.

It wasn't the alley or the Dumpster that drew Tully back to the scene. He found and planted himself in the same spot where Samantha Ramirez had been when she shot the footage of the photo he had in his hand. Broken glass glittered on the ground. Most of the debris — the big pieces — had been raked and sifted. Small piles littered the cordoned-off sidewalk where investigators used the concrete as a flat, hard place to sort.

Tully held up the eight-by-ten photo Nadira had given him. He tried to match the photo's background to what remained. Ramirez had shot this footage before the second blast, so the scene in the photo looked different from what surrounded him now.

He lined up street signs and corners of existing buildings until he was certain he had the correct angle. Then he paced out measured steps toward the area where the man was last seen.

Tully kept the photo in front of him while he walked slowly, step by step, examining the surroundings. He glanced at the grass, then the curb and street, focusing only on what was directly in his path.

After a few minutes he thought he had gone too far and started to backtrack. He stopped to study the photo. He pushed up the bridge of his glasses. In the photo, right behind the man's right shoulder, was a light post with a flyer taped to it. Tully couldn't make out the details on the flyer but he could see that someone had used thick swatches of duct tape to attach it to the post.

He looked around him and saw what had to be the same post. The flyer and tape were still attached but both had been pelted with debris. He stepped onto the curb and positioned himself in the exact spot where he believed the man had been standing. He checked over his shoulder to make sure the street sign was where it was in the photo. Then Tully took a deep breath.

Okay, where the hell did you go, mister?

He began a slow circle, taking in everything from door wells to fire escapes on the buildings. In the photo there were no vehicles close by for the man to duck under or hide behind. Tully made a full circle before he saw it.

Three feet to his left, steam puffed out from a manhole cover.

CHAPTER 42

Everything Cornell Stamoran had left in the world was in that red backpack. Why the hell did he toss it at that guy?

Instinct had taken over — fight or flight — and of all the things he had done or been in his life Cornell was *not* a fighter. But he was good at running away.

Since the fire, all he had thought about was running. He maneuvered his way through the underbelly of the city, back and forth, memorizing pipes and valves while wading through crappy water. He didn't mind the smell. You couldn't live on the streets if you couldn't stand the smell. Even his body odor no longer repulsed him.

What bothered Cornell were the noises. The echoes freaked him out. So did the clanks, the drips and hisses, the whines and hums. He couldn't tell what the hell was happening around him, if he heard footsteps chasing him or if it was just his imagination. Except he was fairly certain that someone was following him.

At first he worried it was the man he'd seen pouring gasoline in the alley. He couldn't forget the look on that guy's face when he saw Cornell slipping and rolling in the trail of fuel. That twisted grin when he lit the match. If Cornell hadn't scrambled and found the manhole when he did, he would have been toast.

But that wasn't the man following him.

Then Cornell thought it might be a co-incidence. He saw the same man in different places, and only at a distance, but the guy was always watching him. Cornell had no clue why the man would bother to follow him.

That's when he started to vary his exits and entrances to the underground. From below he could look up through the grates or holes and almost always determine when it was safe to come up. Ironically it was best at the busiest times and at some of the most crowded intersections, where people hurried by and couldn't be bothered with someone crawling out of a manhole.

Of course, it helped that Cornell had found an abandoned city maintenance vest and hard hat — both fluorescent orange. Instead of attracting attention they seemed to make him invisible. The vest and hard hat quickly became his most valuable possessions. They not only gained him unfettered access to the city's underworld but also bought him a surprising amount of leverage and respect on the streets. When he finally remembered he had more than thirty dollars in his buttoned cargo pocket he treated himself to a bowl of soup and a sandwich at the same diner where he'd eaten the night of the fire.

The same waitress took his order. She was the one who had looked at him suspiciously the other night and then grudgingly given him change back as he requested, in one-dollar bills. Only this time she smiled when she set his plate in front of him. Refilled his coffee. Even asked, "How's it going?"

And he knew he smelled worse today than he had that first time he'd been in. Although he had tried to clean his jacket and the vomit and gasoline fumes had finally aired out a bit, he knew he couldn't travel through the sewer and not have the stink cling to him.

But put on a fluorescent orange vest and hard hat and it all became acceptable.

He ate at the diner's counter again and watched out the window. He still couldn't believe he had tossed his backpack. He had gone back to the alley to see if he could retrieve anything from his Maytag box. He thought all the cops had left. At least the alley. Once the body was gone he had seen the remaining investigators pack up and then either leave or focus on the rubble inside.

He should have waited longer. Even after he tossed his backpack and took out the tall guy, that broad had kept coming after him. He couldn't shake her, couldn't outrun her. But he knew how to drop out of sight. That threw her off but it didn't lose the bastard who kept finding him.

If he wasn't the man who started the fire, who the hell was this guy?

He didn't think he looked like a cop or a fed. He wore blue jeans, a nice pair of work boots, a ball cap, and brown suede jacket. Hell, he looked pretty ordinary, nothing menacing about him except that he was always there. Cornell would see him leaning against a lamppost or sitting on a bench. Once at a Metro bus stop. Buses came and went but the guy stayed. Sometimes he saw the man downtown, but then hours later he'd see him walking back by the same warehouses where the fires had been. There was no reason that he could think of for this guy to be in these two very different places in the city unless he was following Cornell.

A couple of times when Cornell traveled underground he could swear he'd seen the shadow of someone behind him. Lighting was crap down there. Long stretches were pitch black. He tried to avoid those. Even the best stretches were limited to a bare lightbulb tucked into the maze of pipes.

The first time he noticed the man was right before he tossed his backpack. Though he didn't look like a cop, Cornell had thought maybe he was part of the investigating team, but only because the guy was inside the barrier of yellow tape. He had been leaning against one of the vehicles, watching and smoking a cigarette.

Maybe he knew the dead woman. A shiver slid down Cornell's back and a sudden bout of nausea made him put down his spoon. He sipped his water, waited for it to pass. He didn't like thinking about the dead woman. Didn't like remembering that battered face, pounded and ripped like ground beef.

Cornell grabbed the little package of saltine crackers. His fingers shook and he struggled to tear the plastic, suddenly desperate to get at them. He crunched a piece out and quickly put it in his mouth, holding it on his tongue and sucking off the salt, waiting for the nausea to pass. It didn't seem to be working.

He stuck another piece in his mouth. Weren't saltines supposed to help? Probably not if you had wrestled a dead body with your bare hands. He still couldn't believe he'd touched it.

When Cornell looked back up, the man in the brown suede jacket was standing just outside the diner window. And he was staring directly at Cornell.

CHAPTER 43

By the time Maggie arrived, the cross at the top of the steeple blazed against a smoke-filled sky. She could see a second black plume several blocks away.

She showed her badge at the first barricade, a half block from the fire. The uniformed officer lifted the yellow tape for her and pointed out Detective Racine. Here across the river, Racine would be out of her jurisdiction. That was the only reason she stood back and tolerated the man beside her. Maggie recognized Brad Ivan, the ATF fire investigator.

"Were there any church services being held?" Maggie asked as she joined them. There were three ambulances parked at odd angles. One had driven onto the church lawn.

"No services," Racine told her, "but there was an altar society meeting in the basement of this one."

"Fatalities?"

Racine didn't answer, looked instead to Ivan. Technically ATF would be the point agency now that the fires had moved out of the District.

"We don't know yet. They're still inside," Ivan said as he hitched his trousers up, then stopped almost abruptly and kept the belt just below his waist.

Maggie guessed the gesture was an old habit but that a new paunch still surprised him. Ivan looked like a man who had kept himself in shape until recently. Maybe a change of schedule or, Maggie speculated, a change in living routine, perhaps a separation or divorce. Curious to prove her theory, she glanced at his left hand and saw a subtle streak of lighter skin where a ring had been.

Maggie waited for Ivan to continue filling her in, but there was nothing after the pants hitch. She couldn't see his eyes behind the mirrored aviator sunglasses. Odd that he'd need sunglasses, since the smoke blocked out the sun.

"The middle of the afternoon goes against his MO," she said. "How do we know this is the same guy?"

"It would be nice if we had some kind of a profile."

His sarcasm surprised Maggie. She didn't

240

think the man had it in him to muster up something as complex as sarcasm. Racine raised an eyebrow. Looked like he'd surprised her as well.

"The murders at the last scene throw off any typical profile of a serial arsonist." Maggie told him this as a matter of fact. "If you remove the two victims from the equation, he becomes a repeat nuisance offender."

"Yeah, under twenty-five, male, white, history of family dysfunction, father abusive or absent, blue-collar job if he has a job, low self-esteem, low IQ, social misfit, yadda yadda. I've seen these profiles before. They don't tell us jack-shit."

"Sounds like you already have your own profile," Racine said, but Maggie could see Racine's sarcasm was lost on Ivan. She even thought she saw the detective take a step forward as if in Maggie's defense. Maybe she could hear the throbbing in Maggie's head. It had started as soon as she'd left Ganza.

"I think he's older," Maggie said when she knew Ivan wasn't expecting her to say anything. Maybe that's why she continued, "The fire chief's report mentioned a chemical reaction being the starting point."

"That's right. The fires have been too quick and the heat too intense. There haven't been any other accelerants used."

"But it smelled like gasoline was poured in the alley."

"That's the exception. Incidentally, he didn't start the fire on that side of the building. He uses materials he finds at the site. But he brings whatever the hell he's using to start the chemical reaction."

"No timing device?"

"Haven't found one yet. But all that fits a pyromaniac's profile, right?" Ivan said with a smirk, as if goading Maggie. "Goes along with an impulse disorder. He gathers whatever he finds to start the fire — rags, newspapers, garbage. Doesn't really think about it or plan it. Just needs to satisfy his impulse, relieve his sexual tension and his desire for the thrill."

Maggie suppressed a sigh of frustration. Was he serious or simply having fun with her? She studied his face and decided he was making fun of her and of profiling. "Pyromania" was a term psychiatrists and defense attorneys loved to use. In reality, few arsons on this scale had been blamed on an uncontrollable impulse or an irresistible urge to start fires to "relieve sexual tension," as Ivan put it.

"But you said he has to bring the chemicals," she pointed out. "Hardly impulsive if he's toting around whatever it takes to create such a combustion."

Ivan shrugged. "So what's your profile?"

He looked pleased to put her on the spot, shifting his weight and crossing his arms. Behind them sirens wailed along the streets. Police whistles directed traffic. Overhead, they could hear a helicopter, still too far away to tell if it was a life flight or cable news crew.

"He's educated," Maggie said. "A chemical reaction that includes that sort of timing, as well as the correct proportions, is not something he learned in the Boy Scouts or surfing the Internet. I'd guess it was part of his job at one time. Maybe it still is. He's someone who doesn't attract attention. He can blend in. He looks like he belongs."

"Right. And what kind of job combines chemicals to start fires?" Ivan was skeptical.

This time Maggie shrugged. She wasn't the arson expert. She wanted to say that perhaps someone with the ATF — perhaps a fire investigator like himself — should be able to examine and determine that part of the puzzle.

"So what does he drive?"

She almost rolled her eyes. They were always so hung up on a vehicle that they could stop by throwing up blockades. Maggie shook her head. "It won't matter because I think he parks away from the site and walks several blocks."

"Humph. You're not giving me anything."

"Okay, here's something. Have you checked the surrounding ERs?"

"Emergency rooms?"

"Check for chemical burns. Whatever he's using might burn his skin or even discolor it."

"Great. So we look for a guy older than twenty-five who's educated, in good enough shape to walk several blocks, and maybe has — what, like purple fingers or something? That's supposed to help me?"

"Hey," Racine said. "It's more than we had an hour ago."

"Except these two fires change things a bit," Maggie continued.

"What are you talking about?"

"Churches instead of warehouses. And in the middle of the day. If he knew there were people inside he's no longer a nuisance offender who likes to stand back and watch the chaos or read the headlines the next day. The fact that there were people inside changes his motive."

"What about the victims in the last fire?" Ivan asked.

"He may not have known about the person

inside." Although Maggie knew that if the skull was bashed in the way the woman's face was in the alley, then chances were the victim inside the building was not an accident.

"We still haven't figured out who the woman was," Racine added. "She definitely wasn't killed there. Her murder may have had nothing to do with the fires."

"Interesting," Ivan said, shifting his feet again and practically stomping them. "But you still haven't given me a solid description of this guy."

"What exactly do you expect?" Maggie asked. "That I tell you he wears double-breasted suits and talks with a stutter? That he walks with a limp and drives a white paneled van?" She purposely mixed several famous profiles. First, the Mad Bomber of the 1940s. Second, the vehicle that was supposed to lead them to the Beltway sniper.

Ivan stared at her — or, rather, his mirrored glasses did. Then recognition came as a smile crept over his lips. "That's right. The profile of the Beltway sniper was totally wrong. The type of vehicle was just one mistake. You're only proving my point, Agent O'Dell."

"You need to give me some facts, too, Investigator Ivan. Agent Tully and I were asked to profile this case, but we were given very little information from your department. By now you must know or at least can speculate what chemicals are being used to start the fires."

"Wait a minute," Racine said. "The District PD is under the impression that the ATF and FBI are coordinating this effort and working together."

Maggie saw Ivan clench his teeth and suck in a breath as his head swiveled away from her. In the mirrored reflection she watched flames dance where his eyes should have been. There was something unsettling about the sight.

"Our lab's still working on that."

"Tell you what. I'll make you a deal."

The mirrors came back.

"Send whatever trace you've collected to Keith Ganza. When he tells me what the chemicals are, I'll have a detailed profile for you within twenty-four hours."

Another fire engine wailed to a stop about a hundred yards behind them. In Ivan's glasses Maggie could see two firefighters jump out. Ivan was still stonewalling when Maggie heard someone call her name. It took her almost a minute to recognize the arriving firefighter in his full gear, his hat brim pulled down low over his brow.

It was Patrick.

CHAPTER 44

"That hot cop is your sister?"

"She's not a cop. She's an FBI agent." Patrick hauled his equipment to the curb.

"Looks familiar. Hey, wait a minute. Last night on TV. Wasn't she on *Larry King Live*?"

"Larry King's not on anymore."

"Really? What happened to him?"

Patrick wasn't in the mood for this. It was bad enough to run into Maggie here. He didn't need Wes Harper's ridiculous chit-chat.

"Is she married?"

"Divorced."

"That's even better. You know what they say about divorced women?"

Patrick didn't know and didn't want to know.

"What did you do to your hand?" he asked, changing the subject. He pointed at a fresh scar on the back of Harper's right hand. It still looked a bit raw.

"Nothing." But he pulled his glove up quickly. "So maybe you could introduce me to her."

"Don't you think we should get our equipment ready?"

"Hey, chill out, dude. You're not the team leader on this one."

Harper gave Maggie another look before he turned his back to get to work. "There're three buildings in between the fire and our client's building." He kept his voice low. "Not like it's urgent. Probably won't even need to foam it if those guys take care of their business."

By "those guys" Patrick knew he meant the real firefighters. He stopped to watch. They had a hell of a job on their hands. Hoses were still being attached to fire hydrants. A second engine screamed two blocks away. The siren faded, then stopped when it arrived at the other church. Two blazes spewing black clouds of smoke and yet Patrick and his partner weren't here to help on either blaze.

For Patrick, this was much worse than being five miles away, like the last assignment, spraying down a house and watching from afar. To be here — right here — to feel the heat of the flames and fill his lungs with smoke and just stand back and watch. It was wrong. It went against his basic instinct.

Patrick twisted his gloves in his fists instead of putting them on. He felt helpless, shackled. He glanced at Harper, who had pulled out a computer tablet but was staring up at the flames.

"It's actually pretty, isn't it?" Harper said, and smiled at Patrick. "It takes on a whole life of its own, swallowing up everything into red and gold flashes of light."

Patrick had always thought fire was fascinating, but he couldn't say he'd use the word "pretty."

"Sometimes," Harper said in almost a quiet confession, "even when I'm not on duty I'll go to fire sites just to watch."

"Really?"

"Oh yeah. Got my police scanner on to see if there're any close by. I've always had a thing for fire. My nickname growing up was Matches." He laughed, but Patrick didn't join him. "My parents were very relieved when they heard I wanted to be a firefighter instead of a fire starter."

Harper stared at the blazing steeple for a few more seconds, then, as if he'd flipped a switch, he went back to the computer and started tapping. He started to go through their checklist, completing the required form that their client — a group of law offices, three buildings down — would need to sign off on when they were finished.

Patrick glanced over to where Maggie stood with Detective Racine. Harper's admission reminded him of Maggie's Christmas dinner last year and how Racine had asked him why he wanted to be a hose monkey. He didn't take offense at the term. He knew cops and firefighters had a love-hate relationship and that Racine didn't mean anything by her comment.

Firefighters axed and stomped and crashed their way through a fire, their minds set on rescuing anyone inside. Get in quick. Find survivors and get them the hell out. Then put the fire out. It was messy. No doubt about it. But the cops, the detectives, the investigators, and the crime scene technicians hated that evidence got trampled, sometimes destroyed, and often washed away.

Patrick suspected that Maggie thought he wanted to be a firefighter only because their father had been one. He had to admit, when he found out his father had died saving others, he did think that was pretty cool. He never knew the man. Thomas O'Dell died before Patrick was born. He probably did have an inflated super-hero image of the man. And so what if he wanted to follow in his father's footsteps? What was so wrong about that?

Patrick knew he had the raw instincts needed to be a good firefighter. It became obvious to him a year ago when he and some friends were at the Mall of America on the day after Thanksgiving. Three bombs blew up and ripped through a portion of the mall.

Patrick could have easily made it to safety, but without hesitation, without even thinking, he turned around and went back into the devastation. While other people's instincts were to flee from danger, Patrick's was to run toward it and see how he could help.

"I think it's what I'm supposed to do," he had told Racine.

"You mean like God told you?"

By then he had already been warned about Racine's smart mouth. He remembered smiling politely and saying, "Exactly. Just like God told you to be a homicide detective."

Suddenly the church's stained-glass windows burst into a rain of colored glitter. Three firefighters were caught under the spray of shattered glass. They stopped to shield themselves, then immediately hurried into the building.

Patrick stood back and watched. He felt his gut twist and his fists continue to ball up around his gloves. He should be following them instead of sitting on the sidelines preparing to hose down a building that wasn't even on fire.

A firefighter in front of him struggled to unwind more hose. Another shouted at the guy to hurry just before he disappeared inside the building. Patrick didn't even look over at Harper. He secured the chin strap on his helmet and pulled on his gloves. Then he hurried over to help the firefighter with the hose, knowing full well he was probably walking away from the best job he'd ever get in a long time.

CHAPTER 45

"It bothers you," Racine said as soon as Ivan left, right after the windows exploded.

It took a second or two for Maggie to realize that she was talking about Patrick. When she didn't answer Racine continued, "Tate Braxton's an asshole but his firefighters are highly trained and certified."

"How do you know Braxton?"

"Just by reputation. He's a businessman. In it for the almighty dollar. But he does a good job making sure his people are qualified."

They stood side by side watching the flames. A stretcher with a body on it had just been hauled to the first waiting ambulance. They sighed in relief when the body raised an arm and they realized the person was alive. Still, Maggie could sense Racine's frustration at not being able to help. Her impatience and tension radiated off her.

"I dated one of Braxton's firefighters a few

254

years ago," Racine added.

Maggie recognized the idle chatter the detective resorted to when she hated waiting, when she felt sidelined.

"She didn't make it to Valentine's Day either, huh?"

Neither of them shifted or looked at each other.

Racine said, "Nope."

But she could see the smile at the corners of Racine's lips.

Maggie felt her cell phone vibrate in her pocket and she pulled it out. "This is Maggie O'Dell."

"Maggie, it's Tully. I just heard about the fires. Do I need to be there?"

"Not unless you want to stand around with Racine and me."

"How bad is it?"

"Bad. We have casualties this time. There was a meeting in the basement of one of the churches."

"And it's the middle of the day. He's getting cocky."

"Or reckless."

Racine's phone started ringing. She pulled it out of her pocket and walked away from Maggie as she answered.

"The guy with the backpack," Tully said. "He was there during the warehouse fires.

The film footage shows him in the middle of the bystanders before the second building blast."

"Doesn't mean he started the fires."

"No, but get this. Instead of just walking away? He disappears down a manhole."

"That's weird. Are you sure?"

"I went back to the site. Yeah, I'm sure. So why travel through the sewer system unless you have something to hide?"

"Or maybe you don't want to be seen. Any idea who he is?"

"No. I don't even know how to find him without staking out all the manholes in a ten-block radius."

"That's not a bad idea."

"You're joking, right?"

"Not in a ten-block radius, but maybe around the fire site. He stuck around during the fire and then came back at least once. Maybe he was looking for something in that alley. Something he left behind. Something that could incriminate him."

"Good point."

He sounded tired. She wanted to ask if he was okay. If his shoulder was okay, but she knew he hated such questions as much as she did.

"What time will you be finished with Dr. Kernan?"

Kernan. She'd almost forgotten.

Her grip tightened on her phone. She rubbed her eyes and let her fingers find the scar at her temple. She didn't realize she'd taken too much time responding until Tully said, "Let me know if you need anything, okay?"

She smiled, told him she would. Then she clicked off just as Racine finished her conversation. She didn't look happy. She avoided Maggie's eyes the whole time she came back, glancing at the fire, the ambulances, everywhere — except at Maggie.

"They finally released the information on that breast implant," she said, still not looking at Maggie. "The manufacturer has privacy rules. Said we needed to contact the surgeon."

"Was that the manufacturer?"

"No. It was her surgeon. Our Jane Doe was Gloria Dobson, a breast cancer survivor. She's a mother of three from Concordia, Missouri. She was supposed to be at a sales conference in Baltimore all this week."

Maggie noticed Racine's eyes were still preoccupied. She held her jaw like she had something that tasted bad in her mouth. She was trying to keep her tough-guy exterior from revealing that this piece of news didn't sit well.

"Did you ever notice," Racine said, "that it's always women in Dumpsters? Men rarely end up in Dumpsters."

Maggie stayed quiet when she could have reminded Racine that Gloria Dobson was actually found beside the Dumpster, not inside. It was a detail that didn't matter when struggling with the brutality of a senseless murder.

"She survived cancer," Racine continued, "just to end up in a fucking Dumpster."

CHAPTER 46

Sam noticed him first on the other side of the crime scene tape. When he saw her, his grin — all dimples and white teeth — made her insides flutter like an annoying teenage girl.

What was wrong with her?

She shot a quick glance at Jeffery to see if he'd noticed. Thankfully he was too busy being Jeffery Cole to notice anyone else. Which always seemed a bit odd to Sam. Weren't investigative reporters supposed to be observant? Ever since they had heard there were people trapped in the church basement Jeffery had been transfixed on the side door he expected them to come out of. They had rescued only one person so far. Jeffery made Sam hold the camera on the door, though she had sneaked a few sweeps of the crowd when he was preoccupied.

He wanted an interview with one of the fire personnel. Every one of them ignored his shouts. When Sam realized Patrick was coming over she wanted to wave him away. She caught his eyes and gave a slow, subtle shake of her head. He stopped in his tracks, his face completely changing as if he'd been caught doing something inappropriate. What was worse — he looked hurt.

It was too late anyway. Jeffery saw him and immediately shot a look back at Sam, with the question he left unsaid, *You know this guy?*

Before Patrick could turn around, Jeffery hurried over, microphone in one hand, the other hand straightening his tie. Sam knew to follow, though she didn't want to, her feet almost dragging along. The camera suddenly felt heavy, making her arms ache. She noticed a slight tremor in her fingers.

"Jeffery Cole." He introduced himself to Patrick. "Can you tell us how everything is going? Any news on the rest of the people trapped inside? Did this fire start like all the others?"

Sam winced. She couldn't look Patrick in the eyes. For a split second her fingers found the camera's OFF switch and she almost hit it. But the light would go off and Jeffery would know immediately. He'd just insist she turn it on again. Still, it might give Patrick a chance to escape.

"I'm not with this crew," Patrick said, standing exactly where he'd stopped. Not retreating but no longer coming forward.

Sam felt his eyes searching her face. She focused on the viewfinder and avoided looking at him even through the camera.

"You're all dressed up for a fire." Jeffery's voice took on a hard edge. "Who exactly are you with? You must have some idea of what's going on."

Sam cringed and her back went rigid and straight. She pulled in a deep breath, waiting for Jeffery's combative persona. Light and dark, up and down — there was no in between for the man. She felt her senses preparing, standing guard. She let her hand slip down and with a sweep of her thumb she cut the live feed.

"I'm on standby," Patrick said.

Sam saw Patrick go into defensive mode. His jaw went taut. His gloved hands balled up. His stare hardened and went wide, away from her, away from the camera, and away from Jeffery.

"On standby?" Jeffery laughed. "Seriously? You mean like a rent-a-cop? Only a rent-a-fireman? How interesting. Who exactly do you work for?"

"I'm not obliged to answer that. In fact, I need to get back to work." But he didn't turn to leave.

"Oh yes, of course, we wouldn't want to keep you from standing by. So you know nothing about the fires? You're just sort of here in case they need you?"

Then Jeffery must have realized he would lose his only opportunity, because Sam saw him switch back from antagonist to newscaster. "Certainly you must have heard something. I mean, you are on the inside of the perimeter. What's the mood? They must be frantic to get those people out. Or do they already know it's hopeless?"

Sam shifted the weight of the camera and in doing so adjusted her finger until the viewfinder went black. Her thumb found the MUTE button. The lights stayed on as if nothing had changed.

"I'm not authorized to give you any information."

"What's the harm in giving us a general sense of the mood? What it's like to be behind the scenes?"

"I believe he already said he had nothing to tell you," a woman's voice said.

Jeffery's head snapped to see the woman approaching them.

"Special Agent Maggie O'Dell. So pleased you can join us today."

Sam moved the camera at his instinctive

wave, but kept her finger in place. She was going to be in such trouble. Already her mind scrambled for an explanation. She had managed to get footage while sliding down a wall of mud during a hurricane. There would be no believable explanation for this blackout. And unless Jeffery heard the thumping of her heart, he seemed totally unaware of her secret.

"Mr. Murphy's not authorized to give you a statement."

In the back of her mind, Sam's inner voice prayed, *Please don't say he's your brother. Please don't say I know him.*

"I was just leaving," Patrick said. He looked over at her before turning and Sam saw Jeffery notice. If there was any doubt that he recognized they knew each other, his smile wiped that doubt away.

"So Agent O'Dell, perhaps you can tell us what's going on? Are there any fatalities? We've been waiting for some word to let our viewers know if everyone in that basement is okay."

"I have no idea." And she started to turn to follow Patrick.

"Maybe you'd like to comment on the profile piece we aired about you last night."

Sam could see the agent's shoulders push back, but she continued to leave. Sam hoped O'Dell wouldn't unleash her anger. Sam would never be able to compensate for not getting it on film. Jeffery would certainly fire her.

And now Jeffery, ever the performer, turned so the camera captured a better angle of him before he delivered his blow. "Perhaps you'll offer some comment after the interview tonight with your mother."

O'Dell stopped this time. "Excuse me?"

CHAPTER 47

The last time Maggie sat in Dr. James Kernan's office she had been even more on edge. Her world had been turned upside down by a serial killer named Albert Stucky. Several years before, he'd gotten away, leaving her cut and bleeding in a Miami warehouse, but only after making her watch while he gutted two women.

Albert Stucky ended up in prison, but during a transport he managed to escape, killing his two security guards. For his second rampage he decided to kill women who had the misfortune of simply coming into contact with Maggie: the pizza delivery girl, Maggie's neighbor, a waitress.

It had been his sick game of cat and mouse, seeing to it that she received or found pieces of the women — a spleen in a cardboard pizza box, a kidney on a hotel room service tray. How could anyone blame her for being on edge? For feeling the need to be on alert 24/7, constantly looking over her shoulder?

Her old boss and mentor, Kyle Cunningham, had pulled her from the field, his idea of protecting her, not punishing her. Though at the time it certainly felt like punishment, working the teaching circuit. Talking about killers instead of tracking them, instead of hunting down Albert Stucky.

Jeffery Cole's profile included some of the very things she had worked so hard to compartmentalize. But the exposé wasn't the only thing conjuring up old memories and fears. If Ramirez had seen a man behind Maggie's house last night, who was he? And why was he there in the middle of the night, in the middle of an ice storm? Was it the same man in the tunnel? She had no evidence, nothing to support her suspicions except a gut instinct.

It would sound ridiculous if it hadn't, in fact, happened in the past. All of her memories of the Stucky murders came back to Maggie as she sat in her old professor's office, waiting for him. In some ways it seemed like a lifetime ago. Right now it felt like yesterday, listening for the shuffle of his footsteps as she breathed in the remnants of cigar smoke, Bengay, and old leather.

She had been in a much more fragile place

in her life back then. She and Greg had just separated. She had bought the house in Newburgh Heights and had just moved in. It hadn't even been a week when Stucky took her new neighbor. Days later he took her real estate agent. The only good to come out of the ordeal was Harvey. While Maggie hadn't been able to rescue her neighbor, Harvey's master, she had rescued him.

Yes, she had been in a much different place then, her frame of mind much more volatile than ever before. And sitting in Kernan's office brought it all back. It didn't help that the constant ache in her head had made her feel as vulnerable about her body as Stucky had made her feel vulnerable about her mental state. Without warning, the ache could turn into a dull throb, sometimes escalating to a jackhammer drill against her temple. The throb had come and gone throughout the afternoon, and it was back now.

How could she keep Kernan from seeing it?

Even with his thick Coke-bottle glasses he'd spot a wince or a twitch. The man definitely had the power to see things no one else noticed. Perhaps that explained his office decor.

She looked around the small space at his

strange collection of paraphernalia. A Mason jar with the frontal lobe of a human brain acted as a bookend. It held up leather-bound volumes of what Maggie knew were rare first editions that included Freud's *Interpretation of Dreams* next to Lewis Carroll's *Alice's Adventures in Wonderland.* The latter appropriate because Maggie could easily envision Kernan as the Mad Hatter.

Displayed on the credenza were antique surgical instruments. One in particular Maggie recognized as a tool used to perform lobotomies. She knew, because Kernan had brought it to the abnormal psychology class that he taught years ago at the University of Virginia. Maggie had been one of his students. One of thousands, and yet he still remembered exactly where she had sat in his classroom.

She heard his shuffle down the hall and caught herself sitting up straight in the hardback chair, the only chair, incidentally, that he had in his office for guests or clients. Another sound accompanied Kernan, a *click-pat, click-pat-patter* on the hallway's linoleum floor.

"O'Dell, O'Dell, the farmer and the dell." He began his ridiculous chants before he entered the room.

Maggie's back was to the door. She tried

to stay quiet, tried to shrug off what sounded like the rants of a senile old man. He played word games, using silly rhymes to throw off his students and now his patients. He'd probably been doing it for more years than Maggie was old. It broke down anyone's focus, little by little, and dismantled his opponent's thought process, putting them on guard for the next slew of unpredictable phrases instead of thinking about a response to a question he lobbed into the fray. It wouldn't work with her this time. She was prepared for his mental duels.

It was the dog that surprised Maggie, coming in first. A small brown-and-white corgi who touched his muzzle to her hand as if to warn her of his master's entrance.

Directly behind, connected by a leash, Kernan shuffled past her, his short frame a bit more hunched, his thick hair completely white, his suit wrinkled, and his thick, black-framed glasses at the end of his nose. He didn't even glance at her and continued to his chair back behind the desk.

The corgi settled in a corner before Kernan sat down.

"So O'Dell, Margaret," he said, his back still to her as he eased into his high-backed leather chair. "Premed. The little bird who sat in the back left corner of my classroom taking very few notes. Miss FBI Agent with yet another scar to heal."

Maggie gripped the seat of her wooden chair. There was nothing to dig her nails into.

The bastard.

She wouldn't let him get to her. *Bring it on.*

"I thought I already fixed you once," he said as he turned to face her.

Even through the thick lenses she could see his eyes roam well over her head. She glanced at the dog and back at Kernan. The watery blue eyes weren't focused on her face and tracked just a bit to the right of her.

Maggie couldn't believe it. The old man had actually gone blind.

CHAPTER 48

Sam felt relieved, even though Jeffery was in a foul mood. It had turned black — directly to black, no gray — as soon as they brought the last person out. Alive!

Seven survivors. No dead bodies.

Jeffery's immediate response: "What a fucking waste of a day."

Sam realized she was probably just as bad as Jeffery, because her relief didn't come from the news that everyone had escaped safely, but rather because Jeffery wouldn't be using any of her footage. Especially not the footage she had purposely messed up of Jeffery's exchanges with Patrick and Agent O'Dell.

"Big Mac will cut this entire afternoon to a couple of minutes," Jeffery huffed as he yanked his tie loose and almost snapped off the top button of his shirt. "He's already said, 'No dead bodies, no story.' Doesn't even matter that it's churches. Or that you'd need a chemistry course to time these sons of bitches."

"Are you sure he's not interested? Two churches in the middle of the day? And in Arlington? It's not like the warehouses in a homeless district that nobody cares about."

She stopped herself as she broke down her equipment. Did she really just say that? Jesus! She really was starting to sound like Jeffery.

"I talked to him earlier. Said he needed something to keep this story alive."

Jeffery stood watching her. Usually he'd leave her to do this by herself, but he needed a ride back to the diner where he'd left his car.

"He loved the crap out of my profile on O'Dell," Jeffery said. "Wait till he sees the interview with the mother."

Sam felt a momentary twitch. Would he be wanting the nonexistent footage after all? She hadn't known about the interview. Jeffery had invited O'Dell's mother to come down to the news station, so he hadn't needed Sam.

"Hey, maybe I can help you out."

She and Jeffery both startled. Neither of them had noticed the firefighter come over to them from behind the crime scene tape. He pushed back his hat and the first thing

Sam noticed was how clean he was — no black smears on his face, no sweaty hair, no smoke or soot anywhere on him. Even his boots were dry.

He looked about Sam's age — around thirty — short and muscular, though the latter was difficult to judge under his heavy uniform. He had a square jaw, a nose that looked like it might have been broken at least once, and narrow, deep-set eyes that traveled too slowly over Sam's body. Usually that sort of thing didn't bother her. She wasn't sure why it did now. What was it about this guy that didn't feel right?

"From what I hear," Jeffery said, "there's not much to tell."

"I recognized you when you were talking to my partner earlier. You're Jeffery Cole from CNN."

Sam almost laughed. She should have looked away. She already knew what Jeffery's response would be.

Too late.

She saw him smile and his chest practically puffed out as he straightened his tie.

"What is it you think you can help us with, Mr. Firefighter?"

"Actually my name's Wes Harper. I'm a private firefighter with Braxton Protection Agency."

"Private? I didn't realize there was such a thing. That's interesting, but I don't think we need any more footage."

"I saw that piece you did last night."

Now that Jeffery had decided this guy wasn't one of the "real" firefighters and that he wasn't interested, he had started to shut down, like an actor done with his role and donning his own persona. Even his smile waned, polite because he couldn't resist a compliment and would certainly wait for this guy's, but beyond that Sam could see he was no longer interested in resuming his role as Jeffery Cole, investigative interviewer.

"I know you'd probably rather interview my partner, but since he turned you down maybe I could fill in."

"That's nice of you, but I think we're good."

"Aren't you doing like a part two on his sister tonight?"

Sam almost dropped the lens she had taken off and was carefully putting into its sleeve.

"Excuse me?" Jeffery said, stepping closer to Harper as if he hadn't heard him. "That young guy, that rent-a-fireman, is Agent O'Dell's brother?"

"That's right," Harper said with a smile, not the least bit bothered by the derogatory remark about his occupation.

"Well, well," Jeffery said. "It's certainly a small world, isn't it?"

CHAPTER 49

This would be a piece of cake, Maggie thought. A disabled Kernan wouldn't be able to see the reactions his insults and swipes registered. She saw his head tilt, his chin track up — signs of a man depending on what he heard and smelled rather than saw.

"Once again," Maggie said, "I'm here only because my superior insisted."

"Oh, that's right. And they're always wrong. Aren't they?"

"They have rules and regulations they need to follow. I understand that."

He leaned back and his head cocked to the side as if gauging her response. He intertwined his fingers and laid them on his thick chest. That's when Maggie realized his tie was navy blue but his suit was dark brown. He had no one to help him dress. No one to offer advice before he went out the door. Just the dog, who although he rested in the corner, still kept his eyes trained on his master. But a dog couldn't tell you that your tie doesn't match your suit. And suddenly Maggie wanted to kick herself, because she actually felt sorry for Dr. James Kernan.

"But you still believe they're wrong? That you shouldn't be here?"

She sat back in the chair, fingers no longer clenched and now resting in her lap. She stared at him and wondered what it was like to be cunning and sharp-tongued, to be brilliant and to win every mental game, and yet be totally alone in the world. No, she didn't feel sorry for him, she felt uncomfortably *like him.*

Was this her future? Instead of the paraphernalia from the history of psychology, she'd have strange tokens and memorabilia of the serial killers she had tracked.

Then Maggie thought of Lucy Coy, the old Indian woman she had met in the Sandhills of Nebraska. She'd be content to be like Lucy, surrounded by dogs and quiet and a beautiful landscape.

"Have you become hard of hearing, Ms. O'Dell?"

She'd forgotten to respond and now Kernan would read something into that hesitation.

"You'd much rather be shooting some killer between the eyes. Isn't that right?"

Ordinarily that jab would have made her wince, but now Maggie caught herself smiling. Kernan's power to intimidate and humiliate, to make her question herself — all of that was gone. The only thing she saw now was a pathetic, white-haired old man who couldn't even see her smile.

"I'm a different person than I was five years ago, Dr. Kernan."

"Is that right?" He smacked his lips together and did his trademark "Tis tis," which announced he couldn't be fooled when, in fact, he already had been.

Maggie was about to remind him that he also was a different person than when they last met, but he cut her off by asking, "How long have you been getting the headaches?"

Maggie hadn't told anyone about her headaches. She knew it wasn't in the ER report. Sometimes when a person loses one sense the others become more alert. Was that what had happened with Kernan?

"How did you know?"

This time it was his turn to smile.

"You just told me," he said.

She felt the blood rush to her face. It was the oldest trick in the book and she had fallen for it.

"Now we're even," Kernan said. "Perhaps we can start over. I may have lost the better part of my sight, O'Dell, Margaret, but do not underestimate me. Never underestimate your opponent, no matter what you perceive to be his disability."

"Perhaps this would go much better if you didn't perceive me as an opponent." She said it out of anger, but it was exactly how she felt. Wasn't that what this session was supposed to be about? How and what she was feeling.

She steeled herself for one of his silly, cutting word plays. Instead, he said nothing and stared at a spot over her head, his watery blue eyes magnified behind the thick lenses. He pursed his lips then blew out air, sending his lips vibrating and making a sputtering sound.

Finally his eyes came close to where they might meet hers and he said, "Fair enough."

CHAPTER 50

Sam understood exactly why Jeffery had suggested Old Ebbitt's when he offered to treat them to dinner. The restaurant was a favorite of politicos and the District's movers and shakers. Every time they walked through, it would take three times as long to get to their table because Jeffery had to stop and chat, shake a hand or two, or wave to anyone who recognized him. He even insisted on having a table instead of the high-backed booths that Sam loved. She wanted the quiet and privacy. Jeffery wanted to be at a table where he could be seen and be on display. But first he wanted to stop next door for a drink.

Sam understood all this. She knew Jeffery too well. She could predict and anticipate his actions. What she didn't understand was why he had invited Wes Harper to come along with them. She didn't like the guy. There was something about him that creeped her out.

"He's an interesting guy," Jeffery had admonished her. When she rolled her eyes, he added, "You could do worse."

Of course Jeffery hadn't noticed the lurid body swipes Harper's eyes had been giving Sam. Jeffery rarely noticed anything that didn't involve him. And Harper was sly enough to know that. He had been lavishing Jeffery with compliments, laying it on thick. And Jeffery appeared mesmerized by all of Harper's talk about fire.

Sam had agreed to have one drink, then she wanted to go home. She made it plain she wouldn't be joining them for dinner next door, telling the men that she had spent too little time with her son this week. The comment, meant to dissuade Harper, only seemed to encourage him.

"Divorced?" he asked, not just in a hopeful tone. Instead, he made the word sound sexy, but in a naughty way. There was something about the way he stared at her with gray eyes that reminded her too much of a wolf. It made her skin crawl. Maybe he'd missed her mention of a young son. Usually that had the same effect as throwing cold water on men.

They ordered drinks and, thankfully, Jeffery steered the conversation back to the fires. He and Harper talked as though they were experts comparing notes.

"These have been intense, white hot," Jeffery said. "Most chemical reactions are."

"Who said they were started by chemical reactions?" Sam asked. She couldn't recall the real experts saying a thing about chemicals.

"Someone mentioned it." He dismissed her with a wave of his hand, like he couldn't be bothered with such trivial details at the moment. To Harper he continued, "Accelerants don't matter. You can pour all the gasoline you want but you still need a spark. A chemical reaction provides a spontaneous ignition. It's ingenious, wouldn't you say?"

"Oh, absolutely." Harper sipped his Grey Goose vodka.

Jeffery lifted his index finger from his chin and gave a signal that always managed to get instant attention. He could get a cab with a subtle gesture, too. It was one of the things Sam admired about him — that air of confidence that grabbed attention with a nod or a flip of a finger. A waiter arrived and Jeffery pointed to all three glasses for seconds, though Sam hadn't yet taken a sip of her Bud Light.

"I've either put out or tried to light just about any kind of fire you can think of,"

Harper said.

"So you like to light them as well?" Jeffery asked. "A firefighter?"

He grinned at their reactions. "My momma is very glad to know I decided to make a career of putting them out instead of starting them. But I learned a great deal from lighting fires. For instance, you know you can tell what's burning by the color of the flame."

"That right?"

Harper took a generous sip of the vodka while nodding and taking his time to respond. "Reddish yellow is usually wood or cloth. Yellow white is kerosene or gasoline. They burn at different temps. I still think there's nothing prettier on a cold night than bright yellow and red flames dancing in the sky."

The waiter delivered the drinks and Harper slung back the remainder in his old glass before he surrendered it. He pulled the fresh drink from the center of the table and set it protectively in front of him.

"It's interesting what fire does to a body, too."

He was looking directly at Sam now. She knew what this was — he wanted to see if he could make her squeamish. There was a whole class of assholes who liked to make women squirm over grotesque subjects, usually sexual, sometimes just violent. Harper looked like the type who combined the two.

When neither she nor Jeffery responded, Harper took it as license to continue. "The arms and legs are the first to go. They're like kindling, thin and surrounded by oxygen. Easy to ignite and quick to burn."

She refused to let him see her flinch. Besides, she'd heard worse. Been through worse. She held his stare and tried to ignore the grin beginning slowly at the corner of his mouth.

"Skin blackens pretty quickly. Fat sizzles." He hissed out the "z's," his voice a bit lower now. He was clearly enjoying himself. "Usually within minutes the skin splits open. That's when the body starts to clench in on itself and the legs start to spread apart and the knees —"

"Yes, yes, we all know about the boxer stance," Jeffery said, waving his hand at Harper, indicating that anything beyond this would be boring. Sam held back a sigh of relief. Now if Jeffery could just get Harper's eyes off her.

"Pugilistic posture," Jeffery added. "The fire dries out the muscles and the tendons shrink."

"That's right. Where did you learn so

much about fires?" Harper asked.

Jeffery sat back and Sam could see he was pleased with the question. Pleased with drawing the attention back to himself. And for once Sam was glad to have him back in control of the conversation.

"I wasn't always a newscaster. I did have another life before this. And I do copious research for my features."

Sam restrained a smile. How many real people actually used the word "copious"?

"I interview a variety of people," Jeffery continued. "I did a documentary — perhaps you've seen it — *Life Behind Bars*. Fascinating stories. Simply amazing what some of these criminals have to say. Of course, you have to wonder whether or not some of their stories are anywhere near the truth."

He laughed his best fake laugh and Sam held back from reminding him that whether or not the stories were accurate didn't always stop him from using the tall tales and sometimes sensationalizing them. With the exception of Otis P. Dodd. She still didn't understand why Jeffery had been so quick to dismiss the man.

"So you interviewed some fire starters? A chem guy, huh?"

"Yes. Big-time arsonist. Not as big as this current guy will be. This case certainly gives you a new respect for your ordinary under-the-sink solutions or swimming pool cleaners."

Both men laughed while Sam sipped her beer. The only arsonist on the list had been Otis P. Dodd, and Jeffery hadn't asked him a single question about his arson adventures. But then she remembered that Jeffery had received detailed letters from Otis P. long before they met with him.

A man appeared at their table.

"Wes, what the hell are you doing here?"

Sam almost didn't recognize Patrick Murphy. In jeans, a black turtleneck, and a leather jacket, he looked like he'd stepped off the cover of *GQ*. Even as he addressed Harper, his eyes found and settled on Sam's as though he were really asking what *she* was doing here.

Jeffery obviously didn't recognize Patrick at all. His first response was to be perturbed, and he played the role well. He pushed back his chair with an impatient sigh. He didn't like sharing the limelight.

"You know what, guys?" Sam announced. "I've got to go. Jeffery, thanks for the drink. You boys enjoy dinner."

She slid her bag onto her shoulder before Harper or Jeffery noticed.

"Yes, hug that boy of yours," Jeffery said,

looking around for the waiter.

Just when Harper looked like he might protest Sam's leaving, the waiter brought more drinks, giving him what looked to be a difficult choice.

"I'll walk you out," Patrick said quietly, setting her pulse up a notch and making her wonder if staying may have been safer.

As she stood and tried to ignore Patrick's eyes, she glanced up at one of the televisions over the bar. Something, or rather someone, on the screen caught her eye. Peter Sanders, a network news reporter and someone Jeffery considered his competition, was doing a live broadcast from the middle of some dark wooded area.

The sound was turned down but there were closed captions running along the bottom of the screen, and as Sam started reading them she felt her stomach slide to her knees.

Jeffery glanced up to see what had captured her attention. He did a double take and then he got quiet and stared at the screen.

They watched while Peter Sanders directed his camera technician. The picture focused in on a culvert under an old dirt road and the three people hunched over — two men and one woman — with the white letters "CSI" on their jackets. Floodlights had been set up, casting shadows. Sam didn't need to see beyond them. She didn't need to see anything more. She couldn't take her eyes off the swatch of orange peeking out from under the leaves and mud.

"That son of a bitch," Jeffery said under his breath as he stared up at the television. "He was actually telling the truth."

CHAPTER 51

"What was that about?" Patrick asked Sam as they stepped outside onto the sidewalk.

"The prison documentary Jeffery and I have been working on. Yesterday one of the guys told us he knew where there was a body."

Her eyes left his, wandered away. He could tell this was unsettling for her, but she wasn't willing to share that part. He knew Sam Ramirez was the type of woman who didn't reveal her feelings or her vulnerabilities.

"He said it was a young woman. That the killer left her in a culvert. He said the guy didn't take off her orange socks."

"How did he know so much? Was he there?"

"He claims the guy told him after a couple of whiskeys in a bar one night."

"Wow. Interviewing murderers. Your job is more dangerous than mine."

She finally smiled.

He walked alongside her as she led the way to her parked car.

"I just wanted to tell you I appreciate what you did at the fire site."

"I didn't do anything."

"You backed me out of what could have been an embarrassing interview."

"I think you would have handled yourself just fine."

"For a minute back there I thought you were with Wes."

"So what if I was?"

He heard a slight bit of irritation in her voice, and he glanced over his shoulder to make sure Wes Harper hadn't decided he wanted Sam more than he wanted the expensive vodka. Patrick tried to remember if he had told Harper anything he'd regret, anything Harper would tell Jeffery Cole.

They hadn't partnered up by choice. Braxton Protection Agency assigned teammates. Patrick didn't trust Wes Harper from day one. Turned out his instincts had been correct. Last job, Harper couldn't wait to rat him out.

Finally he looked back at Sam, standing in front of him, tapping her foot, waiting for a reply.

"Sometimes he's not a very nice guy."

"Really? Seems like an odd thing to say about your partner."

"We're not partners by choice," he said, but he didn't want to go into the long explanation. He looked back over his shoulder again. "I'm supposed to meet Maggie. Should I warn her that Cole is here?"

"Don't worry. If he doesn't have a camera on him" — and she tapped her shoulder bag — "he's pretty harmless." She seemed to reconsider that, then added, "But you might want to keep her from seeing the second part of his profile later tonight."

"Why did he decide to target Maggie?"

Sam shrugged. "You'd have to ask him."

He was sorry he'd asked because now she glanced down the street like she couldn't wait to escape from him. Maybe she was keeping someone waiting.

"I know you must have someplace to go, but would you like to join us? Get a quick bite? Didn't look like you got anything to eat."

"Thanks, but I need to get home to my son."

"Oh sure. Ignacio." He tried not to sound relieved that it wasn't a date she was running off to.

"You remember my son's name?"

"I remember a lot of things if given a

chance." He said it and immediately wanted to kick himself.

He had never been good at flirting. The remark, however, registered a slow smile from Sam as she glanced away and shook her head. But she made no attempt to walk away.

"Maybe another time, Murphy."

CHAPTER 52

Tonight's motel had a large flat-screen television. He made sure of it before he checked in, looking inside a window after he saw the maids leave. He didn't mind that this one was an extra twenty bucks a night. Money wasn't a concern as much as privacy and, now, a big flat-screen television.

He was tired after a full day of work. He'd stayed out most of the night, blowing off steam, driving in the sleet, and finding the right place to lie in wait for just the right target. He was so good it wasn't much of a challenge anymore. He constantly had to add something to the mix, change things up. Last night's kill had calmed him, but it wasn't as satisfying as the doubles he had pulled off just days ago.

It didn't matter. He was finished with this job. He wanted to go home. He would get back on the road after one final task.

He hauled in his treasure trove from last

night, everything fitting nicely in a small black garbage bag. It had leaked in his vehicle. He had to throw out the brand-new liner. He had chosen a Dumpster behind a truck-stop diner that was already ripe and foul smelling. No one would notice his addition. For now he'd set the sticky bag in the bathtub. He'd get to it later.

He took out his burger and fries and arranged them on the greasy paper bag they'd come in. He made himself comfortable on the middle of the bed, where he could lounge, eat, and watch part two of Margaret O'Dell's life.

He had been looking forward to seeing Cole's next piece, though he didn't like the man interjecting so much of his own opinion. Cole pretended it was journalism, but he'd do better by sticking only to the facts. Still, it was extremely enjoyable.

He'd gotten delayed in traffic on the interstate, so by the time he found the channel Cole was already asking Kathleen O'Dell about her daughter's childhood.

He saw the resemblance. The same auburn hair and brown eyes. He was hoping there would be more photos. Maybe some of Margaret as a child. A teenager.

"Her father called her Magpie," Kathleen O'Dell was telling Cole. "He died when she was twelve. Sometimes I think she loved him so much that when he died she didn't have any more love to give."

He didn't hear what Cole asked next. All he heard was "magpie" and his mind went into a tailspin. His own mother had all kinds of superstitions that she tried to instill in him and his brother. He remembered her story about the magpie. It was the only bird that refused to enter Noah's ark and preferred instead to perch on the roof. It was bad luck to see one when you set off on a journey. And if you dared to kill one, misfortune would strike you down. It was best to treat a magpie with respect.

From the first time he saw Margaret O'Dell, he felt there was something special about her and now he knew.

By the time his mind came back to the television the interview was over. Someone else had replaced Jeffery Cole. His burger was cold and his fries were hard. He lay on the bed and began flipping channels, trying to clear his mind. He breezed over a news alert on one channel and then backtracked out of curiosity.

He didn't recognize the setting at first. He saw the State Patrol jackets and dark woods and suspected a dead body had been found. He was relieved that it didn't look anything like the rest area he had been to last night. But there was something familiar about the winding road. Then he saw the culvert and he knew they had found one of his after all.

He sat on the edge of the bed, his hands on his knees, and he tried to steady himself. That's when he noticed there was blood splattered along with river mud on his work boots. He'd spent the day working with blood on his boots.

Damn! He was getting reckless.

Of course, anyone else would see only the mud. He yanked the boots off. He'd have to clean them.

He padded in his socks to the bathroom to look into the black garbage bag he'd left in the tub. A ring of blood pooled around the bottom, a pretty crimson against the white porcelain. He tugged open the plastic. The smell was no longer rancid to him. Instead, it reminded him of raw meat in various stages of spoiling.

He was always so careful, leaving the ones he wanted found and tucking away the ones he wanted to hide. How the hell had they found the girl with the orange socks? And why now, when he just happened to be back in the area? Was his bad luck already beginning?

■ ■ ■ ■

SATURDAY

■ ■ ■ ■

CHAPTER 53

As soon as Maggie walked into the forensic anthropologist's lab she remembered how much she hated the smell of boiled flesh. Not that burned or putrefied flesh smelled much better. Somehow it seemed more rancid when it was done on purpose like the scientists did here.

Several pots and one huge roasting pan sat on the industrial stove's burners. Maggie could see the rolling boil in the roaster, and whatever was inside was producing the worst aroma.

Despite the smell, Maggie welcomed the distraction. She had been avoiding her mother's phone calls since last night. This morning she listened to only two of her dozen or more voice messages.

"That Jeffery Cole twisted everything I said," her mother whined. "He made me sound so awful."

Of course she'd make it about the injustice

done to her rather than admit she had been wrong. And forget about an apology. Odd as it seemed, Maggie would even trade listening to her mother's pathetic excuses with the smell of boiling flesh.

"You must be Agent O'Dell." A small Asian woman in a white lab coat greeted her. "I'm Mia Ling."

She was standing over a wide stainless-steel table under a hanging fluorescent light. Her purple-gloved fingers picked at a piece of bone.

"Detective Racine is on her way. I hope you don't mind if I don't shake your hand. I'm almost finished with this piece."

"No, of course. Please continue."

Maggie glanced in one of the other boiling pots as she made her way over. Maggots squirmed and rode on the greasy film. Several made it to the wall of the pan and tried to scale the metal only to die with a sizzle and a pop. Maggots were one of the few things that truly creeped Maggie out.

During autopsies they appeared indestructible. Even freezing them only slowed them down. Once present on a corpse, they couldn't simply be removed without also destroying valuable evidence. An autopsy with maggots became a race, the morgue's bright lights churning them up. Sometimes they shoved each other out onto the floor, where they'd search for the closest warm, moist place, often crawling up a pant leg. She found it morbidly satisfying to see them in hot water, finally something that could destroy them.

It only then occurred to her that Gloria Dobson's body didn't have any maggots, even though it had been dumped in the alley.

"I would be doing that with your victim," Ling said, indicating the boiling pot, "if you hadn't been able to identify her. It'd certainly be easier to boil away the flesh than to pick at it." She held up a bone in her fingers. "Funny how family members don't really appreciate us cutting off a victim's head just to figure out what happened. So I'm left to pick off the brain tissue from the bone by hand."

Maggie liked Mia Ling even before she added, "And my family doesn't understand why I won't eat meat."

"So this is Gloria Dobson's?" Maggie pointed to the tray with bits of bone and what looked like several teeth.

"Yes, what pieces we have. There are a lot of bone fragments missing. They probably were left at the crime scene." She poked at the teeth. "I found these down at the base of her skull and in her neck. Some pieces of her face were smashed into her brain."

Maggie pulled up a stool to sit down and to get a closer look.

"I'm trying to clean these pieces and sort them before I pull her out of the refrigerator."

Maggie could see the fragments Dr. Ling had already cleaned and processed. She arranged them like pieces of a jigsaw puzzle.

"Will it be at all possible to guess what kind of weapon caused this damage?"

Ling's hands stopped. She put down the bone she had been working on and picked up the biggest fragment from the tray. She turned it, found what she wanted, then leaned over to show Maggie.

"Can you see these crisscross fracture lines?" Her long index finger moved along what looked like scratches in the bone.

"Yes," Maggie answered.

"And see how the bone is sort of warped?" She held it up to the light.

It was subtle, but Maggie nodded.

"Bone literally bends when you hit it really hard. It'll bend before it breaks. If the warped area was dented and rounded, I'd guess something like a ball-peen hammer, which incidentally seems to be a favorite of skull bashers.

"The instrument used to do this had a larger surface area, it had a wider impact area. It had to be something larger and heavier. And because it also scratched the bone, I think we might rule out any shaft-like weapon, like a tire iron or a golf club. Those usually leave a long, narrow groove.

"Whatever he used — and I'm simply guessing that he didn't stop and use more than one instrument — it had a considerable head or end on it to inflict tremendous trauma. It also had some sort of claw or a sharp hooked end to cause the scratches and nicks I'm seeing in some of the bones."

"Stan said the tissue looked like it had been ripped out."

"If you had the crime scene to process, I bet we'd see a lot of flyers. Without the crime scene, we're doing a whole lot of speculating."

Flyers were the blood and tissue trails flung on walls and ceiling as the weapon is raised for the next blow and then the next. In this case, Maggie realized both experts were saying that the weapon not only broke and shattered bone and splattered blood and tissue, but also dug into and ripped out pieces.

"What about a crowbar?" she asked Ling.

"It would need a long enough handle to

create this kind of force. And I'm thinking wider. Maybe like a pry bar."

They sat quietly for a minute. Dr. Ling's hands were still.

"What about the other victim, the burned skull recovered from inside the building?"

"I spent almost five hours at the site sifting through the ashes. There were no other bones."

"Is it possible the rest of the body was destroyed in the fire?"

"It's pretty difficult to burn up a body entirely, even when accelerants are used. Cremation will even leave portions of bone that require mechanical pulverizing. This was an intensely hot fire, but not hot enough to destroy everything but the skull. I would have expected to find some long bones, or at least pieces of them. Also the teeth were smashed, but I didn't recover any and teeth don't burn."

"Sounds like you're saying this person was murdered somewhere else as well?"

"That would be my guess. The trauma sustained, as well as the decapitation, most likely did not happen in that building."

"Same weapon?"

"I can't make that determination at this time."

"Male? Female?"

"Male. Caucasian. That's really all I can tell you right now."

Silence. Maggie could hear the boiling water gurgle. Somewhere a machine clicked on and hummed.

"This was a brutal murder," Ling finally said, her face expressionless, her eyes trailing to the tray of bone and teeth, fragments of Gloria Dobson. "Some of the bones were congealed with blood and shoved into the brain."

Ling didn't need to explain that meant Gloria Dobson was still alive — hopefully unconscious — but her heart still pumping blood when she sustained some of the most vicious blows.

Racine chose that moment to stroll into the lab and call out, "Hey, Doc, whatcha got cookin'?"

CHAPTER 54

Sam's one day off and she spent the entire morning at the news station. Abe Nadira showed her to an empty editing booth. He helped her access the files she was looking for, then hesitated like he didn't want to leave her alone with them. Thankfully he was too busy to stay. She immediately locked the door behind him.

Last night Wes Harper's description of what fire can do to a body had freaked her out more than she liked to admit. What bothered her the most was how much pleasure Harper seemed to take in telling all the gruesome details. She also didn't like the fact that he and Jeffery seemed awfully chummy for having just met.

Just how did Jeffery know so much about these fires and about this fire starter? Yes, he did a ton of research, a habit he claimed was left over from his high school teaching days. So Sam was never surprised by the things he knew or remembered. He was one of the brightest guys she knew. And he could have learned things from Otis P. Dodd's personal letters, but they wouldn't have told Jeffery any details about these fires.

She couldn't remember any one of their interviewees or sources mentioning that the fires were started by a chemical reaction. Yet Jeffery appeared certain. She wanted to check some of their film footage. And she needed to check the films' date and time stamps. How did Jeffery know about the fires so early?

She wondered if someone was tipping him off. He often joked that he had more contacts and informants than the CIA, and Sam had always been amazed at the network of people he knew, not just across the country, but across the world.

Why Big Mac hadn't given Jeffery his own show always baffled Sam. Except that he didn't have the "look." Jeffery Cole was a bit too ordinary looking.

Sam jotted down names as she watched the taped segments. Was it possible one of these criminals had been paroled since the interview? There had to be a way she could check.

After two hours she was certain no one on

the list, other than Otis P. Dodd, had been charged or was serving time for arson. Of course that didn't mean arson wasn't in their background. Most of these guys were charged with multiple offenses. And they weren't choosy about what the offenses were. But if there was a connection between one of these criminals that Jeffery had interviewed and the fires from the past two weeks, she couldn't find it. Even Otis's "mystery man," who had killed the woman with the orange socks and stuffed her into a culvert, didn't show up anywhere else.

She was convinced, however, that Jeffery had inside knowledge. If not directly from the arsonist, then from someone who knew when and where the fires would happen. But who? And what kind of dangerous game had Jeffery gotten himself into this time?

Sam pulled up the footage from the warehouse fires, the footage she had taken before the fire trucks and rescue crews arrived. She remembered thinking it odd that no one else was there, and yet at the same time she had been excited about getting the exclusive. Agent Tully had been interested in this same footage but only until he found the man with the red backpack. Sam started watching from the point where Agent Tully stopped.

It was boring. Slow going. She clicked up the speed. Paused it when the crowd began to grow. Zoomed in. Panned the faces. Nothing. She wasn't even sure what she was looking for. Did she really expect to recognize anyone?

She sent it speeding along again. Just after the second explosion, she stopped the film. Hit REWIND then PLAY, and let it move in regular time. She grabbed her cup of coffee and sipped, keeping an eye on the computer monitor. She glanced away to look at her watch. When she looked back up she noticed several more people had joined the crowd. Just before the time stamp where she knew the second blast occurred, Sam paused and zoomed in again. She started panning the new crowd. Then suddenly she recognized someone.

She reached up so quickly to tap STOP that she knocked over her coffee cup.

What in the world was *he* doing there?

CHAPTER 55

Maggie listened while Dr. Ling went over all the same information with Racine. The detective, however, didn't appear all that interested. Maggie knew Julia Racine well enough to know something was up. She was patient and polite but she asked few questions. Dr. Ling started talking about the skull found inside the burned building. Then Racine became a bit agitated.

"But you can't be sure he was killed in the same way or even with the same weapon?" she asked.

"Yes, I'm simply speculating. Although the fractures to the top and to the side of the cranium look similar, you're correct, they are not conclusive."

"Is it possible he fell during the fire and bashed in his own head?"

"No." Dr. Ling smiled before she added, "He would also have had to decapitate himself."

"Stan told us that pressure builds up inside the head during a fire. You know, from the blood and brain starting to boil." Racine looked from Dr. Ling to Maggie and back to Dr. Ling like she was asking for backup. "And that pressure could literally blow a head off a body. That's what Stan said."

"It's possible," Dr. Ling said. "But not in this case."

Ling went over to another counter. On her way she changed out her purple latex gloves for a fresh pair. Then she carefully picked up the skull from a deep tray that Maggie thought looked too much like an ordinary baking pan. Ling brought the skull over to Maggie and Racine.

"I've cleaned it as best as I could." She flipped the skull upside down. It still had a muddy brown color to it, but the fracture lines were visible. Ling pointed to the base. "Do you see the cuts and scratches in the bone here? Right at the base? This one is what I call a hesitation mark. He started cutting and stopped. Perhaps whatever he was using didn't work as well as he wanted. Here and here."

She turned the skull as her finger traced the scratches.

"The fire dulled the effect a bit. These are

311

chops, not cut marks."

"Guess no chance of an accident, then." Racine appeared visibly disappointed. "So what the hell did he use?"

"Anytime you chop, the instrument must be heavy and big enough to contribute to the impact. My early guess is some kind of large bladed weapon. Perhaps a machete."

Maggie watched Racine. Clearly all of this had blown one of her theories.

"You mentioned earlier that Gloria Dobson's murderer did *not* change weapons in between blows," Maggie said. "Is it possible this victim may have been killed by someone else? Maybe even another time or another place?"

"The bashed-in skull is quite similar to Mrs. Dobson's."

"But she wasn't decapitated." Racine sounded hopeful again.

"True enough." And Dr. Ling nodded, but allowed a smile when she added, "However, you could say he tried very hard to knock her head off."

"Dr. Ling?" A tall young man called to her from the door. "That delivery you've been waiting for has just arrived."

"Thanks, Calvin. I'll be right there." She returned the skull to its tray. "Will you both excuse me? I'll be only five or ten minutes."

"No problem."

Ling had barely cleared the door when, like a mother with a child, Maggie pulled Racine's elbow away right before she poked one of the bones with brain tissue still sticking to it.

"What? I just wondered what it felt like."

"You know something new?"

But Racine wasn't ready to talk about whatever it was and tried to change the subject. "That interview last night with your mother — that was brutal."

"It must have been. She's been leaving voice messages for me all morning wanting to explain. Quit changing the subject. Tell me what you found out."

Racine got quiet. She was still eyeing the bone Ling had left on the tray.

"I thought I had it figured out," she finally said. "I talked to Gloria Dobson's husband last night. A male colleague was supposed to be making the trip with her. He said it made him feel better that she wouldn't be driving the eleven hundred miles alone. He liked the kid. Said he was a good guy."

She pulled a small notebook from her jacket pocket and flipped pages.

"Zach Lester, twenty-eight, five nine, a hundred and fifty pounds, light brown hair, blue eyes. Mr. Lester didn't show up at the sales conference either. I put out a BOLO for him and for Dobson's silver 2007 Toyota Highlander."

"You think Lester killed her and took her vehicle?"

"Sometimes the simplest explanation is the correct one."

"When did Mr. Dobson talk to his wife last?"

"Three days ago. She and Lester were on their last leg of the trip, almost to Baltimore. He said it wasn't that unusual that he hadn't heard from her since. The sales conferences were busy and he liked her to feel like she didn't need to check in, give her a break from him and the kids."

"What motive would Lester have for killing her?"

"Coworkers, road trip away from everyone. Maybe there was a thing between them. Maybe he hit her on the head when she rejected him."

"Would he have been mad enough to bludgeon her to death?"

Racine shrugged. "We've both seen people do worse for less reason. Makes more sense than a stranger. Someone bashes in another person's face like that, it's usually personal."

"But the skull inside the building complicates your theory."

"Only slightly. It could be two separate killers. You've been saying all along that you didn't think the arsonist was the same guy who murdered Dobson."

"He didn't bother to burn her body."

"But the victim inside was toast."

"Dr. Ling said she didn't find any other bones from the rest of that body."

"Could they have burned up?"

Maggie simply shook her head, not wanting to go into Dr. Ling's long explanation.

"Guess we'll have to wait and ask Zach Lester what happened as soon as the Virginia State Patrol finds him and Dobson's SUV."

"There's something I should probably tell you." Maggie waited for Racine's attention. "The other day when I went down the manhole? I think someone followed me down."

"What do mean? Followed you down?"

"I heard footsteps in front of me. Then all of sudden there were footsteps behind me. Someone started smashing out the light-bulbs in the tunnel before you called down and scared him off."

"And you're only telling me this now?"

"That's not all. That night someone was seen back behind my property checking out my backyard."

"Could be some crazy who saw Jeffery Cole's profile."

"I've taken a lot of precautions to not be found."

"Property taxes are all online now."

"Mine's not listed under my name."

Racine raised an eyebrow but didn't ask. She crossed her arms over her chest and Maggie waited for the lecture. None came. Instead of anger, Racine looked concerned. Very concerned. And that was more unsettling than having the detective angry with her.

CHAPTER 56

Sam tried not to jump to conclusions. Seeing Wes Harper at the scene of the warehouse fires wasn't all that incriminating. After all, he was firefighter. But why was he dressed in casual clothes and standing back with the crowd of bystanders? Did he just show up to watch? Or was he already there, waiting to witness his handiwork and watch the real firefighters try to put it out?

She spent the next hour looking up everything she could find on Harper, using the news station's access to Internet databases. She found no criminal record except indication that there was a juvenile case that had been sealed when Harper was a teenager. But then he had admitted last night that he had been a firebug in his younger days. Youthful indiscretions hardly resulted in a repeat felony arsonist. It was probably nothing. From what she found about Braxton Protection Agency, Harper would never have been hired if there was something questionable in his past. Maybe she just wanted him to be guilty.

Sam slipped the film footage into her bag and left the station, avoiding Nadira and Jeffery, sneaking through the hallways as though she were the one who had something to hide. She made it to the elevator bank almost home free when one of the doors opened and out came Jeffery.

"What are you doing here?"

"Just checking on something." She brushed past him to get inside the empty elevator.

"Something I need to know about?" He held his hand over the elevator door so it wouldn't close.

"No. It's no big deal." And she wondered if Nadira had tattled on her. Why was her pulse racing? She hadn't done anything wrong. Jeffery was the one keeping secrets.

"Did you hear that O'Dell's mother called Big Mac complaining about our interview? She's insisting on a retraction. Says we cut and edited it to make her look bad."

Sam didn't have anything to do with the interview, hadn't even seen it, but she knew how Jeffery could edit a version so that even Sam didn't recognize an interview after she stood by and filmed it.

"Remember I said you shouldn't mess with an FBI agent."

Jeffery shrugged, but he was still smiling when he dropped his hand away and let the elevator door close. Controversy pleased him, excited him. And Sam could tell by his expression that he viewed Kathleen O'Dell's complaints as accolades. She knew the profile piece was getting all kinds of attention, the exact kind that Jeffery — and even Big Mac — thrived on. Sometimes she wondered just how far Jeffery was willing to blur the line between news and sensationalism. There seemed to be nothing that couldn't be "touched up," "edited out," "beefed up," or "deleted." No wonder she was starting to feel like a paparazzo.

Finally back home, Sam watched her son and mother making cookie dough. Her mother explained the instructions to Iggy in English and he would repeat them back to her in Spanish. It was their way of helping each other learn. It would take them a couple of hours, rolling out the dough, using the heart-shaped cookie cutters, baking, then frosting and decorating them. Her son wanted to make enough to take to school. Sam left them downstairs to take a long bath and read in the bathtub — a rare treat.

The week had taken its toll. She immersed herself in the warm water and felt the tension start to slip away from her muscles. Without effort her mind drifted to Patrick Murphy — his soft brown eyes, the sexy dimple in his chin, his thick hair with the spiky cowlick that gave him that reckless, boyish charm.

It was ridiculous for her to be thinking this way. He was too young for her. There was no doubt about that. Barely out of college and starting his career, his life. Sam had lived a lifetime of experiences already. At thirty she felt far too old and too cynical for someone like Patrick, who was just beginning his career. Nor did she have the patience to entertain a fling. It was best to get him out of her mind.

She lay back and closed her eyes. She lost track of time and started to doze. She wanted to soak out the tension from the week, relieve her senses from the smell of smoke and the sounds of sirens and glass shattering. It would take more than a warm bath to settle the chaos that stayed with her. In fact, she could still smell the smoke as if it radiated off her body. Then she remembered what Wes Harper had said about burning flesh: "The arms and legs are the first to go."

Something was burning. She really could smell it. It wasn't her imagination.

She bolted upright, sending water over the edge of the tub. Something inside the house was on fire.

CHAPTER 57

Sam found her mother on a chair, trying to hit the screaming smoke alarm with the handle of a broom, only she kept missing and smacking the wall. Her son stood in the corner of the kitchen, his hands over his ears, but he was laughing at his nanna despite the smoke still belching from the oven. If Sam hadn't been dripping wet in only her robe, if her heart hadn't been racing out of control, she might have laughed, too. Her mother did look like she was trying to swat down a piñata.

"It's not funny," Sam told her son, sounding too much like her mother. She put her hand around her mother's waist. "Momma, leave it."

"It so loud."

"We'll clear the smoke and it'll stop."

Her mother didn't look convinced, but she let Sam help her down off the chair.

"What happened?"

"We were watching TV," Iggy confessed, no longer laughing and watching his nanna to see if it was okay to tell.

They had become close these past years while Sam trudged around the world with Jeffery. Sometimes she found herself jealous of their closeness. Even now he wanted to protect his grandmother and didn't like tattling on her, even when the entire house smelled of burned cookies.

Sam opened the window. Cold air filled the room but the smoke and smell lifted quickly.

"It's okay," she told them both when the alarm finally stopped screeching.

Her mother pulled out the cookie sheet and shook her head. "Such a waste."

"Leave it," Sam said. "I'm taking you both out to dinner."

They stared at her like she was speaking in a foreign language neither of them understood. She realized she couldn't remember how long it had been since the three of them had eaten out.

"I get to choose the restaurant."

Iggy and his nanna exchanged looks.

"Go on." Sam waved her hands at them. "Go get cleaned up. And dressed up."

Sam was ready before they were. She had found a skirt she hadn't worn in years and put on a long sweater and high boots. When her mother came down the stairs in a burgundy knit dress and the peacock-print scarf Sam had brought her from Italy, Sam hardly recognized the beautiful woman before her.

"This is all right?" her mother asked, worried by Sam's dumbfounded stare.

She kissed her mother's cheek and said, "You look so pretty."

Her crusty, nagging mother blushed like a schoolgirl.

Sam was going to check on Iggy, thinking the boy might need help. But her mother had told her, "Leave him be. He's fine. He said he's a big boy now."

He came marching down the stairs, watching his feet as though he didn't trust the rarely worn leather dress shoes. Sam swallowed hard, but the lump stayed in her throat. He looked like a little man in his trousers and white button-down shirt with red suspenders that matched his red bow tie.

"I tie it for him," her mother said, then shook her hands in a go-away gesture.

Sam's cell phone rang and all three of them froze in place as if the ring had stung them. The two people she loved most in this world looked at her briefly with an innocent anxiousness before their eyes automatically switched over to disappointed resolve.

Sam glanced at the caller ID, though she already knew it had to be Jeffery. She closed her eyes and took a deep breath. In all the years as his camera technician she had always been there. Jeffery was just another reporter without a camera on him, but Sam knew he could replace her tonight and all the nights to come with a snap of his fingers.

Of course, no one would put up with him as much as she did or for as long as she had. Sam and Jeffery had become like an old married couple, ignoring each other's idiosyncrasies, taking the good with the bad. It had been Sam's experience that marriages and relationships usually ended up with one person taking the brunt of the bad. Her mother and son certainly had in the last few years of her relationships with them.

Sam's finger hovered over the phone as it continued to ring. She saw her son put his hands under his suspenders, getting ready to flick them off his shoulders, and she put her hand up to stop him.

"Don't you dare," she said to him, then moved her finger over the phone's faceplate, taking Jeffery's call and sliding it to Ignore. Before it could start ringing again, she shut the phone off.

"Let's go," she said, but neither her son nor her mother moved. They stared at her, almost as stunned by what she had just done as Sam was.

CHAPTER 58

Patrick opened the door and recognized the woman without an introduction. By the surprise on her face, he knew she recognized him, too.

"She said you looked exactly like your father."

"Maggie said that?"

"No. Your mother."

"So you're Kathleen O'Dell?"

"And you're Patrick."

"Maggie's not here." But he opened the door and invited her in anyway.

She hesitated, but only for a second, staring at him as if she were seeing a ghost.

"I know she's not here. I didn't come to see Maggie."

Now Patrick wished he hadn't been so quick to open the door. Maggie had a security camera. He could have easily avoided this and just pretended to not be here.

"You keep in touch with my mom?"

"From time to time." She made her way into the living room. "Don't look so surprised. How do you suppose we kept the two of you from finding out about each other all these years?"

He didn't like the sarcasm in her voice. She might resemble Maggie in looks, but her brusque manner was nothing like Maggie. Not two minutes after their introductions and Patrick could detect a cruel edge to this woman.

"What is it that you wanted to see me about?"

"My, I don't recall your mother mentioning how rude you are."

He felt the flash of heat crawl up the back of his neck.

"Perhaps you could get me something to drink?"

She followed him into the kitchen like she knew her way. Stopped at the island counter and watched him take out two glasses from the cabinet and open the refrigerator. Before he brought out the pitcher of ice tea she stopped him.

"You must have something a little stronger than ice tea. I know you were tending bar at college, so you must be old enough to drink."

"You know exactly how old I am," Patrick told her, allowing his irritation to show.

She looked at him for a second and he saw a deep sadness in her eyes as she said, "Yes. Yes, I do know exactly how old you are."

It had taken Patrick's mother a lifetime — Patrick's lifetime — to admit that he was conceived during a three-month affair with Thomas O'Dell. Growing up, he knew little about his father except for the bits and pieces he kept in a Nike shoe box. It wasn't until five years ago, when Maggie came looking to meet him at the University of New Haven, that Patrick learned the secret that Thomas O'Dell's wife and mistress had kept for more than twenty years. He wondered what Kathleen O'Dell hoped to accomplish by coming here today.

He pulled out the bottle of wine that he and Maggie hadn't finished the night he fixed them dinner. He exchanged the tea glasses for goblets, popped up the cork, and poured. At first he was going to stick with tea for himself but then he decided this conversation might go down better with some wine.

There was only half a bottle left. He emptied it into the glasses and slid hers over to her side of the center island, where she

329

had already made herself comfortable on one of the bar stools. Patrick remained standing, taking his old bartender stance, and then remembered how Maggie and Sam had taken these exact positions during their midnight confrontation.

"Maggie has a misguided sense of obligation to you," Kathleen O'Dell said, taking a healthy gulp of the wine.

"Unlike you and my mom."

"Why in the world would I feel any obligation to a bitch who tried to steal my husband?"

Patrick kept himself from flinching at his mother being called a bitch.

"What is it that you want to talk to me about, Mrs. O'Dell?"

"I want you to leave. Pack up and get out of Maggie's life."

"Maggie invited me to stay here. I didn't ask her for a place to stay."

"But of course you jumped at the offer."

"I'm pretty sure this isn't any of your business."

"So what will it cost?"

"Excuse me?"

"What will it cost to get you to leave?"

"I think you're the one who needs to leave, Mom," Maggie said from the doorway.

Neither of them had heard her come in. Patrick had forgotten to lock the door and set the alarm. Maggie must have recognized her mom's car in the circle drive.

"Patrick's a guest here. I suggest if you want to continue to be one, you'll leave right now."

"I expected you to be curious about him. Maybe even want to meet him. I didn't expect you to drag him into our lives."

"My life. Not yours."

Kathleen O'Dell slid off the bar stool and stood in front of Maggie. That's when Patrick realized she was a bit wobbly on her feet. She may have had a few drinks before she arrived.

"So you're choosing this bastard half brother over your own mother?"

"I'm not choosing anyone. You want to talk about choice, Mom? Maybe you should tell me how you *chose* to give a tell-all interview to some two-bit reporter."

"Jeffery Cole is an award-winning journalist. How was I supposed to know that he would twist my words?"

"Right, he twisted your words to make it sound like you were betraying your daughter."

"Betraying? You see that as a betrayal? But this — inviting him into our lives — that's not a betrayal?"

Kathleen O'Dell waved her hand at Maggie like she thought she was being ridiculous. She shook her head, a slow side-to-side motion that Patrick thought looked melodramatic and perhaps even practiced. She made her way to the door without argument, either anxious to escape or simply needing the last word. Either way, Patrick realized she was willing to leave without further explanation or apology.

Before she left she mumbled something that sounded like "You'll be sorry."

From the disappointment on Maggie's face, Patrick thought she already looked like she was sorry.

CHAPTER 59

Tully wore jeans, an old gray sweatshirt, the grimiest pair of high-tops he owned, and a threadbare jacket he'd bought earlier from a Salvation Army thrift shop. Last night when he carefully went through the red backpack he had found an interesting assortment of worthless junk. Or at least he had believed it to be worthless. Then he discovered that whoever had been using the backpack had one of the same habits Tully had — pocketing an extra napkin or two from whatever fast-food joint or vendor he ate at.

Tully took out all of the napkins — eight different ones, plus four from the same place. Then he bought a tourist map of the District and started highlighting all the napkin food stops.

More than half of the food places were around the fire site and close to the Martin Luther King Jr. Memorial Library, where the homeless buses picked up and dropped off passengers. The others were downtown. The four duplicate napkins were from a small corner shop called Willie's between the library and the fire site on Massachusetts Avenue.

The guy who tripped Tully and ran away from Maggie, only to drop down a manhole, had looked homeless. Maybe it was just a disguise. If he was the arsonist, maybe that's how he managed to blend in. Both Tully and Maggie suspected that the fire starter walked to the sites. How better to get away than to drop underground and make your way safely home?

Of course, the church fires in Arlington threw Tully's hunch way off. Still, he had a gut feeling that this guy — whoever he was — knew something more. Maybe he had seen something or someone. After all, why disappear down a manhole the night of the fire when he could have easily walked away without notice? And was it a coincidence that he disappeared before the second building burst into flames?

Between the corner shop named Willie's and the fire site, Tully had narrowed it down to three manholes that could easily be accessed without much notice or without traffic running over them. Then he found a place where he could watch all three.

Along with the napkins he had found several store receipts smashed into the bottom of the backpack. Most of them were from Willie's. And all of those had time stamps between five and seven o'clock in the evening.

Tully bought a sandwich and coffee from Willie's and found his place. It was ten minutes before five. He figured he could kill a couple of hours hanging out. He sat down on the cold concrete, realizing quickly why most of the steamy grates were already occupied.

He ate his sandwich, sipped his coffee. He had memorized the blown-up photo he had of the guy. Although the features were mostly shadows, he thought he would recognize the guy's build, shaggy hair, and pointy beard. But it didn't really matter. How many guys would be coming up from a manhole after five o'clock?

He sat and ate and sipped and watched. Thirty minutes later his butt felt numb against the cold concrete. He thought about moving to one of the grates, but there were no vacancies and he worried he might not be able to see all three manholes. The sun had disappeared behind the buildings and from the sidewalk. It would get damp and chilly very quickly.

Tully pulled himself up and leaned against the building, looking for a warmer place. He was a bit distracted when suddenly an orange hard hat popped up out of the manhole farthest away on the other side of the street.

CHAPTER 60

Maggie watched Dr. Mia Ling clearing her credentials with the uniformed cop at the first checkpoint. For Ling to be here instead of Stan Wenhoff, the medical examiner, or one of Stan's deputies, meant the bodies inside had been reduced to very little flesh and mostly bone. Pathologists worked with tissue and organs. Anthropologists were called in when there wasn't much left to recover.

Just before Ling ducked under the crime scene tape she saw Maggie. She didn't bother to hide the obvious relief on her face.

Maggie wished that all it took was a familiar face to make her more comfortable. The fire had already been put out, the building no longer in flames or spewing black smoke. Firefighters had pulled back their equipment. A rescue crew of paramedics was treating three firefighters at the mobile unit. One sat with an oxygen mask.

Another's head had been wrapped, the gauze already soaked with blood. The third was bent over beside the tire well and it looked to Maggie like he was throwing up.

She tried to ignore her own nausea. She had just taken three ibuprofen, hoping they might dull her headache. No luck yet. In the short time it took for her to walk the hundred feet over to Dr. Ling, she noticed the woman's look of relief change to one of concern.

Before Ling could ask if she was okay, Maggie held up her hands in surrender.

"Just a bad headache," she told the doctor, deciding not to share the fact that her stomach had started to roller-coaster on her.

"You don't have to go inside."

Maggie hadn't gone into the previous buildings. Ling was right. She didn't have to go into this one either. But this arsonist was accelerating at an unpredictable speed. If she wanted to understand him and know how to catch him, she would have to look at the crime scene herself.

"I need to see what he does."

Dr. Ling stared at her for almost a minute. Then she nodded and headed for the burned-out entrance. Before going in, Ling stopped, opened her duffel bag, and pulled out two pairs of tightly rolled up Tyvek coveralls. She handed one to Maggie.

"I always carry extra."

A firefighter had given Maggie a pair of fire boots when she arrived. She had slipped them over her leather flats and they still felt like clown shoes on her feet. She kicked them off to pull on the Tyvek coveralls.

Both women rolled up their sleeves and pant cuffs. Maggie folded and placed their jackets in the duffel bag. She stuffed her feet back into the boots while Dr. Ling tugged on a pair of her own. Ling continued her preparation, slipping on a pair of goggles and letting them dangle from her neck; then came thin leather gloves and knee pads, the latter making her look like a baseball catcher.

Maggie slapped on a navy-blue FBI ball cap just as Ling asked, "Ready?"

Inside, ATF investigator Brad Ivan stood between the fire chief, who towered over him, and Julia Racine. When Ivan saw Maggie, he tucked his chin and shook his head like somehow this was all her fault. Maggie followed Ling's careful steps to the pile of rubble that had attracted the investigator's attention. In the middle lay what looked like a thick wood door.

The fire chief looked at Ling and immediately began in an apologetic tone, "We came in this way. I'm afraid we stepped right on top of them."

The debris still smoldered and it took Maggie a moment to make out shapes. A skull with hollow eye sockets that stared up at the ceiling. Beneath the charred piece of wood Maggie could see a long, blackened bone. Then suddenly she could differentiate others poking up out of the rubble.

Flashes of light startled her. Ling had a camera and was busy carefully maneuvering around the group. Quietly and patiently nudging them back without saying a word.

"We didn't lift anything off the bodies yet," the fire chief said.

"That's great. You did good." And even in her own zone, Ling remained polite. She pocketed the camera and looked up at the fire chief. "Can you help me move this large piece of wood?"

No one moved while the two slowly lifted the charred and crumbling wood. Before they set it down, Racine let out a gasp.

"Jesus! How many people do you think are under here?"

"They were trying to get out through this exit."

Maggie counted four more skulls. One body was contorted into what she knew was called the pugilistic posture, a boxer on his side. Muscles reacting to being sucked of oxygen pulled the arms up toward the shoulders, leaving the hands fisted and legs bent at the knees, like a boxer ready to deliver a punch. She had only read about it until now. It meant the victim was still alive when the flames burned through the skin, making it tighten and split open, causing the muscles to clench. Alive but overcome by smoke inhalation. Thankfully carbon monoxide builds up in the blood rapidly and causes loss of consciousness.

Again Maggie caught herself thinking of her father. This was what he would have looked like had one of his fellow firefighters not pulled him out. As a child she didn't understand why he looked the way that he did in his coffin. His face looked painted and his eyebrows were gone. He seemed peaceful except for the crinkle of plastic underneath his suit. It wasn't until years later than she learned that when most of the skin and muscle have been burned away, morticians have to wrap the body — arms and legs — in plastic to keep the embalming fluid from leaking out.

Dr. Ling took her last photo, the flash bringing Maggie's focus back to the pile of bones and ash.

"I need to do this slowly," Ling told them,

ready to begin and ready for them to leave. She started bringing out plastic containers and paper bags, a garden trowel, a short-handled whisk brush, and an ordinary dust pan. "A couple of technicians will be joining me."

"Can we help you bag the larger pieces?" Ivan offered, while Maggie had already started stepping back, ready to escape.

"Actually, I save the torso for last. Taking the big pieces first tends to break up and disrupt the smaller ones."

Ling brushed at the closest skull, revealing more pieces of bone. She carefully picked up each and placed them in a plastic box she had already labeled. Maggie had become so focused, so fascinated, by Ling's small gloved hands, their movement confident and intent, that she had almost forgotten about her own purpose for being here until Racine tugged at her elbow.

"The chief's ready to show us the start point."

She turned to see the fire chief and Ivan going back outside. She glanced at Ling, who no longer seemed to notice anyone else. As Maggie walked past her she noticed the small child's skull Ling had just taken up out of the debris and into the palms of her hands.

Chapter 61

Cornell didn't make a fuss this time when the tall guy in the ratty-ass green jacket asked to talk to him. Even after the man mentioned a red backpack Cornell hadn't recognized him. He pulled out what looked like a wallet and Cornell thought he might offer him some money until he remembered he was wearing the hard hat and bright city maintenance vest. Probably wanted to complain about some potholes or sewer backup. Cornell had gotten several of those. So he was taken off guard when the wallet opened, revealing a badge.

"You're the guy I tripped up."

"Agent R. J. Tully. And you are?"

"Busted."

But he didn't make a run for it and Agent Tully looked surprised, almost disappointed, like he had waited for it all day long. Maybe like this would be an opportunity to pay back Cornell for sending him facedown onto the pavement.

Cornell didn't remember how the police cruiser appeared out of nowhere. One minute Agent Tully was telling him he wanted to ask him some questions and the next minute a cop was there snapping handcuffs on his wrists.

"Am I under arrest?" Cornell had to ask three or four times before Agent Tully admitted he just wanted to take him in for some questions.

Before his life on the streets Cornell had been arrested once for drunk driving. That time he had been scared shitless that his clients would find out. Funny the direction life took and how circumstances could change a person's perspective.

This time all Cornell thought about was how warm a holding cell might be. He knew they'd have to feed him. Maybe even give him a clean orange jumpsuit. He found himself getting excited at the possibility of a shower and the availability of a toilet. It would certainly throw off the bastard who was following him. He almost laughed, thinking about the son of a bitch watching him slide into the backseat of the police cruiser.

He'd answer questions all night or maybe not at all. Whichever one got him a holding cell. He could outsmart these guys. His job used to have him chewing up and spitting out guys like this over lunch, sending them into tailspins with all kinds of bullshit. No problem.

Although it would certainly be easier with his friend Jack Daniel's.

CHAPTER 62

Maggie needed to breathe. She took her time following Racine, Ivan, and the fire chief. Just a half dozen deep breaths of clean, fresh air would help. That's all she needed, but soot and ash still filled the damp night. The oversize boots made her feet heavy, like lifting blocks of concrete while trying to be careful.

The skull in Ling's hands had looked so small. It had to be a baby, no more than a toddler. When Maggie got the call earlier, Racine had said this one might be bad. The shops below had closed for the evening but Racine had warned her that some of the shop owners lived in apartments above. This family had come down through the shop, hoping to escape. Why hadn't they considered using the outside fire escape? She was about to find out why.

"There was a pile of old rags and news-papers," the fire chief told them, pointing to a black-and-gray stack of ash now on the pavement in the alley, but then the chief was pointing up to a landing. And Maggie immediately noticed that the fire escape was pulled down.

"He probably soaked the newspapers with gasoline. He used a piece of wood to make a little platform on top of the flammables. Then he put the chemicals on the platform. It allowed him some time to climb down and just walk off. Maybe as much as five to ten minutes."

"Do we know what the chemicals are yet?" Racine looked at Investigator Ivan.

"We sent the sample residue to the FBI lab."

The chief continued his assessment.

"I'm thinking one's a solid, perhaps in crystal form. The other must be a liquid. He might even place something between them so when he pours on the liquid it has to soak through that barrier before it's absorbed by the first chemical. When the two mix, there's an intense reaction. A white-hot flash that immediately ignites the stack of flammables underneath."

He pointed his flashlight back up at the landing and moved the beam over the side of the building, showing a black smudge that rode up the wall from the fire escape landing to a hole that used to be a window.

"The entire windowsill was splattered with gasoline. He didn't need to break in or enter the building at all. The fire broke in for him. There were curtains hanging in the window. After the glass broke, the curtains ignited and suddenly the fire easily spread inside. It's similar to the warehouse fires. I don't know much about the church fires in Arlington yesterday but I understand they were started from the outside, too."

"I'm sorry," Racine said, "but it seems like a lot of hocus-pocus to me. How did he know it would work?"

"Just between us, I'd say he knows what he's doing."

"Wait, what do you mean? Are you saying it could be a firefighter?"

The chief shot a look at Ivan like maybe he had already said too much or, worse, offended the ATF investigator.

"It wouldn't be the first time," Maggie said. "I'm thinking of Benjamin Christensen in Pennsylvania. I think he was a volunteer firefighter. No body count but at least a dozen fires, some landmarks."

"John Orr in Southern California," the chief said.

"That was a long time ago," Ivan said with a scowl.

Maggie remembered the case. Although it was thirty years ago, it had come up when she began researching serial arsonists. Orr had been a fire captain and arson investigator and had even been assigned to one of the fires he started.

She wasn't surprised Ivan didn't like anyone bringing up the criminal behavior of a fellow arson investigator. Surely they had their own version of the thin blue line.

Maggie considered Brad Ivan. There was something about him that bothered her, but she hadn't wasted time trying to figure it out. He hadn't been happy about the FBI's involvement, to the point of withholding information from her and Tully. From the beginning, Brad Ivan had struck her as someone who didn't play well with others, nor did his confrontational manner fit in with other law enforcement officials.

He listened to the fire chief with his arms crossed over his chest and she noticed that his coat bulged tight across his midsection. She remembered his hitching up his trousers yesterday and then looking almost surprised, like a man who was used to being in shape and suddenly finding he was no longer.

He scratched at his steel-gray hair and swiped back the swatches that climbed over his ears like he was well past a haircut. She realized all the extra weight and need for a haircut could just mean he was putting in some unexpected long hours. Which would account for his irritability. But there was something that made Maggie wonder if he was disgruntled or just exhausted.

He was standing behind the fire chief when she saw him frown at something the chief was telling Racine. Maggie decided she needed to take a look into Ivan's background. She found herself wondering whether he could have followed her down the manhole, hoping to catch a fleeing arsonist and maybe scare the crap out of her just for good measure. Teach the profiler how much she doesn't know. Was that something he was capable of? Was he the man she'd seen outside her property? As an ATF investigator he could easily get access to federal employees' information, including her private home address.

She was considering all this when something across the street caught her attention. An empty lot had been gouged out. Stacks of concrete and piles of dirt were all that remained except for monster yellow equipment with claws and dump wagons, all parked and quiet for the night. There were construction sites all over the city, but two of them right across from arson sites? Was it a coincidence?

CHAPTER 63

About an hour ago Sam had been laughing with her son, watching her mother struggle to pick up a fried dumpling with chopsticks. That's when she had heard the first siren.

It had stopped blocks away, but she felt her body tense up. She had forced a smile so her family wouldn't notice that her pulse had started to race. She didn't want them to see the slight twitch of panic as her eyes darted around the restaurant in search of the nearest exit.

A few minutes later she had heard a waiter tell someone that the shops just five blocks away were on fire. And Sam thought immediately about Jeffery. She knew he'd be frantic to get in touch with her. She had reached for her cell phone to turn it back on. Had it out of her purse and in her hand when she caught herself. Across the table her mother and son had been giggling over each other's fortune cookies.

"Momma, read yours."

Her palms had started sweating. The phone felt heavy in her hand as it slid from her fingers back into her purse.

It had been the purest choice she had made in a very long time.

Now when she saw Jeffery's Escalade in her driveway a lump gathered in the pit of her stomach and she reminded herself that the right decision is not always the easiest. Nor would it be the best for her career, if she still had a career.

"It's my boss," she told her mother.

"Your boss here? On your day off?"

Instead of explaining, Sam asked her mother to take Iggy into the house and put the leftovers in the refrigerator.

"I'll be just a few minutes," she told them, hoping the alarm going off inside her head hadn't affected the tone of her voice.

She watched them scurry around the big SUV that left only two feet between her garage and its bumper. Sam almost smiled at the scowl her mother was giving Jeffery, despite the dark and despite the tinted windshield. Her mother's defiance helped fuel Sam's courage. Still, her knees went a bit weak as she climbed out of her vehicle and went to stand in front of the garage, keeping a safe distance between herself and

Jeffery and choosing someplace where she didn't think he could run her over. She also knew that where she was standing she couldn't be seen from inside the house.

She stood and waited.

She would not get inside his SUV. If he wanted to rip her a new one, he'd have to do it where her neighbors might watch or call the cops.

The engine started, a quiet hum. The driver's-side window slid down. Jeffery's face looked calm. His eyes did not.

The glow of the interior lights gave him an eerie blue sheen, as if the illumination came from under the surface of his skin. His tie had been yanked loose and his white collar smudged. His jacket had been tossed aside and his shirtsleeves were rolled up in haphazard folds. His face didn't look angry, but everything else about him looked enraged.

"There were bodies tonight," he said in a casual tone that sounded odd considering the context. "Just what Big Mac ordered up."

She felt his eyes bore into her but she didn't flinch or look away from them.

"Do you have any idea what you cost us, Sam? I hope your little chop suey dinner out was worth it. Don't you dare turn your back on me again."

The SUV's window hummed back up as Sam's stomach crashed down.

How had he known where they had gone for dinner? Had he followed?

Then she remembered that her mother had carried in the leftovers. Of course, the bag must have the restaurant's logo stamped on it. But when Sam walked into the kitchen she saw the plain white paper bags still on the counter. There was no logo, no indication of a Chinese restaurant.

CHAPTER 64

Maggie reeked of smoke but at least she didn't look as bad as Tully.

"What happened to you?"

He came into the conference room and dropped into the leather chair across the table from her.

"I finally got that backpack bastard."

"Is he our guy?"

Tully shrugged, looking defeated, tired.

"I think he's some homeless drunk who's paranoid and maybe a bit schizo. What do you have going on?"

He pointed to the file folders and maps she had scattered on the large tabletop. Instead of going home, she'd come back to Quantico to pull some files and access some databases. She was screening her calls, still avoiding her mother's voice messages, when Assistant Director Kunze called, insisting she and Tully meet him in the conference room in an hour. Never mind that it was late on a Saturday night.

"There was a construction site across the street from the shops that burned down tonight."

"Okay."

"And there was a construction site just down the street from the warehouse fires."

"Same contractor?"

"That was my first thought. Unfortunately no. Two separate companies. But here's something interesting — both projects are federally funded. The one across from the shops is going to be a food pantry. The one in the warehouse district is something called the D.C. Outreach House. It's going to be a community and sleep shelter for the homeless. Both are HUD projects."

"Can we access employee lists to see if there's anybody working on both sites?"

"I'm trying. There's more red tape than even my clearance can cut through."

Tully laughed.

"There's more," Maggie said. "I talked to the owner of the construction company working in the warehouse district."

"I bet he was pleased to get a phone call on a Saturday night."

"Actually he didn't seem surprised." Irritated was more what Maggie had detected, but Mr. Lyle Post had treated her phone call as if it were only one in a long run of federal interruptions into his business.

"Can he get you a list of his employees?"

"Said it would be tough."

"Because of privacy issues?"

"No, that wasn't the problem. He doesn't keep track of the names of all his crew members."

Tully blinked and sat up like he hadn't heard her correctly and needed to get a closer listen.

"Said he's had to hire a lot of private contractors because the project got fast-tracked. Someone at HUD told him they needed the job done sooner than they needed to know every single person who was working on it."

"He told you this knowing you're an FBI agent?"

"I didn't exactly tell him who I was." It wouldn't be the first time she or Tully had withheld information in order to get information.

"So someone could be working on both projects."

"Or someone could think the fires would get more attention because they were close to federally funded projects."

"Could be why Kunze has his panties in a twist."

"It's taken you both this long to figure that out."

Assistant Director Raymond Kunze stood in the doorway of the conference room. Tully sat up in his chair, a flush of red running up his neck. Maggie dropped her hands into her lap and restrained a smile. Kunze looked like a linebacker but dressed like a nightclub bouncer. The blazer he wore was probably a rust color, but under the fluorescent lights it looked orange.

"I've got one senator and the director of HUD kicking my ass until you two catch this frickin' firefly." He started into the room but stopped halfway. "Tully, you look like crap. And O'Dell" — he sniffed the air — "you stink."

If Maggie didn't know better she'd guess Kunze was finally joking with them like they were part of a team. It certainly was the first time he'd admitted to the politics of his actions.

He threw what looked like a faxed document on the table. The pages were the old flimsy paper of antiquated fax machines that curled.

"I just received the ATF's report on the church fires." He sat at the head of the table, tapping the top of the papers he'd thrown down. "Gasoline was poured at the

359

threshold of the door to the basement. Not only did this bastard know there was a meeting being held down there, he was hell-bent on killing someone. Tonight he finally did. He murdered an entire family by setting fire to — of all things — the fire escape *and* the back door, their only other way out."

Maggie hadn't known about the back door. She watched Kunze. She was used to seeing him angry, but there was something different tonight, emotion she didn't recognize. He appeared shaken by these latest deaths.

"There was an eighteen-month-old child," Kunze said quietly. "My ass is so going to get kicked when this hits the news." He looked up at the two of them. "And so are both of yours if you don't catch this bastard."

■ ■ ■ ■

SUNDAY

■ ■ ■ ■

CHAPTER 65

In the security camera outside her front door Maggie watched the woman fidgeting on the portico. Her first reaction was that at least this time Samantha Ramirez had decided to come to the front of the house instead of the back.

"I know I should have called first, but I didn't think you'd agree to see me." Ramirez blurted it so quickly a slight Spanish accent slipped out.

"What makes you think I will now?" Maggie blocked the open doorway while Ramirez continued to shift from one foot to the other.

"Because I have something I think you'll want to see." She opened the flap of her shoulder bag to show Maggie the camera inside. "I need to run the footage for you to take a look. It's from the warehouse fires."

"What's going on?" Patrick asked from behind Maggie.

At the sound of his voice she noticed Ramirez's demeanor changed. At first Maggie thought the woman was disappointed she didn't catch Maggie alone. But at second glance she saw that wasn't the case. It wasn't disappointment that had suddenly struck Ramirez and dismantled her composure, but rather what plainly looked like a physical attraction to Patrick — an attraction that caught Ramirez off guard so much she hadn't been able to control her reaction.

Maggie glanced back at Patrick. His hair was dripping. He must have jumped out of the shower to come to her defense. All he had on was a towel around his waist. She tamped down the urge to roll her eyes, but couldn't stop a smile. No wonder Ramirez was blushing.

"Everything's fine," Maggie told him. "Ms. Ramirez has something she needs to show me at eight o'clock on a Sunday morning."

"Actually Patrick may want to see this, too."

Maggie stepped aside and waved Ramirez inside, enjoying her obvious discomfort as she passed by Patrick.

"Let me grab some clothes." And he disappeared down the hallway.

"I thought Agent Tully already went over

the footage from the warehouse fires?"

"We stopped when he found the man with the red backpack."

Without waiting for permission, Ramirez started unloading the camera, adapter, cords, and cables.

"Agent Tully didn't ask to see any more after that. But I noticed something."

She stopped herself. Looked up at Maggie. Her eyes flicked to Patrick, who had returned, now wearing blue jeans and a T-shirt. She quickly looked back to Maggie.

"Actually I noticed *someone* in the crowd. He wasn't there until after the second blast."

She pointed at Maggie's television. "If I can plug it into your TV we'll have a much better and bigger view."

"Here, I can help you with that." Patrick slipped past Maggie and held out a hand for the cable.

Maggie stood back and watched the two of them. She admitted electronic gadgets baffled her, but these two knew exactly what they were doing. And now she saw that the attraction went both ways — a graze of a hand, eyes trying to avoid but stealing quick glances.

Without warning she thought about Ben. She certainly understood that uncontrollable physical reaction. Her body wanted what her mind told her she couldn't have. Telling herself that she couldn't have Ben only made her want him more. Would she ever get it right? Would she ever fall for a man who was emotionally available at the same time that she was emotionally available?

Patrick turned on the TV. Ramirez pressed some buttons on the camera and suddenly the blaze from the other night filled the big screen.

"This is right after the second blast."

Ramirez had swept the shaky camera across the grounds in front of her. She must have just been getting up off the ground. Maggie recognized Tully on his hands and knees, Racine beside him. And to his left she realized she was looking at herself. She hardly recognized the woman lying face-down, flat on the ground, pulling herself up onto her elbows. Back behind them was the perfect shot of the second building engulfed in flames. Ramirez couldn't have positioned herself better without planning it.

"Watch carefully. He'll be up on the far left of the screen."

The image jerked around again. Ground then sky, like an airplane nose-diving before pulling up.

"I was a bit unsteady on my feet," Ramirez

apologized. "It gets better."

The camera moved off Maggie, following Racine, who was on her feet and rushing to help a group of people beyond the crime scene tape. Several were still sprawled on the ground.

The camera paused on them, then continued tracking. In the background Maggie could hear a low voice — Jeffery Cole narrating the scene, frame by frame. Ramirez had turned down the sound.

The camera's view swung back a little farther, taking in the crowd gathering on the sidewalk across the street. It panned the length of them, and halfway through Ramirez punched a button and froze the image. She put the camera down and walked to the left side of the television.

"Right here." She pointed at a man standing in the middle of the crowd, hands in his pockets, face expressionless. On the screen the image was big enough and focused enough to recognize, and although Maggie thought he looked familiar she couldn't place him.

Ramirez, however, wasn't interested in Maggie's reaction. Instead she was looking at Patrick.

"Who is he?" she finally asked.

"Wes Harper," Patrick told her. "My partner."

And suddenly Maggie became interested. She walked across the living room to stand in front of the television, taking in as much of Wes Harper as she could.

"It's probably no big deal," Patrick said. "He told me he likes to go watch other fires."

"Watch them?" Sam said. "Isn't that a little weird?"

"Tell me about him," Maggie asked Patrick without taking her eyes from the big screen.

"I really don't know him that well."

"But you spend a lot of time together. Is he married?"

"No."

There was something about the delivery of his "no" that made Maggie glance at her brother. He was staring at the screen, too, but to avoid her eyes.

"What is it?"

"He asked about you. It felt a little weird."

"About my being an FBI agent?"

"No. About whether or not you were married. He's a player. He likes women."

She could see he was uncomfortable talking about this with her. "What exactly does that mean?"

It was Ramirez who answered. "It means every woman he meets he thinks about screwing her."

"Did he hit on you?" Patrick wanted to know.

"I can take care of myself."

Maggie studied the man. Ramirez had left the film frozen on an excellent view of Wes Harper. While others around him displayed that wide-eyed look of shock and awe — one with a furrowed brow, another held a hand over her mouth, still another bent over with hands on his knees — Harper stood straight, hands in his pockets and a placid, almost content look on his face.

He looked to be in his thirties, square jaw, medium height, thick-chested, and muscular. He wore trousers, not jeans, and a nice jacket. Maggie stepped closer to examine the logo on the pocket.

"Is that a Members Only jacket?"

"Yeah, he loves that jacket." Patrick came up beside her. "I don't know how many times he's told me that the company's tagline was stolen by a condom manufacturer. Laughs every time he tells me. Thinks it's pretty cool."

"What's the tagline?"

Patrick hesitated, uncomfortable again. " 'When you put it on something

369

happens.' "

"Does he have a degree in fire science?"

"He started a program but said it was lame. Quit after a year."

"The other night he was telling Jeffery and me what fire does to a body," Ramirez said, and Maggie could see the woman was uncomfortable even with the memory of this. "He seemed to take great pleasure in describing it. It was almost like he had seen it himself and . . ."

"And what?" Maggie asked.

"And that he enjoyed watching a body burn."

Maggie pulled out her cell phone as she told Patrick, "I need you to tell me everything you can think of about Wes Harper." Then she punched in Racine's number.

"Hey, I was just getting ready to call you," Racine answered. "Virginia State Patrol just located Gloria Dobson's SUV."

CHAPTER 66

Virginia

Maggie was surprised to find the rest area backed to woods. No meadow or pasture with the funky yellow weed that Ganza had found. But it did look like a place deer would frequent.

She and Tully had made the hour-and-a-half drive while Racine put out another alert on Dobson's travel partner, Zach Lester. She also had started a background check on Wes Harper. Maggie had to stop Racine from bringing Harper in for questioning, telling the detective, "We don't have enough and you don't want to tip him off."

They parked at the far end of the rest area and got out to walk.

"The State Patrol already towed the car to their crime lab," Tully told her. "I'm not sure what else we'll find."

"He had to have taken her from here. It's a crime scene."

"The car may have been the only crime scene."

Maggie stood on the edge of the sidewalk and took a good look around. Down here she could barely hear the interstate traffic. The exit divided cars from trucks right before they drove down into the rest area surrounded by beautiful and remote woods. Even the brick building with the restrooms was nestled in the trees. Well-kept sidewalks meandered all around, leading separate paths from up above where the trucks parked. She could hear the faint hum of their engines running. Through the trees she could see only five semitrailers occupied the area that, by Maggie's estimate, could accommodate at least a dozen big rigs comfortably. She also noted that there were mulched trails leading into the woods.

"If it was her coworker, Zach Lester, why leave her car behind?" Maggie asked. "And how did he take her to the District?"

"Maybe he has an accomplice."

"So they meet out here?"

"Or he called him. It's possible. Might explain why the car doesn't show any sign of a struggle inside. The State Patrol will be able to tell us if her car had been tampered with. He could have done something to it. Made her believe they were stranded."

"So where did he take her to bash her face in? He couldn't have done all that in a vehicle. Ganza found deer hair and weeds attached to her clothing. Dr. Ling made it sound like the killer used a large, heavy weapon."

"If he had another vehicle or an accomplice, he could have taken her anywhere." Tully was watching Maggie instead of studying the surroundings. "But you're thinking it was here."

"Just a gut instinct. I expected it to be secluded like this, but with an open field somewhere close by."

"Because of Ganza's weed?"

She nodded and started walking. Tully followed.

"Depending on what time of day or night they stopped here there may have been no one else."

"He could have easily taken her into the woods," Tully said. "Maybe convinced her to go stretch her legs with him."

"I have to tell you I've looked over the file Racine has on Lester and he sounds squeaky clean. He doesn't sound like a killer."

"How many times have we heard that? It's always the ones nobody suspects," Tully said. "That quiet neighbor. The helpful janitor. Remember what people said about Ted

Bundy. Such a nice guy. How about the BTK killer? Wasn't he on the church council or something?"

"I've also read all the information on Gloria Dobson and she certainly doesn't sound like the type of woman who would walk into the woods with someone suspicious. And she would have fought for her life. She has three kids. She's a recent breast cancer survivor."

Maggie continued to walk all the way up to where the trucks were parked. It was high enough to see over some of the trees that surrounded the lower half of the rest area. She studied the parked trucks.

"Ganza told me there's a whole subculture to truck stops and rest areas. A whole world no one sees unless they know where to look. Prostitutes come knocking on the doors of the big rigs while they sleep. Drug dealers, too. Where do they go in between tricks and deals? Do they have their own vehicles? Why doesn't anyone else see them?"

Tully was quiet for a moment, looking around. "Maybe no one else notices them because they blend in."

She turned to examine the paths below and take another look at the travelers going in and out of the restrooms. That's when the birds caught her eye.

She hadn't noticed them before. The angle of the setting sun transformed their circle above the trees into a halo, the tips of their black wings highlighted by brilliant yellows and oranges. She heard Tully's intake of breath and she knew Tully saw them, too. And he was thinking exactly what she was.

Without a word or a glance they started down across the parking lot, across the brown lawn, not even using the sidewalks. There were dirt paths going into the woods. They took the closest one. It narrowed immediately but Maggie kept going, ducking tree limbs and ignoring the dried brush that scraped her arms.

Several hundred yards into the trees she could smell it. Rotting meat. Several days old. Not the pungent coppery smell of a fresh kill. Whatever had captured the birds' attention had been dead for a few days.

She looked up to the birds for direction. She slowed her pace so she wouldn't lose her footing. Inside the canopy of trees the shadows of dusk threw off her depth perception. She looked for the birds, but what she saw stopped her dead in her tracks. Tully bumped into her.

"What is it?"

She pointed up into the branches of a huge maple that stood about seventy-five feet in front of them.

This time she could hear Tully gasp, "Dear God."

Though they were dried now, Maggie could still recognize the streamers that decorated the lower branches. She wondered if she would have recognized them as easily without seeing the gutted body that lay at the base of the trunk.

"What sick bastard have we found?"

Immediately Maggie saw that the body didn't include a head.

"I think we may have found Zach Lester," she said.

CHAPTER 67

Mutilations always caught Tully off guard. It didn't matter how many he saw. He stood back and tried to make his lungs inhale despite the stink that already permeated the lining of his nostrils. He knew there was an initial shock, as if his eyes had to convince his brain that, yes, indeed, there were no limits to evil.

Maggie moved forward already examining, analyzing, shifting smoothly into gear. She swatted blowflies, swarms so slow and unwilling to leave their treasure that she could knock them to the ground with a simple wave of her hand.

Tully didn't see any of the hesitation in her, none of the fear he had witnessed the other night at the warehouse fires. He kidded her once about becoming a specialist in dismembered bodies. The parts seemed to appear on cases she was assigned, whether in take-out containers, Mason jars, or fishing coolers.

"Should we call the State Patrol guys to come back?"

She squatted down about three feet away from the corpse, careful not to touch and even more careful where she stepped. She seemed so intent he didn't think she had heard him. He looked down at the pine needles and soggy maple leaves, some embedded in the mud. He moved closer, keeping to the same path Maggie had used.

"He crossed state lines," she finally said. "And the interstate is federal property. Are the rest areas?"

Tully had no idea.

"Technically it's our jurisdiction," she said.

He closed his eyes and let out a breath. Too many times law enforcement agencies fought over jurisdiction. He never understood it. Opening his eyes and following the trail of what was once Zach Lester's intestines, Tully found himself wishing they could hand this off to someone, anyone, else.

"The state of Virginia's crime lab is top-notch," he said, giving it another try.

"One of the best," Maggie agreed.

He saw her glance at her watch as he pulled his cell phone from his jacket pocket.

"Ganza should be able to get a unit out here in forty, forty-five minutes," she said.

Ganza. Tully bit back a response, not surprised that she'd choose to hand it over to their FBI crime lab. And it was probably a smart choice, even the correct choice. But it meant they'd be out here, stranded, until almost every last piece of evidence had been collected.

Still, Tully made the phone call without question or comment.

The whole time he talked to Ganza he watched Maggie. She had started taking pictures with her smartphone. A good move, considering there would be little sunlight by the time Ganza and his team made it to the scene.

He slipped his phone back into his pocket, his fingers lingering. He wanted to call Gwen, the urge something fierce. Even though and maybe because she wasn't expecting a call.

Maggie stopped and Tully watched her slowly turn, taking in the surroundings as if for the first time really seeing them.

"Do you think he killed Gloria Dobson here, too?"

Tully listened now that his breathing had returned to normal and his heartbeat had settled. He couldn't hear the interstate traffic. He couldn't hear any traffic or car doors being slammed or voices calling to each other back at the parking lots. A breeze rustled branches overhead. The birds cawed and squawked at each other. If the killer had timed it right and no one had been at the rest area, these woods would have absorbed the victims' screams.

"Ganza should be able to figure that out," Tully said.

But as he looked around he wondered how difficult a job it would be. Outdoor crime scenes were always challenging and this one was days old, contaminated by the birds and other predators. Pools of blood that seeped into the ground would need to be dug up. Leaves and debris would have matted on top. The wind may have blown away fabric and hair.

Tully remembered Gloria Dobson's face — or rather what was left of it — in that dark alley. If pieces of her had been splattered and left here on the tree bark or stuck to blades of grass, Keith Ganza and his technicians would find it.

"I don't think he killed her here," Maggie said. "It'd be too far to drag her body back. He had to take her someplace where he could bring a vehicle close."

"Maybe she didn't make it this far into

the woods."

He tried to imagine a pursuit and found himself looking for broken branches, skid marks in the mud, a drag line. He remembered it had rained the other night, not hard but enough to disrupt evidence. Did it rain here, too?

He glanced at Maggie and saw she was thinking along the same lines. She was scanning the path they had taken.

"Why would he take on two? And how was he able to do it? Did he plan it or was it an impulse that got terribly out of hand?"

"Either way, we're dealing with one sick bastard."

Maggie stared up at the streamers of intestines. Ripped and ravished by the birds, they still looked to Tully too much like human guts. The large intestine retained its dark red color, the small a grayish purple.

"The average small intestine is twenty feet long," Maggie said, and he knew she wasn't spouting off trivia. Then she added exactly what Tully was thinking. "He's done this before."

Tully took three steps for a closer look. He agreed. The streamers were intertwined on the low branches of the maple tree like someone would hang a strand of lights on a Christmas tree. It took some time and effort and expertise. This wasn't the chaotic frenzy of a madman, ripping and tossing.

Maggie's phone started ringing. She glanced at the caller ID and answered, saying, "You're not going to believe what we found."

But the person interrupted her and Maggie went quiet, listening, her eyes darting around before settling on Tully.

After a few seconds she whispered, "I'll be there as soon as I can."

CHAPTER 68

Cornell had talked them into holding him another night in jail. He insisted he had some valuable information for Agent Tully. Only problem was that Agent Tully, he was told, was out of town and couldn't talk to him until Monday morning.

What a shame. What a lucky shame.

The wafer-thin cot was softer than the pavement and a blanket — hell, he didn't even need a blanket it was so much warmer in the holding cell. He tried his best to not let them know that this inconvenience was like a vacation. Although not quite a vacation. He missed not having a shot or two of whiskey. And the headache was not a picnic, but the food was lukewarm and he even got a couple rec hours in the TV room.

It had been so long since he'd watched TV he didn't recognize any of the celebrities or pundits. Though Cornell had never been much interested. Reality shows —

what a bore.

Tonight a thin, washed-out druggie had control of the remote and Cornell knew not to challenge the man. Glassy-eyed and leather-skinned, this guy looked like he had climbed out of a Zombies-R-Us ad. And for some reason the guy appeared fascinated by cable news. No channel surfing, no checking sports scores or weather.

The next show was supposed to have a feature on the fires and that caught Cornell's attention. So he sat patiently. What else did he have to do? Oh, that was another thing — the drug zombie kept the volume to a whisper, so Cornell spent most of his time reading the crap at the bottom of the screen.

He pulled up the chair closer to the TV just as an interview started. Two men were identified at the bottom of the screen as Jeffery Cole, journalist, and Wes Harper, private firefighter for Braxton Protection Agency. Cornell was so busy reading, it took him a minute to look at the two guys and when he did he couldn't believe it. Without a doubt he recognized the guy from the alley. The guy who had poured the gasoline.

CHAPTER 69

Maggie had turned down Tully's offer to drive her to the hospital. Someone needed to wait and secure the crime scene until Ganza's crew got there. Besides, it wasn't the first time her mother had attempted suicide. In fact, Maggie had lost track of how many times Kathleen O'Dell had tried to kill herself.

The first time it was sleeping pills. Then pills and alcohol. Five years ago when Maggie was in Nebraska, working a case, Kathleen decided to use a razor blade for a change of pace. Her therapist at the time called the cuts hesitation marks. After all, if she was really serious she would have cut vertically, slicing the veins open instead of across.

It had been three years since her last attempt. Julia Racine had been there that time, too. At a restroom sink in a Cleveland park, just before a rally for a religious organization.

Later Maggie asked Racine what it was that she said to convince her mother to stop. Racine told her, "I said I was already in a shitload of trouble with her daughter and maybe she could give me a break." Of course Kathleen had laughed at that. She could relate. For the last twenty years she had felt like she was in a shitload of trouble with Maggie, too, because she had constantly let her down.

Maggie realized that ever since her father's death, her mother had exchanged and swapped out her addictions like they were fashion trends, from Johnnie Walker to Valium to sex, then religion and health food and back to Johnnie Walker. The other day when Maggie walked in on her mother trying to get rid of Patrick, she recognized the signs that her mother was drinking again without needing to smell it on her breath.

When Maggie finally got to the hospital, a nurse in the ER directed her to intensive care. In intensive care a unit secretary told her she'd need to wait for the doctor and pointed out a lounge at the end of the hall. In the lounge, Maggie found Julia Racine.

Her sweatshirt had so much blood on it that Maggie thought Racine had been injured, too. Even when she realized it all belonged to her mother, when Racine looked up, Maggie asked, "Are you okay?"

It was the first time she had caught Racine speechless. The younger woman simply nodded and ran her fingers through her hair, leaving it more spiked than usual.

She shrugged and said, "I hate hospitals."

CHAPTER 70

Sam knew she had done the right thing, telling Agent O'Dell and Patrick about Wes Harper. After Jeffery's fit in her driveway last night something still nagged at her. Especially after she listened to a couple of his voice messages. The time stamps with him asking her to meet him at the shop fires last night were long before Sam heard the sirens while at the restaurant. How did Jeffery always know so far in advance?

After her mother and Iggy were in bed, Sam had plugged in the tape from the warehouse fires and started reviewing the footage, wanting to make sure it was Wes Harper in the crowd. That's when it all seemed to come together. Harper was the firefly, and somehow he'd been getting messages to Jeffery. Maybe Jeffery didn't even know it was Harper. Whatever was going on between the two of them, Sam was glad she'd shared the film footage with

Agent O'Dell.

She wasn't sure why she didn't tell Jeffery about Harper. Even when he called her, excited — saying they were "back in the saddle," was how he put it. He had managed to get an exclusive interview with someone who Jeffery said had intimate details about the fires.

This "someone" wanted to meet Jeffery in a remote place, "a safe house" was what Jeffery called it. And he was willing to go on camera, but only with Jeffery and Sam present. No one else. Jeffery said he wouldn't even give him the address until they arrived at the location where he insisted they leave their cars.

Sam was certain Jeffery's "someone" was Wes Harper. And as she drove and started seeing familiar territory, she wasn't surprised at his choice of meeting place.

Although she arrived early, Jeffery was already parked exactly where he'd instructed her. When she pulled her car up behind his SUV, he had the liftgate up but he was in the backseat. It looked like he was changing his shoes. He was in shirtsleeves, rolling them down and buttoning his collar.

As she got out of her car, he stuck a hand out the door to wave his acknowledgment. She pulled out her shoulder bag and waited at the front of her car. When he stepped out of his vehicle, he still didn't even have a tie on yet and she saw him unzipping a garment bag. Why had he waited to get dressed out here?

With the SUV parked right under a lamppost and with the liftgate open, she could see the mess inside. It looked like he had, at least, put down black trash bags to line the inside of the trunk space. Evidently he had spent the weekend doing some yard work, gathering up his recyclables, and washing his SUV. He had several stacks of newspapers, aluminum canisters, the jug of pool cleaner Sam had noticed the other day, a pile of old rags, and a red five-gallon can of gasoline.

Funny, she hadn't thought of Jeffery as doing those kinds of household chores, but it made sense. The man was so picky he'd never find anyone to do the job to his satisfaction.

"I've got the address," he told her, holding up a piece of paper. "It's only about two blocks from here."

The day had been sunny but the night was crisp. The walk would be no problem but Jeffery seemed out of breath already. As they got closer to the meeting house, Sam realized why Wes Harper had picked this spot.

Patrick had said Harper had asked about his sister. Now Sam realized it had probably been more than a casual inquiry. Was Harper the man in the ball cap Sam had seen stalking Agent O'Dell's house that night in the rain?

The homes in this neighborhood were on one- to two-acre lots, treed lots with huge pines that offered enough privacy that Sam couldn't really see O'Dell's house, though she knew it was right next door.

CHAPTER 71

Maggie sat on the sofa next to Racine, leaning forward, elbows on her knees, her body tense, nerves twisted, head pounding.

"Hospitals remind you of your mother," Maggie said, and Racine nodded again, staring at the muted television in the opposite corner.

Maggie tried to remember what kind of cancer had taken Julia's mother from her when she was nine or ten. She did remember that the woman had died in a hospital.

"I don't understand why she called me," Racine said, almost in a whisper, all the typical smart-ass wisecracks tucked away. This was Racine raw, unguarded, her defense barrier destroyed by exhaustion and perhaps a bit of shock, though Maggie knew she'd never admit it.

"Because she knew you'd call me" was Maggie's only response.

She wasn't sure she understood why her

mother did what she did, let alone could she explain it to someone else.

"There was so much blood." Again a quiet, calm tone. "I beat the frickin' ambulance there. I tried to clamp her wrists with my hands. Then I tried to use hand towels as tourniquets."

Racine was staring at her hands like she could still see the blood, though it had obviously been washed off. Maggie understood the shock of it — someone you know. Her blood still warm and splattered on your skin, your clothes. Both she and Racine had witnessed countless bloody murder scenes, and yet nothing prepared you for finding someone you knew — a colleague, a friend, a family member. Nothing prepared you for that moment, that helpless feeling.

"I remember the first time I found her," Maggie said, elbows still on each knee, but now her chin rested in her hands, her pounding head suddenly heavy. "She had just taken a bunch of pills and washed them down with vodka. I didn't know what was wrong with her. She was unconscious on her bed. One side of her face was caked with vomit. I'm not sure how I even knew to call 911."

With little coaxing that night could come back to her as vivid as if it were last week, and Maggie didn't want to revisit it just now. Nor did she want to tell Racine all the details. Like the fact that it wasn't her mother's first attempt and she wasn't alone. One of her male friends practically knocked Maggie over trying to leave their apartment. He hadn't called 911 or considered the fact that Maggie was only fourteen. Some things were better left hidden in the dark corners where they belonged.

All her mother's therapists — and there had been too many to count — always said it was a scream for help or attention. That Kathleen really didn't want to kill herself. Maggie disagreed. Her mother wasn't looking for attention. She was looking to punish herself.

It had taken Maggie years to understand that, because for a long time it felt like her mother was trying to punish her. And no matter what the reason or excuse for Kathleen O'Dell's suicide attempts, there was one thing Maggie was certain of. One of these times her mother would probably succeed by sheer accident.

Maggie took a deep breath and sat back. She desperately wanted to change the subject.

"How's your dad?" she asked Racine, staying on common ground. While Racine had saved Maggie's mother from self-destruction, Maggie had once upon a time saved Luc Racine from a serial killer. She thought about the kind, gentle man often but hesitated to ask about him, knowing his Alzheimer's disease rarely brought good news.

"He's starting to forget my name." Racine crossed her arms and slouched down even more into the sofa next to Maggie.

"It's the disease. You can't take it personally," Maggie said, now regretting her cheap excuse to change the subject at the expense of Racine.

"He never forgets the fucking dog's name."

This time Maggie didn't say anything. Instead she put her arm around Racine, squeezed her shoulder, and pulled her in against her. Racine's body went limp as if finally relinquishing the tension of the day, and she slid down enough to lay her head on Maggie's shoulder.

They sat there quietly, side by side. The beeping of monitors from the intensive care unit stayed muted in the background.

"You think maybe you should call Ben?" Racine asked, again almost a whisper.

"I don't know what to do about Ben," Maggie said, a bit surprised with herself for letting her guard down. She discussed her personal life with only two people — Ben Platt and Gwen Patterson. Julia Racine was nowhere near the list of possible additions. At the moment she was too exhausted to care. "Ben wants kids."

"Just because his ex-wife started a new family." A statement, not a question. Racine had met Ben's ex. Maggie shrugged, even though Racine couldn't see it. "You don't want kids?"

"I never imagined myself a mother."

"Me either," Racine said, easily and without hesitation. "Rachel says it's because I never got a chance to be a kid."

"What do you think?"

"I think it's because I hate kids."

Maggie smiled and contained a laugh because she knew Racine was serious.

"Doesn't Rachel have a daughter?"

"Yeah, CariAnne. She's a pain in the ass. Always has too many questions. Always on my case about using the fucking f-word. Last fall she puked all over my favorite shoes. Cole Haan, driving loafers. I loved those shoes. Couldn't get the smell out of the leather. Had to throw them out."

"So what happened?"

"Bought a new pair."

"No, silly. I mean what made you change

your mind?"

Racine's turn to shrug. "She's a part of Rachel. How can I love Rachel and not love her child?"

A man appeared, filling the doorway. He was dressed in khakis and a sports jacket.

"Are you Kathleen O'Dell's daughters?"

His voice was deep and authoritarian but his eyes gentle. His hands were the size of catcher's mitts and Maggie caught herself staring at them, thinking they could have easily clasped around her mother's wrists and stopped the bleeding.

"I'm Maggie," she finally said, standing. "This is Julia."

She didn't bother to correct him, that they weren't both Kathleen's daughters. After stopping one suicide attempt and witnessing the aftermath of a second, Julia had earned the right to be called Kathleen's daughter, though it came wrapped in burden rather than honor.

She offered her hand to shake his and immediately saw his eyes take notice of the scars on her own wrist.

"No, it doesn't run in the family."

He didn't look convinced, but Maggie didn't think she needed to explain how months ago a killer had tied her hands together with zip ties. How the plastic had cut deep into her skin while she tumbled down rock ledges and ran through a dark forest at night. So deep had the ties cut into her wrists that when she finally sliced herself free she had to dig the plastic out of her flesh. Of course, it left scars and she didn't need to explain.

"How is she?" Racine asked, standing up beside Maggie.

"I gave her something to help her rest. She asked not to see anyone right now. She'll be groggy, but in an hour or so I think it would be a good idea for one or both of you to sit with her for a while. You're welcome to stay here in the meantime or go home and come back. There's coffee in the reception area outside of the ICU. Cafeteria's downstairs."

He went on to tell them how to contact him and what to expect. Maggie tuned him out. She'd heard the litany too many times before.

He left and Maggie and Racine had just sunk back into the sofa when a dog — a brown-and-white corgi — sauntered in.

Maggie looked up to find Dr. James Kernan with two foam cups, which he handed toward them, arms stretched out in front of him.

"Coffee's awful," he told them, "but it helps pass the time."

CHAPTER 72

Sam had the camera set up on a tripod. It made interviewees less nervous when she stood beside a stationary camera than when she held it and pointed it at them. She and Jeffery had found the door unlocked and the house empty except for some trash in a corner, a stack of newspapers, and something that looked like a tray of rat poison on top.

Only one lamp on a timer lit the interior from the middle of the living room floor.

Sam had switched on a ceiling light only to have Jeffery flip it off immediately.

"We're going to need more light. I didn't bring backup lighting."

Still, he insisted she keep it off.

She finished the rest of the coffee Jeffery had brought for her. She hadn't needed the caffeine. Her adrenaline was enough to keep her going. But for some reason she felt a bit blurry, unfocused. It was funny she hadn't even noticed Jeffery's pacing. It was odd that he might be nervous to the point of a sweaty forehead and a tie let askew. This would be a big interview but the two of them had done bigger — several prime ministers, a congressman on the eve of his resignation, and a couple of Taliban leaders.

"I know that you figured it out, Sam."

Her hands stopped. She thought her heart may have, too.

"Nadira told me about you taking the tapes from the warehouse fires."

His voice remained calm, but he continued to pace.

Had Jeffery closed all the blinds or were they closed when they came in? She tried not to panic. So what if he did know it was Wes Harper? But maybe he and Jeffery had a deal. He wanted his own show so badly and he was so close to getting it. This one huge feature exclusive could seal his fate.

"What tipped you off?" He was still pacing.

"You knew about the fires so quickly." He didn't seem enraged; instead he was almost too calm. "I figured someone had to be tipping you off."

He stopped in front of her and cocked his head as if he didn't think he had heard her correctly. His hands had balled up and there was a brown stain that covered one.

"Tipping me off?"

"I saw Wes Harper at the warehouse fires. In the crowd after the second blast."

He stared at her. His eyes hard, cold blue. And suddenly he laughed. "That's what you saw on the tapes?"

"It's okay, I won't tell anyone he was in touch with you. But how can you be certain he won't? Especially if he's ready to talk."

He laughed again and shook his head. "Sam, Sam, if only you hadn't turned your back on me Saturday night."

"I know you don't think you can trust me, but this interview —"

"There's no interview, Sam."

"But Harper —"

"There's no Harper. The reason I knew about the fires, my dear Sam, is because I started them."

CHAPTER 73

Sam had not even thought about Jeffery.

How could he have started the fires?

"This isn't funny, Jeffery," she told him while she gulped lukewarm coffee, hoping the caffeine would kick in and dissolve her blur of exhaustion.

"No one tipped me, Sam." He was pacing the room, checking the windows. "I stumbled upon a ratings bonanza. Why wait for some huge news story when I simply could create one?"

He couldn't be serious. The room tilted and Sam leaned against the tripod. She closed her eyes for a second, waited for her head to stop spinning. It had to be a joke, a prank.

"Big Mac kept wanting bigger and bigger stories," Jeffery was saying. "We interview dictators. Not good enough. We almost get killed in the middle of those crazy-ass protests in the Middle East. Not good enough. We get awards for that Afghanistan exposé, and yet nobody thinks that's good enough."

She opened her eyes, only her eyelids were heavy and for some reason she was seeing three of Jeffery. She blinked several times but she still couldn't focus.

"Otis taught me a hell of a lot in those rambling letters of his. He gave me the idea. I thought you figured it out that night with Harper. I screwed up and said something about chemical reactions."

"But how . . ." Her thoughts slipped away.

"You knew I taught high school. What you didn't know was that I taught chemistry. Basic stuff. Kid's play. It was so incredibly perfect," he continued his rant. "I could time it. Control it so we had every exclusive. But then you — you, Sam — you fucked up."

She felt her body sliding. Saw the tripod fall. She tried to put out her hands to brace herself but they didn't work.

"The biggest fire of all and you decided to have a little Chinese with Mama and Sonny Boy. You shut me out." His voice sounded hard now, like staccato punches. "A whole family died and I missed the exclusive of a lifetime. I had to sit on the fucking sidelines because of you. *You,* my dear Sam."

The coffee. He must have put something in her coffee. She stared up at him from a heap on the floor. Her body had become paralyzed, her vision swirled, and her mind screamed because her mouth couldn't.

Her cheek lay against the cold tile while he paced. All she could see now were his shoes, shiny leather. That was Jeffery, so neat and clean. He was still lecturing her but the words were getting garbled. Something about opportunities he had given her. How he couldn't let her ruin things for him.

He had a plane to catch. Nothing made sense. His voice came to her in a low monotone, muffled and slurred. She caught words and phrases. A story to cover in the Middle East. He'd miss not having her with him. But he'd make sure everyone saw him grieve when he heard the news about her unfortunate demise.

"I saw the way you looked at him," Jeffery was saying, but she had no clue who he was talking about.

What was that smell?

"They'll think you were lovers. That you were both targeted. Especially since his house is on fire, too. Poor Patrick Murphy. Even his famous FBI sister couldn't save him."

Through a blur she watched Jeffery pour

the liquid on the tray of purple crystals. The trail of smoke was so pretty.

She didn't even hear him leave. Sam had no idea how much time had passed when she saw the white flash of light. The tray sparked and in seconds the stack of newspapers underneath became engulfed in flames.

Whatever drug Jeffery had used, it relieved her of panic. It weighed her down, glued her to the floor. Her vision was blurred, her mind a pleasant haze, almost as if she were dreaming. She simply watched the red and yellow dance up the walls. Even the heat from the flames soothed her, like a warm breeze on a cool day.

Sam closed her eyes. Listened to the crackling and *swoosh* filling her ears. And she thought about Iggy in those silly red suspenders.

CHAPTER 74

Maggie hardly noticed her headache. The rest of her body felt completely drained of energy. So deep was the exhaustion that she drove home with the windows rolled down, hoping the cold night air would keep her awake.

Seeing Dr. Kernan had certainly put things in perspective. The curmudgeon had actually been sweet and gentle with her. He had heard that a Kathleen O'Dell had been admitted and checked to find out if she was Maggie's mother.

"I practically live here, so if you need anything, you let me know."

He didn't need to explain why he rarely went home. Two months ago his wife of forty-seven years had gone into a medically induced coma. Maggie hadn't asked any questions and he wasn't ready to share more details.

This was one of those times when nothing

made sense in the world and she was too exhausted to do anything about it. Racine had left an hour ago, after getting some information on Wes Harper. Tully had called to see how Maggie was doing and to tell her Ganza and his crew had left State Patrol officers to guard the site until morning. There was too much to process to do it in the middle of the night.

All Maggie wanted right now was to go home. Patrick had offered to wait up and she ordered him to bed, promising she'd let him know if she needed anything. And she had finally called Ben. They talked for thirty minutes about how much James Kernan reminded her of Spencer Tracy and then went back and forth with lines from Tracy and Hepburn movies. To others it would be nonsensical and trivial, but it was exactly what she had needed.

In her frenzy to get to the hospital she had parked in the facility's garage without paying attention to the level, let alone what corner, she had left her Jeep. Now she wandered the cold concrete building, which was quiet as a tomb. She thought she remembered being on Level 2, but after a walk clear around the dimly lit area she knew she had to be mistaken. She took the ramp up to Level 3. More cars here and yet she couldn't find hers. Again, complete silence at this time of night. Not even a car door slamming or an elevator binging.

Maybe it was the opposite corner. She turned to circle back and caught a shadow disappearing between cars. Her hand immediately dug into her jacket as she sidestepped and then backed against a wall.

Her pulse raced as she listened. Somewhere above she could hear a faint sound of an engine starting. She stayed close to the wall and started slowly toward the area where she had seen the shadow. She weaved around car bumpers and almost stepped on a discarded fast-food bag. She didn't let her eyes leave that area even as she let them dart around.

There was no one there. Only a doorway, an exit to the stairwell. Could someone have escaped without her hearing the *whoosh* of the door? Maybe she had imagined the shadow.

She continued to the next level, her fingers on the butt of her revolver. By the time she found her Jeep and locked herself inside she was convinced that exhaustion was simply playing havoc with her. She tried to calm herself. Turned on some music and eased her vehicle into the flow of interstate traffic.

When she heard the first siren, she pulled

to the side of the road and waited for it to wail past her. The closer she got to home the more sirens she heard, and her insides clenched. Her hands gripped the steering wheel. With the windows down she thought she could smell smoke. More flashing lights behind her. She jerked the car to the side just in time for the fire and rescue unit to screech by her.

She followed it. Every turn it made was like squeezing her heart, tighter and tighter, a fist in her chest. Each turn took her closer and closer to her neighborhood, inside her neighborhood, up her street. Barricades kept her from driving to her house. She jumped out of her car so quickly she didn't realize she hadn't put it in park until the vehicle started rolling. She slid back inside and slammed the gear shift, crushed the parking brake into place.

Beyond the barricades blue, red, and white lights flashed but farther up the street she could see flames shooting up over the pine trees. She grabbed her cell phone and tried calling Patrick, letting it ring while she sat paralyzed behind the steering wheel. Over the pounding of her heart she heard his voice mail pick up. She pressed End and tried again.

Maggie tried to calm her breathing. Maybe

it wasn't her house. She stopped Patrick's voice mail and punched in the number again.

CHAPTER 75

Maggie's badge got her past the first set of barricades. She stopped herself at the second set, fear turning her knees to mush and panic making it hard to breathe. So much smoke, and the flames kept swallowing more and more. She could see that the house next door was completely engulfed. Her house was filled with angry black clouds of smoke.

"Ma'am, you can't go any farther." A firefighter stood in front of her.

She held up her badge.

"It's still not safe for you to go any closer, Agent . . ." He bent down to look at her ID. "Agent O'Dell."

"It's my house." It came out in a whisper. She wasn't even sure she had said it out loud.

"O'Dell."

She didn't look up at him but she could tell he was putting it together. Every fire-

412

fighter in the area probably knew all the details about these arsons.

"The CNN piece," he said. "Good God, he came after you, too."

"Please, can you tell me if anyone made it out?" Her voice cracked over the lump in her throat. She had been so frantic about Patrick, only now did she realize Harvey and Jake had been inside, too. In a matter of one night, all her prized possessions and companions gone. Up in smoke.

"No one's come out. We're still trying to get inside both houses."

"The house next door is for sale. I believe it's empty."

"That's what we thought, too, but we heard a dog barking, insisting someone was inside. We've got a crew trying to bust in the back."

"Wait a minute. A dog?"

He nodded. "Big black shepherd."

"Jake," she said, and smiled. "Jake made it out."

She saw two firemen carrying a body from the backyard of the empty house. Just then a blast of flames shot through Maggie's roof.

"I've got to go," the firefighter told her, already racing up her lawn.

She sat, actually collapsed onto the curb. She could feel the heat of the flames even from back here. She buried her face in her hands and tried to drown out the tromping of boots, the yells of the rescue crews, more sirens.

She had been worried about shadows following her in the parking garage and all the while the bastard was here. Right here at her house, setting it on fire.

She felt the hand on her shoulder at the same time a wet muzzle pressed under her chin.

"I couldn't save the front. But I sprayed the hell out of the back."

She looked up to see Patrick, his face smeared with soot, his white T-shirt torn and gray, his eyes watery and red. Both Harvey and Jake were with him.

Maggie stood on wobbly knees. "It's just a house," she said and hugged him. "The most important things I have are right here."

■ ■ ■ ■

THREE DAYS LATER

■ ■ ■ ■

CHAPTER 76

Quantico

Maggie and Tully sat on opposite sides of the conference table. Assistant Director Kunze sat at the head.

"There seems to be no evidence to support Samantha Ramirez's claim that Jeffery Cole is a serial arsonist," he told them.

Maggie couldn't believe that no one was taking the woman seriously. She was in intensive care, barely able to speak, and yet she was insistent that Jeffery Cole had lit the fire that almost killed her. That he had admitted setting all the other fires.

"What about the fact that he used to teach high school chemistry? We now know the chemicals used were potassium permanganate and glycerin. Ms. Ramirez said she saw a jug of swimming pool cleaner in his SUV. She saw him pour something on purple crystals. Potassium permanganate is a crystal-like chemical found in swimming pool cleaners."

"This is your evidence?"

"Okay, what about Cornell Stamoran? He recognized Jeffery Cole as the guy he saw pouring gasoline in the alley right before the warehouse fires."

"You said yourself, Agent Tully, that the man appears to be an alcoholic schizophrenic."

"Why not let us question him?" Tully persisted.

"Cole's on assignment in the Middle East."

It was useless. Maggie sat back and let out a sigh of frustration. The man had almost killed her brother, and Kunze was tying their hands. Several days ago he had pushed her and Tully to catch him an arsonist. He was in political hot water if they didn't do so. She worried that now suddenly it wasn't politically correct for that arsonist to be Jeffery Cole. She wanted to tell Kunze that he couldn't pick and choose his madmen.

"How about the fact that the arsons have stopped?"

"Agent O'Dell," he said while he avoided eye contact and shook his head. "We all know that doesn't necessarily mean a thing."

"We have sufficient reason to question

him. Even on foreign soil," Tully said.

Again Kunze shook his head. "That's not going to happen. The Justice Department won't allow it."

So he had checked, was Maggie's first thought. Someone was shutting him down again. And Kunze was shutting them down. He stood and picked up a pile of file folders from a credenza behind him. He dropped the foot-high stack on the table between Maggie and Tully.

"This is where I want your focus to be."

"What is this?"

"Both of you, along with Keith Ganza, have told me that Gloria Dobson and Zach Lester were not murdered by the same person who set fire to the warehouses. Isn't that correct?"

"There's not a way to connect them, that's correct," Tully admitted. "Neither of us believes Jeffery Cole committed those murders."

And neither one of them believed that he had followed Maggie down a manhole or sneaked around behind her house. Cornell Stamoran said a man had been following him, too. He thought he was the same man who dumped the body in his cardboard box, the man who killed Dobson and Lester.

Kunze ignored the mention of Cole and

continued, "Ganza's found three similar murders at other rest areas. Different parts of the country. One of the bodies was just found about a mile off the interstate in a roadside culvert. We think this guy has killed more — many more. You both have heard of the Highway Serial Killings Initiative?"

Maggie and Tully nodded. She remembered Ganza's mentioning it when he talked about prostitutes and truck drivers.

"More than five hundred unsolved murders near interstate rest areas in the last ten years. And that's only the ones we've entered into our initiative's data bank. I think you two may have stumbled onto one of the murderers."

Kunze's phone interrupted them. He looked at the ID and answered immediately.

"This is Director Raymond Kunze."

He was quiet and listening, his face expressionless, and Maggie found herself thinking the man would be excellent at poker. After several nods Kunze said, "I understand." Then he ended the call.

"It appears CNN has just announced they'll be airing an interview with Jeffery Cole."

"About what?" Maggie asked.

"He's confessing to eight counts of arson. He's giving them the exclusive."

CHAPTER 77

He pulled down the bill of his ball cap and walked against the wind. He was glad to have gloves today. Back here along the stream it felt colder. The weather was changing again and he'd be glad to get back on the road. He'd stayed too long as it was, reluctant to leave her behind.

Over the top of the privacy fence he could see parts of the two beautiful houses ravaged by fire. It was a shame the way things turned out. He found a trail in between the two properties. No one was around today. The houses looked abandoned but he knew she came back every day to recover what the fire or the water hadn't damaged.

He actually hated leaving her. He was convinced they were kindred spirits. But he needed to get back home. This magpie was definitely an omen, but not a bad one. Now that her life had been turned upside down he figured she would need something — or someone — to keep her mind off her own troubles.

He made his way up to the front door, or what was left of it. He climbed over the yellow DO NOT ENTER tape and took a look around. There was a good spot — on what used to be a kitchen counter. He set down the torn piece of a map with a red circle in the middle. Then he anchored it with a rock from the stream back behind her house. The map would help her find the garbage bag he'd left there for her.

And when she did find it, he knew he'd see her again.

AUTHOR'S NOTE

Fireproof is my twelfth novel and the tenth in the Maggie O'Dell series. Quite a milestone considering I never intended to write a series. But sometimes being a writer is as much about listening as it is about writing. You might say Maggie prevailed because you readers demanded to see more and more of her. I must confess that I needed to be pushed and prodded in the beginning. I had never read a series and hadn't a clue how to write one. I wasn't thrilled about being saddled with a character I hardly knew. For those of you who have stuck with Maggie and me from the very start, I am forever grateful. You've made an incredible difference in my life. I hope Maggie and I can continue to repay the favor.

Research is one of my favorite parts about writing novels, and although I take pride in combining facts with my fiction, I do allow for creative license. The District does, in fact, have an elaborate underground sewer and water system, though I've taken great liberty in giving my characters unprecedented access to these tunnels. However, much of the homeless situation depicted in the novel is drawn from factual accounts, including the District's separate Metro bus system and the fact that many of the sleep shelters are located five-plus miles away from the city's food kitchens.

As with each of my novels, I have a bunch of people to thank. The experts continue to amaze and astonish me with their generosity in sharing their experiences. I want to emphasize, any mistakes are solely mine.

First, a humble thank-you to the firefighters in my life: Lee Dixon (Pensacola Fire Chief, retired), Terry Hummel (District of Columbia Fire Department, retired), Carl Kava (Omaha Fire Department, RIP), David Kava (Omaha Fire Department, retired), Rich Kava (Omaha Fire Department, retired), and Larry Wilbanks (NAS Whiting Field, Milton, Florida).

My publishing teams: Phyllis Grann, Alison Callahan, Stephanie Bowen, Judy Jacoby, and Kristen Gastler at Doubleday; Andrea Robinson at Anchor; David Shelley, Catherine Burke, and Jade Chandler at Little, Brown UK.

The new guy on my team, Scott Miller at Trident Media Group, and his colleague, Claire Roberts.

Dr. Liz Szeliga for answering all my questions about teeth and fire.

Annie Belatti and Sandy Powers for sharing their experiences with burn victims and all the gut-wrenching details of what fire does to a body.

Cornell Stamoran for his generous donation to Save the Libraries.

Partners in crime and fellow authors Patricia Bremmer, Erica Spindler, and J. T. Ellison.

Ray Kunze, once again, for lending his name to Maggie's boss.

My friends and family put up with my long absences and my inappropriate trivia. They keep me sane and grounded. Special thanks to Marlene Haney and Sandy Rockwood, Patricia Kava, Sharon Car, Patricia Sierra, Leigh Ann Retelsdorf, Maricela Barajas, Martin Bremmer, Cari Conine, Lisa Munk, Sharon Kator, Luann Causey, and Andrea McDaniel.

A personal thank-you to Dr. Nicole Smee and the amazing crew at Kansas State University Veterinary Hospital for taking such good care of my Miss Molly and giving me five extra and priceless months with her.

Last, but never least, to Deb Carlin. I could never do any of this without you.

The employees of Thorndike Press hope you have enjoyed this Large Print book. All our Thorndike, Wheeler, and Kennebec Large Print titles are designed for easy reading, and all our books are made to last. Other Thorndike Press Large Print books are available at your library, through selected bookstores, or directly from us.

For information about titles, please call:
  (800) 223-1244

or visit our Web site at:
  http://gale.cengage.com/thorndike

To share your comments, please write:
  Publisher
  Thorndike Press
  10 Water St., Suite 310
  Waterville, ME 04901